Diary of a Dead Guy

A Country Ghost Story

TY HAGER

ISBN: 978-1492270294
Cover art by Jessica Hall Graphics

TY HAGER

Dedicated to Rachel, Liana, and Ava...my beautiful girls and my beautiful girl's girl.

<u>CHAPTER ONE</u>

Some folks believe that when you die you go to Heaven. I write that with a capital "H" in case it really does exist, and in case there's a chance in Hell I'll ever get to go there. Not real sure why I capitalize "Hell." Maybe for the same reason I capitalize "Oklahoma."

Anyway. Heaven. These folks believe you go to this place which is joyous and infinite and without any of our earth-bound trials and tribulations and those distractions which might lead one down the path to Hell. Which is why, once you get to Heaven, you're for all intents and purposes stuck there. You'll see all of those loved ones who meet the criteria of having gone before you and having led similarly righteous lives. I think of some of my loved ones who have passed before me and are probably in Heaven and, while I still love 'em, bless their hearts, the idea of spending eternity with 'em sounds a lot more like the definition of Hell. More often than not it was a struggle to just get through Thanksgiving dinner, which, as I recall, only seemed to last an eternity. But I digress.

Apparently one of the main requirements for going to this swell place, Heaven, is that you have to believe you're going there. You don't just live a righteous life and wind up there surprised, thinking, well I guess this sure beats the Hell out of nothing! And if I've understood what I've read and been told, believing you're going there sometimes trumps actually living a righteous life, and there's a little loophole whereby you can sin like a motherfucker (even using words like "motherfucker"), torture bunnies, drink, gamble, have sex with hookers, make fun of nuns, maybe even send some righteous folks to Heaven, and, if you ask for forgiveness, you still got your ticket. Seems to me this would kind of give an unfair advantage to those dying long, slow deaths, and leave those who get shot in the head or hit by a train or a falling meteor sucking everlasting hind teat, as it were.

Trust me. I know the taste of hind teat.

Another existential conundrum posed by all this eternity stuff is that no matter how *good a life you lead, how much you abide by all the rules that'll get you to Heaven, there's a better-than-even chance you'll have been abiding by the* wrong set *of rules. While it's generally agreed the world over by those who believe in God that there's just* one *of Him, there seems to be some severe and rather violent disagreement as to just exactly which team He's coachin'.*

For instance, if He's coachin' a baseball *team, you can be the best, most righteous damned* soccer *player in the world, but in that moment when you free up your death bed, you're gonna be in for a rude awakening, or lack thereof. I cannot conceive of a situation more maddening than to know you had spent your entire life forsaking cussin' and bunnie-torturin' and drinkin' and gamblin' – not to mention hooker-fuckin' and nun-ridiculin' - only to find out you could a gone to town on that shit for all the good it did ya. Now* that *would be an eternal aggravation! I think that if Vegas set odds on all this, you'd have a better chance of winnin' sinnin'.*

Which kinda sounds like a country song, don't it?

On the other hand, there are those who believe that death is an abyss, the Big Nothing, *that we make our own Heavens or Hells right here on Earth during whatever amount of time we have allotted. Which is, at the very least, a more* convenient way *to look at it.*

There are even those who believe that life is but a dream, and death is an awakening *from that dream. Not sure I even* understand *that, because it seems it would mean that everybody would be havin' the* same dream, *and I've always kinda liked to keep my dreams to myself.*

Besides, what would be the difference between a dream perceived by everyone as reality and true objective reality (if such a thing exists)? I'll leave that to the philosophers. They've got more inclination to ponder such things, although it seems like I may have infinitely more time.

CHAPTER TWO

Wilson, Tennessee is a small town of about fourteen thousand located in the Cumberland Valley about a half-hour's drive east of Nashville. The seat of Wilson County, it has all the charms of a small Southern town – friendly folk, a town square, a single movie theater (although a full two generations have no memory of it having a single *screen*), and gossip that flies as carefree as the Confederate Flag that waved over the courthouse until almost 1970. While political pressure from Nashville (the threat of withholding *money*!) brought the flag down, *gossip* remains unencumbered.

Northerners like to imply it's a *Southern* thing, but gossip's been around almost as long as people. If they hadn't been *alone* on the planet, surely rumors would've flown about a certain couple having pre-marital sex in a certain garden.

Egyptians gossiped with hieroglyphics, American Indians with smoke signals, frontiersmen with Pony Express riders. One of the driving forces behind many technological advances – if you really study it - has been not only to more-effectively facilitate the slaughter of our fellow man, but also to facilitate the infliction of more subtle (and far more *entertaining*) injuries.

During the late winter and early spring of 2009 in Wilson, Tennessee, rumor had it that Willard Blevins – "you know, *Mack's* boy" – was possessed by a devil in his laptop.

Nobody blamed Mack and Elenore for giving the twelve-year-old a gizmo that came pre-loaded with – in addition to all its other apps – a freakin' *entity*. They were from a different time, a generation that considered programming the VCR and getting the coffee-maker to brew *before* you woke up to be all the technical know-how required of someone without a college degree. And there *were* no degrees in the Blevins family - and none were expected – most likely because the family tree wasn't exactly overrun with branches. Mack's father was Elenore's mother's cousin, Elenore's sister's husband was Mack's uncle's cousin's boy…it didn't make for a high prospect of a bio-chemist in the family's future, but it sure made it easy to find an organ donor. Which was infinitely more practical.

His father got Willard the laptop mainly for its video games, because, as Mack put it, "the little shit's always wantin' to change the goddamned channel from NASCAR." His son's aversion to stock-car racing prompted Mack to wonder on occasion if perhaps the boy wasn't his, but he'd done the bone-dance with Elenore plenty of times, and couldn't for the life of him imagine anyone else wanting to go through that.

It took Willard some time to figure out how to work his new toy. At first, all he could do with it was play *Dungeon Hunter*, which Mack was relieved to discover at least involved *killing*. The boy had always been something of a loner – his weight problem attracted derision from his classmates and eliminated most sports as an activity option – and his parents were both happy to see him while away his free hours doing something he seemed to enjoy more than sitting on the couch, bitching about what was on TV. They often heard him in his room, shouting gleefully at the death of another enemy combatant in the sacred land of Gothicus, and, while they couldn't really comprehend his reports of progress - using words like "Warlord" and "Astromancer" – if it relieved them from seemingly incessant interruptions of watching cars driving around in a circle, they were all for it.

About a month earlier, the joyful sounds of villain-killing exaltation had suddenly ceased. After a few hours of silence from the boy's room, Mack told Elenore he was afraid their son might be burned out.

"Goddammit," he growled. "He's gonna be back in here bitchin' about what's on TV."

Elenore concurred, in the way she'd concurred for years. She silently nodded her head, her eyes glued to the flat-screen. Occasionally she grunted, but mainly reserved such outbursts for family crises.

Mack had hoisted himself out of his comfy recliner. It was pretty much the only exercise he *got* these days, ever since he'd lost a big toe in a drunken bowling accident and got a hefty settlement check. He waddled down the hall to Willard's closed bedroom door, and was about to walk in when he thought he heard a faint but only vaguely familiar sound from inside the boy's room. It was not dissimilar to the sound made by squirrels in the attic, but obviously that wasn't it. A few moments later it dawned on him.

He walked back into the living room, a strange expression on his face.

"Elenore."

Though the tone of his voice didn't seem particularly *urgent*, there was something about it that had pulled his wife's eyes from the TV screen.

"Huh?"

Mack paused a moment, almost as if he couldn't actually commit to words the thought in his head, yet neither could he hold it back.

"I think Willard's in there goddamned *typing*."

Elenore's jaw had dropped and rested on her Titanic-sized bosom.

"Shut the front door."

This was not only as close as Elenore ever came to swearing, it was also one of her rare complete sentences.

"I shit you not. Can't think of what else it might be."

Elenore's curiosity, usually a slumbering, dim-witted beast, overcame her aversion to getting off the couch for anything but going to the bathroom, refilling her iced tea, or popping a snack into the microwave. She gripped the padded arm-rest and lumbered to her feet.

Mack was almost as mystified by this as he was by the goings-on in their son's room.

"Dang, Elenore, it ain't even a commercial."

If looks could slap, Mack would've been smacked.

Without waiting for further reply, Mack turned and walked down the hall, Elenore just behind. The couple paused – as side-by-side as logistically possible with two such bodies in the narrow hallway - just outside the closed bedroom door, listening. Unfortunately, the labored breathing of not one but *two* fat people drowned out whatever faint sounds may have been emanating from the room.

"*Shhh!*" Mack whispered.

" *'Shhh' what?*"

"*Stop breathin'!*"

Elenore back-handed his shoulder, the sound absorbed by Mack's circus-tent-sized flannel shirt.

"You *stop breathin'.*"

With the dual behemoths momentarily completely silent, the only sounds in the house were the faint whirring of the ceiling fan in the living room, barely audible over the TV's inanity.

And the distinctive clickety-clickety-clack of the laptop's keyboard from behind Willard's closed door.

Mack and Elenore exhaled simultaneously, looking at one another wide-eyed, Elenore surprised, Mack with an "I told you so" expression.

"*Shut the front door,*" Elenore whispered.

"*You think he's doing homework?*" Mack whispered back.

It's not an easy thing to whisper a responsive grunt, but that's what Elenore did.

Without awaiting further response or encouragement, Mack quickly turned the knob and opened Willard's door.

"Shut the front door," Elenore said for a third time, and Mack would have thought her incessant yacking nearly intolerable if his attention hadn't been elsewhere.

Willard sat on his twin-sized unmade bed, his pudgy legs stretched out and crossed at the ankles. His back rested against the headboard, his computer opened on his lap as his fingers raced across the keyboard, his eyes staring through his dirty-blond stringy bangs at either the opposite wall or nothing at all.

Mack and Elenore took all this in in exactly the amount of time it took for the sound waves from the opening of the door (and Elenore's "*Shut* the front door") to reach their son's dirty ears. His gaze quickly turned their direction. He slammed his laptop shut.

"I can't believe I fucking lost my fucking capo again," he said.

CHAPTER THREE

Love is only overrated by those who are not in it. Love is a timeless, ageless thing, overwhelming the senses identically at fifty as at fifteen, a meeting of the heart and mind that is not replicated by any other experience – physical, emotional, instinctual, biological. Love is all these things, and the only singularly human phenomenon that absolutely requires reciprocation in order to function at that level which defines it, which makes it the most desirable and aspired-to state of our all-too-short and unhappy existence. Left unrequited, love is a cancer that cannot be cut out, an insidious state of mental and physical anguish curable only by the passage of enough time necessary to return its victim to a state of deluding themselves that it's overrated.

So how does *one separate true romantic love from raw animal passion? Elementary, my dear – one* doesn't. *The latter can thrive without the former, but not vice-versa. At least not until love ages, the maturing of a fine wine, becoming a wiser and stronger and more* comfortable *love, perhaps to compensate for the weakening of physical desire.*

But in the beginning, love needs fucking. And a lot of it.

Angel and I fed our love like a starving puppy, at the very least daily, sometimes hourly, sometimes with scraps under the kitchen table. Not sure what that means *exactly, but we did once make love on the kitchen floor, and wound up under the table. The same one she'd* drunk *me under on more than one occasion.*

From the night we met - at a bar in Nashville where me and my band "The Cowtippers" were playing a gig – I thought her name rather ironic, as she introduced herself to me by showing me the tattoo on her tit, and proceeded from there to introduce me to carnal pleasures that would make Lucifer *say, "That's* nasty," *and spank his monkey.*

I was forty-two, and had been writing and playing songs for over half my life. In that entire time, I'd never got laid as a direct result of playing, which – regardless of what any *lying-ass musician says – was one of the reasons I'd picked up the guitar in the first place.*

After nearly two decades since my initial foray to Music City, I'd got sick to death of the place. The final straw had been (along with a major heartbreak) a big-ass billboard – right outside the window of the Music Row sandwich joint I'd been busting my hiney in for nearly ten years - of the latest country sensation, a teeny-bopper named Billy Gilman, who to me epitomized everything that was wrong *with the biz. I'd always thought country music was supposed to be about the lives and trials and tribulations of the common man, performed and often* written *by artists who you could believe had actually lived and trialed and tribulated. This little Billy Gilman dipstick couldn't write his name in the dirt with a stick if you spotted him the "B," and his greatest tribulation had been his terror over the strange fuzz growing on his peanut-sized marbles.*

So I'd said "Fuck it" and moved to Austin, Texas (my second *journey to the "Live Music Capital of the World). Less than a year-and-a-half later, I'd got signed to a label out of New York City. Guess where they moved me? Yep. Fuckin'* Nashville. *May the circle-jerk be unbroken.*

I wasn't bitching too *much. It was* far *better to live in Nashville as a guy* with *a record deal than it was as a guy* looking *for a record deal. The Prez of the label, Phil, thought I was talented as all get-out, and told anybody who'd listen that I was "a gem." Even nicer than the accolades were the checks he'd send me on those occasions when my day gig didn't quite cover my basic requirements. You know, rent and utilities and bars and beer and cigs and the whatnot. Which was not infrequently. If you've got something to fall back on, you'll always fall back.*

While the first CD had been pretty much ignored (except for some minor airplay which I'll tell you about later), the second one - with some major players on it - had come out and got pretty good press. One national publication said that I "combined

*laugh-out-loud lyrics with solid rhythm guitar and vocals," and
that I painted "a vivid portrait of the dangers of love and
relationships."* I'd *thought I was writing about being a musician
for half my life and* still *not getting laid. I might've mentioned
that.*

*The press had led to more substantial airplay, which had
led to some pretty cool gigs, which had led to Angel. I'd long ago
stopped anticipating anything from playing shows apart from a
good beer buzz and about an hour of feeling like the brightest light
in the room. It's always amazed me how shy I can be for most of
my existence, but how all those deep-seeded insecurities can melt
away with a few beers and my music and applause.*

*And, until Angel, it had amazed me that that shit had never
got me laid. I might've mentioned that.*

*She'd been sitting at a table near the stage with two of her
friends. There wasn't one among 'em I would've kicked out of bed
for eating crackers, but* she *had an aura about her, a spark, a
light.*

*And a helluva set of tits, which she'd flashed at me between
our first and second encore. On her left breast was a tattoo that
said, simply,* **MY FIRST TATTOO.** *In fancy lettering like that. Of
course I damned near shit myself right on stage (which would've
made me feel like somewhat* less *than the brightest light in the
room). Not so much because this beautiful woman had shown me
her beautiful melons (which affected me in a completely* different
way*), but because I'd only seen a tat like that one other place: on
me. It'd been quite the conversation-piece since that Halloween
night I'd had a few too many after work at the sammich shop and
staggered down the street to the "Tattoo Parlor of the Stars". The
guy who did it thought it so damned funny he put it up on their
website, and Phil at the label thought it so typical* me *that it
became the back of my second CD.*

So, needless to say, I figured this gal's titty tat was either a freakish coincidence or an indicator that I had found a really *big fan. I was hoping it was the latter, reasoning that if a woman would put a fella's kinda-trademark on her skin* permanently, *she might allow that same fella's doo-hickey in her giddy-up at least* temporarily. *I also thought "Let Me Put My Doo-Hickey in Your Giddy-up" might make a cute country song.*

After the set, as the rest of the band began tearing down the equipment, I 'd walked to the bar for a much-needed beer, only to find that she'd already ordered one for me. I thanked her. She held out a long smooth hand at the end of a long smooth arm and introduced herself.

"Hi Jared. I'm Angel."

(Don't guess I've mentioned this, by the by, but that's my name. Jared Whaley. Pleased to meet ya, reader.)

I shook her hand and felt a little electrical thrill run up my arm, then zap me in the heart and groin.

"How old were you before your parents realized they'd named you wrong?" I asked.

She'd laughed, all perfect lips and perfect teeth and perfect mouth. Perfect. Hey, she'd already shown me her tits and bought me a beer. Now she was laughing at my first joke. You'll excuse me if I found her flawless.

She was about five-ten, an inch taller than me, but it seemed even more than that because she had good posture, whereas I was a life-long slouch. She had long dark hair and a model's long legs and slim hips and a porn star's fantabulous ta-tas. I guessed her to be about twenty-two, and hoped she wasn't much *younger than that. I've always had a firm rule to not lust after women too close to my oldest daughter's age, which was twenty at the time. But if Angel had told me she was only nineteen, it* probably *wouldn't have mattered. Passion sucks at math.*

"Well, Angel, you've got *to tell me about that tattoo."*

She giggled and took a drink of beer, her hand wrapped sensuously around the bottle, bringing it provocatively to her mouth, her full red lips teasing the opening, seeming to draw the cool liquid to them rather than relying on the natural law of gravity. Hey, if I was that beer, I'd've wanted to be in her mouth too. Even if I wasn't that beer, actually. Which, obviously, I wasn't. But I digress.

"I got it right after I bought your CD, which was right after it came out," she said, setting that lucky-ass bottle back on the bar. "Would you sign it?"

It was my turn to take a drink. Not that we were necessarily taking turns.

"Your CD or your tit?"

She laughed again, and that's when our eyes really met - beyond the glancing perfunctory dance which is a part of the male-female ritual – and I realized that the deep-blue depths of those wonderful orbs were every bit as enticing as her other perhaps more spank-worthy assets. Her gaze was unflinching, magnetic, and gave my own usually-halting stare the gumption to be googly. She seemed to sense this, and a smile played at the corners of her luscious lips, which I only caught peripherally, stuck as I was in those unwavering windows to her soul.

"I just happen to have both with me," she said, her happy hormone-hyping hypnotics broken by the magical mirth of the moment. Geez Louise, I literally love alliteration.

We both laughed, me as much in a "funny ha-ha" as a "funny fucking-awesome" kinda way. Although she was funny ha-ha too.

"Well," I said, after the moment passed and we resumed our eye-fucking. "The guys'll be irate if I don't do a little manual labor."

I'd already noticed a few silent baleful stares between my fellow pickers-and-grinners as they unplugged and wrapped cords and hauled out amps and instruments. They usually only joked about it, but there had always been a slight underlying tension over how little heavy lifting I did, both before and after a gig. Hey,

I was the front man. It was kinda my job *to socialize. Great work if you can get it.*

"Won't take me long. Then I'll get my sharpie," I said, before almost literally dragging my happy ass from her desirable fantasy-inspiring realm for a brief sojourn to the real world.

I felt her eyes on me as I made my way to the stage, unplugged my guitar and put it in the case. As I started wrapping my cord, I didn't realize I had just taken the first step in a not-nearly- long-enough journey that would take me from the pinnacles of both physical and emotional bliss to the fire-and-brimstone-laden depths of despair and back again…and again…and again…*not finally culminating till death did us part.*

I wasn't thinking about any *of that at the time. I was looking around the stage, starting to get a little pissed, wondering where I'd put the little springy contraption that a mediocre guitar player such as myself clamps onto the strings in order to change keys without actually having to play different* chords.

"Goddamn it," I said, as much to myself as to my band-mates. "I can't believe I fucking lost my fucking capo again."

CHAPTER FOUR

"What the fuck's a *capo*, Mack?" Norville asked, adjusting the barber's chair, preparing to give his life-long friend a trim.

Mack settled in for their monthly ritual in this, the only exclusively *male* sanctuary he'd known since that long-ago day he'd misguidedly thought that getting sex on a semi-regular basis was worth actually spending your entire *life* with a woman. Apart from the occasional mother bringing in her son for a haircut, Norville's Barber Shop was about the only place in Wilson free from a daily barrage of estrogen, thus ensuring the town retained a distinctly non-shaggy male population.

"Beats the shit out of me, Norville," Mack replied. "I think it has something to do with the goddamned Mafia."

As a primarily-male domain, it was required that every other sentence or so uttered by its inhabitants contain a swear word. Even Pastor Mike once took the Lord's name in vain while in the solitary chair. He was complaining about his wife, whom he'd been so desperate to escape that he was getting his second haircut in half as many weeks. This particular outburst had set the rumor-mill to overdrive, and in a few days everyone in town was whispering that the Pastor and the Mrs. were heading to Nashville every Tuesday and Thursday for freakin' *marriage counseling*, due to the preacher's wife's new-found affinity for a certain young male parishioner. None of it was true – the reality was that Mrs. Mike was just going through "the change" - but truth has never had anything to do with lubricating the wheels of gossip.

Another misconception about rumor is that it's primarily a *female* proclivity, as if men talk of nothing but sports and sex when they congregate, as if women spend so much time gossiping that they barely have time to comment on one another's *darling* new shoes. Nothing could be further from actual reality. Sports and sex and footwear are only the bridges the respective genders use to get to the main reason for them bothering to speak to one another at *all*. Namely, to talk about the people who aren't in the room, but are actually somewhere else gossiping about *them*.

In this particular instance, the subject of Mack's and Norville's jaw-flapping *was* in the room. Willard sat in one of the waiting chairs, right there but in another universe, his fingers once again typing a mile-a-minute while he stared toward but didn't even seem to *see* the adults a mere six feet in front of his stony face.

"Goddamn, Mack, that's *weird*," Norville said as he snipped, referring to the only fat-kid mannequin stenographer in the room. "I'm pretty sure I've seen *court reporters* type slower than that."

Mack had never had the pleasure of *seeing* a court reporter, but assumed they typed pretty goddamned *fast*, and concurred.

"Yep. Not even sure if he's actually *writin'* anything. Could just be gibberish." Then, as if realizing what he'd just said contained no profanity, added, "Beats the fuck outta me."

"Why don't you take that damned thing from him and see what the hell he's doin'?" Norville ventured, though, truth be told, he didn't actually *care*. Conjecture was more entertaining.

"He never lets go of the fucker," Mack said. "And if you try to look over his shoulder he seems to snap out of his trance and slams it shut."

Norville pulled out his electric razor and shaved the fuzz that had sprouted up on the back of Mack's neck since their last visit.

"Well, maybe it's like you said. Maybe he's just possessed."

"Maybe," Mack said. After a thoughtful pause, he added, "I just hope it's not *gay*."

"Huh?"

"Well, *look*." He indicated the magazine-strewn table next to his son. "There's a goddamned *Sports Illustrated Swimsuit Edition* right there. I don't care *what* kind of goddamned demon is tryin' to take over your soul. How can any non-faggot male not wanna look at *that*?"

"That's a *good* point," Norville replied, brushing the tiny bits of just-cut hair from Mack's neck and shoulders. "Although I'm not sure the devil cares that much about sex one way or the other. Don't believe anyone gets laid in Hell. *Or* Heaven, for that matter."

He giggled, then added, "Unless you're a Muslim. I think they get to fuck a bunch of virgins. That's what makes the fuckers so damned anxious to *die*."

"But what if he's possessin' him with *gayness*?" Mack asked. "Fuckin' fag Satan."

"Huh. Well, I hope *that* ain't it."

Willard suddenly stopped typing.

"Every goddamned dime I *get* from that shit is fuckin' *recoupable*," he said.

Like "capo," neither Mack nor Norville had any idea what "recoupable" meant. But that did nothing to slow the wheels of gossip.

CHAPTER FIVE

"Angel," I said, *my voice taking on this plaintive whining tone I couldn't recall ever having even* known *before I'd started having mind-blowing sex on a regular basis, but with which I had since become all-too-familiar.*

"Every goddamned dime I get *from that shit is fuckin'* recoupable*!"*

We were having one of our increasingly-frequent battles, where I had to explain why - even though my CD had climbed into the Top Twenty of the country charts and you could hardly turn on the radio for more than an hour without hearing my single - my sporadic advance checks from the label and the money from the live gigs were barely adding up to enough to keep us in beer and cigs and food, much less to being able to sustain the kind of high-living she felt was due someone of her status.

We'd been, for better or worse, inseparable since that gig eight months earlier, and it seemed some of the shine was starting to wear off, though I still believed – as I believe now – that she was my soul-mate. I'd moved out of the one-bedroom apartment I'd had since the label had moved me back to Nashville from Austin, quit my day job at that aforementioned sammich shop I'd had to return to, and moved into Angel's *one-bedroom apartment in a kinda-Bohemian area of Nashville known as "Hillsboro Village." Her Dad – an upper-level executive for a large book-publishing outfit - had been paying her rent while she was going to Belmont University, and had thankfully* continued *to pay it after she met me and dropped out. I thanked my lucky stars daily that - even though I was about his age and had led his only daughter down a path of non-educational debauchery - he was a big Willie Nelson fan and therefore considered my long-haired, bandana-wearin', dope-smokin', heavy-drinkin', late-night lifestyle acceptable for the love of his girl's life. Especially since I was getting played on the radio. Music is a powerful thing.*

As Angel sat at the kitchen table and cleaned her gun – a

nickel-plated Smith and Wesson .38 snub-nose revolver her old
man had bought her for protection and which she had a habit of
*cleaning every time we had one of our more heated...uh...*debates -
I explained to her for the umpteenth time that it didn't fucking
matter *how many CDs the label (Phil) said were being sold at the*
various retail outlets, how many songs were being downloaded, or
how many times I was on the radio. In order to achieve all of this
success and feed the music-biz machine, Phil had sunk somewhere
in the area of a hundred grand into me thus far, of which –
compared to the recording and distribution and promotion – my
meager advances were a little drop in a big ol' bucket, and
actually more than he was required *to give me contractually until*
such point as all of his expenditures were recouped by sales.
Hence the word "recoupable." I further explained – again for the
umpteenth time - that I would *get a check from* ASCAP *for the*
airplay *of my song, since I had written it, but that they only*
calculated royalties every six months. So, basically, we were
living like paupers, and would continue to do so, for the next few
months.

    It was like talking to a brick wall I just happened to want to
stick my dick in. One which, for better or worse, I'd got drunk
nine days earlier and married.

    "Jared!" she screamed. "He's making a shitload *of money*
off of your talent! We're drinking PBR *Christ's sake!"*

    Apparently every time I moved my lips to explain the
realities of the music business, I might as well have been Charlie
Brown's teacher. "Waaa waaaa. Waaaaa waaaa." It was like
how goddamned dogs *interpret what we say. Except, again, this*
was a dog I wanted to breed. And, Lord help me, I really like
PBR. The make-up sex with Angel was always fantastic, but damn
it, *I sure had to walk barefoot over a mile of gravel road to get to*
it. Not literally, although I would've.

    "Listen, baby," I plaintively-yet-hopefully-conciliatorily
whined. "We've got the show tonight. My cut'll be a couple

hundred bucks at least, and maybe we'll sell another hundred or so bucks in CDs. I'll take ya someplace really *nice tomorrow."*

We were doing a gig at The Thirsty Turtle, *a joint in Wilson, about a half-hour or so down I-40 to the east. The place held about two hundred people, and I'd been told it was sold out.*

She held up the gun, looking through the thankfully-empty cylinders as she spun the wheel, seemingly satisfied with their cleanliness. They should *be clean. We fought a lot.*

"You never do anything the day after a show but smoke dope and nurse your hangover," she said, reloading the revolver with the cartridges laying on the table (this part for some reason always made me really *nervous), snapping the cylinder-wheel shut, double-checking the safety and returning the now-lethal weapon to her purse, looking at me with an expression that said, "Don't forget it's there."*

"Well, tomorrow *night. I promise."*

"Yeah, right," she said.

CHAPTER SIX

Harvey Boyd was a consummate radio professional, if "radio" could be defined as a 500-watt AM station in a Podunk town, and "professional" could be defined as earning just over minimum wage.

WTOR (Wilson Tennessee's Only Radio) had broadcast on the 900 frequency of the AM band since 1941. In those nearly-seven decades, it hadn't really changed much. It had always played country, had always provided a modicum of local news coverage (in these lean years provided mostly by re-writing the stories printed daily in *The Wilson Democrat*). It had always had its daily buy-and-sell show. And it had always broadcast the death notices, three times daily, brought to you by *Shrum's Funeral Parlor*.

"Helping families in times of great sorrow since 1937," was their *official* slogan. Over the years, Harvey and some of his radio station co-workers had coined a few others:

"Shrum's Funeral Parlor – you give us money, we'll feed the worms," or,

"Shrum's Funeral Parlor - your grief is our bread and butter," or,

"Shrum's Funeral Parlor – because it's illegal to take dead bodies to the dump."

Gallows humor, to be sure, but *fun* gallows humor nonetheless.

Of all the hats Harvey wore, that of "News Director" was the one he most cherished (and the only one he mentally - and in writing – capitalized and put in quotes). While it was true he *did* re-write a lot of the *Democrat's* local coverage, Harvey still always kept his scanner handy, turning it off only during the four hours each morning - from 6 to 10 a.m. - that he had to play stupid records, make stupid jokes, and take stupid requests from mainly the same half-dozen listeners requesting the same half-dozen stupid songs. Harvey did *not* cherish the morning show.

During his tenure as News Director, Harvey could count on one hand the big stories that had broken in Wilson in the seventeen years he'd been working at the radio station.

One was the explosion at the *Hanks Battery* factory that killed four of the plant's twelve employees. Harvey still remembered the frantic call he'd received from Jack Dawes, the station's long-time owner.

"Goddamn, Harvey, I think the battery factory just blew up!" Jack said.

"Already on it," Harvey said, having moments before heard it over the scanner (*"Goddamn, the battery factory just blew up!"* was the actual transmission).

Harvey was the first reporter on the scene that day, and his recorded witness interviews (*actualities* they called them in the radio news biz) had made the state-wide broadcasts. He'd picked up a nice little check for that.

Another was a few years after that, when a Navy pilot taking off from the Nashville airport twenty-odd miles to the east (and showing off for his parents, who were watching), had flubbed up by ascending too fast and at too steep an angle, causing his F-14 to drop an engine and crash on the outskirts of Wilson County.

The pilot safely ejected, but, unfortunately for Carl and Emma Gladstone (who were having their morning coffee), their house had been located at exactly the spot the jet chose to meet the ground at several hundred miles-per-hour. Since Carl was well-known for his sharp criticism of *anything* Emma did in the kitchen, it was widely surmised - falling into the category of accepted fact - that Carl's last words were, "Goddamn Emma, this coffee tastes like shi-."

Harvey remembered the phone call from Jack *that* day as well.

"Goddamn Harvey, I think a plane just crashed!"

"Already on it," Harvey said, having moments before heard, *"Goddamn, a plane just crashed!"* over the scanner.

His actualities were once again used by the state news service, and had even been picked up by ABC Radio for national broadcast. He'd been paid for his recordings of the witness interviews by both, but neither chose to use his full *report* (of which he was quite proud and thought might be his ticket to the big leagues), most likely because it was widely opined that, as nice a guy as he was, Harvey's *voice* sounded like Roseanne Barr doing a bad imitation of Kermit the Frog. Or vice-versa. Behind his back, a variation on the old "face made for radio" insult had not infrequently been bandied about:

"He's got a voice made for print," his critics said.

Now, of course, the "big story" – the one that had made *all* the state and national news agencies – was the murder just over a month ago of rising country star Jared Whaley at *The Thirsty Turtle*. This was not only the biggest thing that had happened in Wilson, it had the potential to become even *bigger*, and for a longer period of time, as the trial for the alleged killer - the singer's wife (her name was *Angel* of all things) – was being held at the dilapidated Wilson County Courthouse, right on the Town Square, where long ago the Confederate Stars and Bars had finally come down, and where Harvey Boyd's own banner might conversely and propitiously rise.

CHAPTER SEVEN

I guess I should tell you about how I got into music, which means telling you about my childhood, which means hopefully not boring you to tears.

I was born in Southern California, but, like most Californians, was raised in neighboring Tulsa, Oklahoma.

That's a joke I used in my first-ever music-biz bio, which I wrote when I was in my early twenties. It was probably about the one million and sixty-seventh thing I wrote.

I absolutely have no recollection of not carrying a notebook around with me, making stuff up and writing it down. It started with little skits I would make my younger sister Sarah perform with me in front of the folks, the neighbors, pretty much anyone we could get to sit still for ten or so minutes. Seems like at first most of my dramatizations centered around Frankenstein or the Wolf Man. I was pretty keen on old monster-movies at that time. Can't figure for the life of me how I came up with plots involving just Frankenstein (me) or the Wolf Man (me) and one other character (Sarah), but they pretty much all concluded with me killing my sister.

So, in that respect, I guess I was a pretty normal kid.

Our father was a piece of shit Elvis wannabe, although he never had the balls to play for anyone but us, and then only when he was drunk. Mom dropped his ass like a red-hot anything-with-a-skirt-poker when I was eight, and we went on welfare and moved probably eight or nine times when I was between the third and sixth grades.

Sometime during that period I became a less-than-normal kid.

I withdrew into myself, fearing all that with which I never had a chance to become familiar – mainly other people – and thriving on that with which I was all-too-familiar – the inside of my own fevered skull.

Mom had it tough. Our father never paid child support (or

even tried to see us), and Mom was forced to work various secretarial jobs while using her significant female wiles to try to attract a man of suitable temperament and means to be a daddy to her kids, while also providing the love she desired and deserved. These failed attempts led to us being graced with the presence of some real losers, but also led to another little sister (Bella), then a little brother (Randall). So, all in all, it was a worthy and justified effort.

Unfortunately - albeit slowly - Mom's disappointments gave way to a bitterness that manifested itself mainly, it seemed to me, in an increasingly acrimonious attitude toward her little rug-rats. Praise and encouragement gave way to disdain and derision. I asked Mom about this one time (I was well into my adulthood and called her while I was drunk), and she defended herself, saying she always only wanted her children "to be the best they could be." When I pointed out that one of my most vivid memories was of her telling me I wasn't worth a shit, and never would be worth a shit, she hung up on me. I was still glad we had the little chat.

Needless to say, this pretty much constant (as I recall it) assault on what was already a pretty low self-esteem took its toll, and I retreated further into myself and my writing. I started a novel at the age of ten. It was a kooky affair having to do with a secret agent (I was hooked on James Bond), and was in my mind, of course, Pulitzer material, although I'm not sure I even knew what the hell a Pulitzer was at the time. When I was about fifty pages into my masterpiece, Mom found where I'd hidden it, and I honestly would have rather she'd discovered a stash of gay porn (although I didn't know what the hell gay porn was either).

"You have much better things to do with your time than to write this garbage," she'd said. I'd of course anticipated such fair and objective criticism – she'd been a lit major in junior college after all – which was why I'd hidden it in the first place. I never added another word to that manuscript.

I caught a break from her well-meaning malevolence a few

months later when I got hit by a car. Or, as the Tulsa World *reported, "stepped into the side of an auto." It ruptured my liver (which is one reason I suppose I so* pampered *that organ in my later years), and I was laid up and lavished attention and affection upon for nearly half a year afterward. My guess is that my coming so close to dying made Mom think that perhaps I* was *worth a shit after all. I spent my time convalescing reading* Mad Magazine, *Edgar Allen Poe, and listening to Mom's Elvis records. Sometime during these six months I developed into a pint-sized Elvis impersonator with a really dark, twisted sense of humor. And* that, *as they say, is when the trouble began.*

CHAPTER EIGHT

"HOLY SMOKES LAND SAKES ALIVE I NEVER THOUGHT THIS COULD HAPPEN TO ME!"

Willard sang from behind his laptop, a plate of pork chops, green beans, and mashed potatoes pushed to the side.

"God*damn it*, Boy!" Mack roared from the opposite end of the dining table, and would've added something equally eloquent had his son not interrupted him.

"Ah ha ha...YEAH! Ah ha ha...YEAH!"

Mack's face reddened and he seemed on the verge of spitting out the mouthful of food he'd managed just moments ago to bellow through, when, just as quickly as he'd started, Willard ceased his performance and quietly shut his laptop.

"Mmmm. Smells good, Mom," he said, setting the computer on the floor beside him and sliding the plate of food where it belonged.

"Thank you, honey," Elenore said, her eyes still glued to a reality show about what were purported to be "Real" housewives.

Mack's disbelieving eyes went from his tube-hypnotized wife to his calmly-eating son then back again.

"Goddamn it Elenore!" he shouted, startling both. "Did you not just *hear* that?"

Elenore seemed perturbed to have her show interrupted. Her gaze flashed briefly to her husband.

"He was singin' Elvis," she said, then, satisfied she'd fulfilled her conversational obligation, returned her attention to the flat-screen. Her fork – on automatic pilot – stabbed a few green beans and transported them to her mouth.

Willard's catatonic typing, punctuated on occasion by sudden non-sequitur outbursts, had, over the last few weeks, become rather the norm in the Blevins household. The abrupt paroxysms still provoked the ire of his father, but not so much because he didn't *expect* them as because he never expected any one *at that particular moment*. They startled the *shit* out of Mack, and it is a well-established male trait to treat any disruption of an unruffled demeanor as something to growl at, bark at, or beat to death with a stick.

But this was the first time the child had burst out in *song*.

"Goddamn boy," Mack said, chewing, looking toward the opposite end of the table as if through the big end of a telescope at his smaller image, also chewing. "Don't think you ever *sung* before."

Willard looked at him with the same expression that swept across his small, chubby features each time he was asked about anything related to what he did with the laptop open. He shrugged his shoulders.

"Dunno."

Mack had grilled his son early on about the strange goings-on between the boy and his computer. Willard maintained he had no idea or even *recollection of* what he typed, or the words he spoke while in the throes of typing, and that closing the gizmo apparently saved whatever he *had* been doing somewhere within its bowels, out of the reach of non-tech-savvy mortals such as the occupants of that particular domicile.

"Well, son," Mack said, "why don't you take that thing to one of your teachers and let *them* find it?"

"I don't think that would be a good idea, Dad," Willard shyly replied.

Mack then threatened to just take the damn thing *away*.

"I think things might *really* get crazy then, Dad," Willard said, his eyes down. Just the *way* he said it, the calm certainty of unspoken malignant ramifications, erased from Mack's mind any notion of going that route.

"All right then, psycho."

Thereafter - much in the way that the Fosters down the street had a kid who saved his boogers and shaped them into small sculptures - the Blevins had a kid who was possessed.

Why *any* spirit (much less the King of Rock – if that's who it *was*) would choose to occupy the laptop and body of his twelve-year-old son was a question for minds more inquisitive than Mack's. Besides, he hadn't missed a single minute of NASCAR in quite some time now.

"Hey Dad, guess what?" Willard asked, with all the enthusiasm of a momentarily *normal* child.

Mack was happy for the respite, and actually smiled. "Hmm?"

"We're going on a field trip Friday."

"Ahhh. Where you goin'?"

"To the radio station!" Willard was beaming, genuinely excited for maybe the first time since he'd made it to "Astromancer" in "Gothicus."

Mack reached with his fork, stabbed the remaining pork chop from the plate near the center of the table, and put it on his own plate.

"Well *that* sounds fun," he said, then picked up the chop with his hand and took a large bite.

"Yeah," Willard agreed, forking in a mouthful of mashed potatoes.

As he chewed, the glow on his face seemed to be replaced by an all-too-familiar blankness, and he spoke without swallowing.

"Gonna need a four gigabyte thumb drive," he said, the voice not his own.

Mack stopped chewing.

"Well fuck a bird."

Elenore seemed sense something out of the norm (*relatively*, that is), but not so much as to require a re-focus of her attention from a commercial for a free credit report.

"Huh?" she grunted.

"He's doin' the shit now without his goddamned *gizmo* open."

This got Elenore's attention.

"Shut the front door," she said.

"You can get one at Radio Shack," Willard-but-*not*-Willard intoned.

"Get a *what*?" asked his mother.

"A four gigabyte thumb drive," he repeated.

"A four what the *what*?" Mack asked. "What the fuck are you talking about, Wil…Elvis…who*ever* the fuck you are?"

Without the slightest change in his stony-faced expression, the boy still managed an exasperated sigh.

"*A four gigabyte thumb drive. At Radio Shack,*" he said, enunciating slowly.

"*Shut* the front *door*," Elenore said.

"Great," Mack muttered. *Now* this bullshit's costing us *money*."

CHAPTER NINE

Two weeks and four days after my sixteenth birthday, I stole my Mom's 1970 Pontiac Grand Prix and headed to Hollywood to be a stand-up comedian.

I'd decided that (and not being an Elvis impersonator) was my life's calling two years previously, when I'd started cracking up my entire ninth-grade Speech class with my funny-yet-twisted self-penned stories.

It wasn't until my sophomore year that I would discover the mind-altering effects of alcohol and marijuana, so - to my relatively pure fourteen year old mind - that laughter and applause, wrought from the adoring semi-masses by words that had come from my own imagination, were by far the most exhilarating phenomena to assail my pleasure-starved senses since I'd discovered masturbation. Which had never got either laughter or applause, thank God.

I'd had the idea of somehow combining my comedy with my Elvis impressions until late one Saturday night when I saw Andy Kaufman basically doing the same thing on national TV. So I'd shelved my mean renditions of "Hound Dog" and "I Got Stung" (complete with well-choreographed thrusts and gyrations) and decided that the stuff I'd made up completely on my own, without the distraction of Elvis, was the way to go. Speech class (and my teacher, Mrs. Stegall) had confirmed those notions, as had my first-place showing the next year in the school-wide talent show. That kinda sealed the deal. Or so I thought.

I started working a few hours on Tuesdays, Thursdays, and Saturdays at a little hamburger joint there in Tulsa. I absolutely hated it, but I was saving a little money, writing stand-up routines, and studying the craft of the comic, all the while planning my escape.

I got my driver's license on my sixteenth birthday, and four days later got a speeding ticket. That Grand Prix was not meant to only go twenty-five miles an hour (as the sign suggested), except as a necessary inconvenience.

The ticket was only forty bucks, but - since I was under eighteen - still required a trip to court. With a parent.

I'd become accustomed to my mother's wrath for things like forgetting to take out the trash, not cleaning all the peanut butter off the knife, and staying out past ten on Friday night, but the idea of confronting her with a speeding ticket - *official, documented* proof *that I was truly and irrevocably* not worth a shit *- sent a terror running through my veins. I don't recall what I imagined the punishment would be for such a transgression, but I wasn't sure it was something from which I'd ever recover.*

So when - on the night before I was due in court - I stole her car and headed west, I swear, Your Honor, it was in self-defense.

It was an interesting trip, an educational and memorable trip. The kind of trip it wasn't *was a trip to Hollywood. Remember when I earlier mentioned something about passion sucking at math? So too, apparently, do sixteen-year-old aspiring comic car thieves. I could've* sworn *that I'd correctly factored the cost of gas (I don't remember), the miles per gallon of the four hundred four-barrel Pontiac ('bout five – maybe eight on the highway), and the miles from Tulsa to L.A. (about fifteen hundred), into an equation that would result in approximately the amount of money I'd need to get from point A to point B, but somewhere along the line I'd stuck a decimal point in the wrong place, or perhaps left it in my other pants. When I stopped to fill up for a second time (not yet even out of* Oklahoma*), the math was easier and* much *more disheartening.*

Another factor I neglected to figure into my calculations was the cost of oil. Turns out, cars need that. I'd noticed a strange clicking *noise coming from under the hood for some time, but since the car was still cruising smoothly along, I figured it was something that didn't make a difference. Maybe I was just low on "anti-clicking" fluid or something like that. As an auto mechanic,*

I made a helluva comedian.

"Fill 'er up," I told the attendant at the little gas station off I-40 about halfway between Oklahoma City and the Texas panhandle. He was a funny-lookin' old fella, seemed to have lost some teeth that weren't important enough to replace, wearing coveralls and a backwards Texas Longhorns baseball cap. Being an Okie, that cap was enough to make me question both his intellect and *moral fiber. Being on E at* his *gas station was enough to make me refrain from questioning them out loud.*

"Sure thing," he said, sticking the nozzle in the gas-hole and clicking that doo-dad on the handle that keeps it pumping on its own. "Want me to check the oil?" he asked.

That didn't seem like a completely *uncalled-for question, and he was the expert, so I said sure.*

He limped a little to the front grill - on a 1970 Grand Prix about a quarter-mile from the gas-hole - and popped open the hood. I heard him whistling an unfamiliar, but more than likely country *song, as he pulled out the dipstick, wiped it with the rag hanging from his back pocket, re-inserted it, then once again pulled it out. I saw his wrinkled, puzzled face appear from around the open hood, look at me, shake his head, and disappear again. He'd stopped whistling.*

"What the...?" he asked out loud, I figured to himself, then heard the dipstick slide back in and out. Once again he peered around from under the hood and looked at me, this time not as much puzzled as annoyed. Then disappeared a third time.

When I saw him next he was walking around the front of the car toward me, holding my dipstick (or, to be more accurate, my Mom's *dipstick), looking outright* pissed off.

"Buddy," he said when he got to the driver's-side door, "You ain't got *no goddamn oil."*

I sensed from both his demeanor and the way he was shoving my Mom's dipstick in my face that this was a bad thing.

"Uh...fill 'er up?"

After paying for the gas, five quarts of oil, and getting (for free) a lecture on the cost of buying a brand-new engine for a 1970 Pontiac Grand Prix, I was once again on my way to Hollywood and the riches and glory anxiously awaiting my arrival. I was pretty sure I didn't have nearly enough money to get me there. I did, however, still have enough of a starry-eyed sense of destiny to believe that, one way or the other, fortune would smile upon me. You know, since it was meant to be. Perhaps I was thinking the rest of the trip was, literally, downhill. Not quite sure.

The next day, after driving non-stop ('cept for pit-stops) through almost equally non-stop rain, I hit the city limits of Albuquerque, New Mexico, about the halfway point between the land of repression and anxiety and the land of milk and honey and fame and fortune. I hadn't slept or showered for nearly forty-eight hours, and that kind of exhaustion and stink can somewhat sap a fella's optimism. Plus, I only had seven bucks in my pocket. So - like the swimmer who gets halfway across the English Channel before realizing he's too tired to make it and turns around and heads back - I conceded to that cruel bitch fate and turned around and headed back.

I ran out of gas somewhere near the Texas border, right where the picturesque panorama of the desert landscape rudely gives way to the boring-ass flatness of the armpit of the Lone Star state. I came to a stop on the shoulder of the highway on the outer edge of the armpit.

The sun was setting and I was too tired to walk anyway, so I crawled into the back seat and got some much-needed rest. I don't know what I dreamed about that night, but it sure the fuck wasn't fame and/or fortune.

The next morning, as I lay in the back seat of the Pontiac crying, contemplating my inevitable intro to the wonderful world of hitchhiking and, possibly, male prostitution, there was a knock on the window. It wasn't – as I imagined - the highway patrol come to arrest me for grand theft auto (I had little doubt my Mom had

*put out a warrant), but was instead the man who owned the
property along that particular stretch of I-40. I don't remember
his name, but he let me work on his farm for a few hours, loading
rotted wood from a torn-down silo into the back of his pick-up,
then gave me a good meal, fifteen bucks, and directions to the
Salvation Army in Amarillo.*

*I called Mom from there, and you'd've thought I'd survived
stepping into the side of another auto, such was the overwhelming
relief and, yes,* love, *in her teary voice. She wired me some money
and I limped home, fame and fortune hidden somewhere over the
horizon, waiting patiently to tease me, tempt me, cajole me, and
basically fuck with my life another day.*

CHAPTER TEN

Spring in Wilson, Tennessee sometimes comes in slowly, the gradually-warming temperatures not so much the advance of the new season as the grudging and halting retreat of the old. Other times – such as the year of the most bizarre trial *ever* - it starts melting Winter not long after the groundhog goes back to bed.

Spring had never been more sprung than on that day in mid-April when opening arguments began in the first degree murder trial of Angel Jessica Whaley. She stood accused of shooting her husband - rising country star Jared Whaley - in the head as he sat in the dressing room of *The Thirsty Turtle* in Wilson some two months before.

In a larger city – say, *Nashville* for instance – such a case would have been postponed and re-postponed, then perhaps delayed a little, until folks had nearly forgotten what all of the hubbub was about.

Not so in Wilson County, Tennessee. Judge Myra Way, the first woman to hold such a position in the county, was not the type to put off till tomorrow what could be done today. Besides, there was an election coming up in November, and *this* was a trial she wanted to be around for, whether it became a campaign tool or just a parting memory. Thus it was that, just over two months after the murder, they were about to get this show on the road.

A couple of things about this trial made it more sensational than your average Wilson, Tennessee courtroom fare: Firstly, no one even semi-famous had ever been *murdered* there before. This was a real thrill for the residents and a boon to the local media, as well as to the area hotels and restaurants that provided shelter and food for the *visiting* press. Secondly, there were some circumstances surrounding this case that either titillated or offended – depending on who you asked - the delicate sensibilities of the small-town South.

For Whaley had not only been shot *in* the head, the fatal

wound had apparently been inflicted as he was – to use a crude vernacular – *getting* head.

Vern Perkins, the Wilson County Sheriff's Deputy who'd been the first to respond to the "shots fired" dispatch (*"Goddamn, somebody's shootin' up the Turtle!"* was the exact communication), testified at the preliminary hearing that "upon entering the dressing room of the establishment," he found the decedent "with a massive gunshot wound to the head, his pants around his ankles, and his…uh…penis exposed."

The County Medical Examiner, Roger Humphries (who was also the town's veterinarian), testified that, yes, there *had* been saliva on the "…*uh…penis*," and that further testing concluded that the saliva did indeed belong to a *female*, which brought a collective sigh of relief from principles and spectators alike. The saliva just wasn't from the *accused*.

The significance of all this (and the factor on which the defense was hanging its hat in attempting to sow the seeds of reasonable doubt) was that – despite the defendant's presence at the scene, despite the murder weapon belonging to the defendant, despite the defendant's smudged *fingerprints* on the weapon and gunshot residue on her hand – no one *knew* who was responsible for the spit-soaked condition of the victim's trouser-trout. *That* particular witness had skedaddled into the melee that invariably ensues following the discharge of a handgun indoors, and hadn't uttered a peep since.

Judge Way ruled that there was enough evidence to hold a trial, and jury selection had commenced the next day.

As the defendant sat without bail in the Wilson County Jail (she'd waived her right to be present), the opposing sides went through the usual back-and-forth, finally selecting fourteen people – twelve jurors and two alternates – to take a couple of weeks off work and maybe get interviewed on TV.

The weigh-in was over. The bout had begun.

Harvey Boyd sat in the section of the courtroom reserved for the local press, listening to opening arguments, staring mainly at the back of the Defendant's head. By mid-afternoon he'd had all he could stand, and his pipe led him out of the courthouse and onto the front steps, where he gleefully lit up.

No recording devices were allowed inside the courtroom, and Harvey had never been much of a *note*-taker. He lived and died by audio, and if he had to leave his digital recorder in the car, he might as well leave his *ass* there too, at least until court adjourned for the day. For that was when County Prosecutor Haywood Brice and Marshall Laughlin - the high-powered Nashville defense attorney whose considerable skills had been purchased at great expense by the defendant's father (some publishing big-wig *also* from the metropolis to the east) - would hold a press briefing, proffering their polar-opposite assessments of exactly the same event.

Besides, Harvey thought as he walked to his car, his ol' buddy Warren Stills from the *Democrat* was there. Warren would fill him in.

Harvey sat in his dirty-red Grand Marquis, tilted the seat back, and turned on the radio. With his half-shut eyes glued to the Courthouse doors, he listened to his recorded voice reading the local news and death notices, wondering where the hell that "Kermit the Frog doing Rosanne Barr (or vice versa)" had come from. He thought his voice distinctive.

As he heard himself report that Monty Clark, 82, was *still* dead, the Courthouse's front doors burst open to an emerging crowd, followed by a staffer with a wooden podium, which he set facing outward at the top of the long flight of concrete steps.

Harvey removed his keys and reached into the glove box for his recorder. He put it into his jacket pocket, then pulled his lanky frame out of the sunken confines of the Grand Marquis' driver's seat, shut the door, and started walking.

He was thirty-eight, but with his boyish looks and short

blond hair (which helped to conceal the gray he knew lurked within), he could have passed for a decade younger. The utmost professional, he'd worn a suit and tie to work every day since he started at the station, with the rare exception of when the scanner awoke him in the middle of the night, and he skipped the tie.

In Wilson, Harvey knew just about everybody, and just about everybody knew Harvey. He was the type who *literally* never said a word about anyone if there was nothing good to say. Unless, of course, it was *news*.

In addition to being an all-around nice guy with a high-profile - if not necessarily lucrative - career, he was a handsome man, and it was widely speculated as to why he'd never married. Despite the rumor-mill being what it was, the gossip-mongers remained fairly civil in their discourse about Harvey, and the whispers of "gay" had died down almost as soon as they began. Further hypotheses seemed to be futile and just plain *boring*, so it was pretty much universally assumed that he simply hadn't found the right girl yet. Some folks are late-bloomers.

Harvey maneuvered around the TV people, overhearing a muttered, "Welcome to Podunk."

Harvey smiled. "Welcome to Wilson," he whispered, his smoldering pipe clearing a path through the crowd to a spot near the front. He retrieved his digital recorder and turned it on.

Marshall Laughlin came out first. He strode confidently, almost elegantly, to the podium, his silk suit impeccable, his longish thick-gray hair only slightly disturbed by the late afternoon breeze. When he spoke, his voice carried well and with authority, and one had a hard time believing – even though he *was* a lawyer – that a word of anything but the Gospel ever made its way past his lips.

"Ladies and gentlemen," he began, and everyone in the audience holding a recorder or a microphone – including Harvey – extended their arms toward him.

"Today is the first day of a trial which is a bold-faced

attempt to perpetuate a gross miscarriage of justice, by a system that places winning above all – and often does so at the expense of the grief-stricken and traumatized innocent."

As he paused to let the import of his words sink in, Haywood Brice, the Wilson County Prosecutor, emerged from the building. He tripped over the door-stop and nearly fell on his face - Jerry Lewis to Laughlin's Dean Martin - eliciting semi-muted laughter from the press corps.

Laughlin remained nonplussed.

"All too often, in this quest for a 'W' masquerading as a quest for justice, it is not the fault of a single individual, but of a system seeking optimum results for minimal effort. Why turn over every stone when what you find under the *first* stone fulfills the primary objectives: *expediency* and *economy*. Turning over stones is neither."

Harvey recognized this speech. It was, basically, a synopsis of Laughlin's opening statement. At least, Harvey *prayed* it was a synopsis.

"Please *God* get to the eyewitness," he muttered, under his breath.

"There is one unalterable fact in this case," Laughlin said, then paused again.

Harvey breathed a sigh of relief.

"We have an *eyewitness*," the lawyer intoned, his somber words blanketing the crowd.

This guy knows how to speak to an audience, Harvey thought, as he heard the reporter from the nearby *Thompsonville Gazette* say to another reporter, "That feller talks *real good*!"

"*We. Have. An eyewitness*," Laughlin repeated, slower, punching each word for emphasis. "How in the *world* can you prosecute a young lady for first degree *murder*, try to take away her *freedom*, maybe even send her to her *death*, when you *know* without a *shadow of a doubt* that there was someone *else* in that room who *knows exactly what happened?! How do you do that?!*"

Laughlin was getting worked up now, pounding the podium to underscore his main points, his hair only slightly more ruffled with each emphatic outraged jerk of his large head.

Then he paused yet *again*, this time to regain his composure.

"I'll *tell* you how," he said quietly. "You don't turn over *every* stone." He shook his head sadly. "Because you found all you need under the first."

There was a silence when he finished – extremely *rare* among the press. Harvey wondered for a moment if there might actually be a round of *applause*. Then – much more *common* among the press – every member of the throng (except Harvey himself) seemed to shout out simultaneous questions.

"Mr. Laughlin, what about the fingerprints?"

"What about the gunshot residue?"

"What about the murder weapon belonging to the defendant?"

"Is that hair for *real*?"

Harvey didn't know *where* that last came from, but none of the questions mattered anyway. Laughlin was gone, waving off a few of the more persistent reporters as he made his way down the sidewalk to his Lincoln Town Car.

Leaving Haywood Brice to follow.

Kinda like the Beatles opening for Tiny Tim, Harvey thought, and almost snickered. He'd never cared much for Haywood.

The County Prosecutor walked tentatively to the podium.

He was a wisp of a man in his early fifties, probably five-four, a buck twenty soaking wet, wearing a cheap suit and a bowtie, his wardrobe seeming to *beg* for a pocket protector. His hair was dark but thin, and he probably would have gladly welcomed even a few *gray* hairs to cover those parts where his scalp showed through.

He placed his briefcase atop the podium, allowing him to

hold on with both hands.

Harvey recalled that Haywood had let his assistant prosecutor - a newly-hired snazzy young man with an air of confidence, perfect teeth and perfect hair – deliver the opening statement that morning, but apparently the powers-that-be had deemed it prudent that the Brice be the face of Wilson County Justice to the media.

As Haywood began to speak, Harvey couldn't imagine *that* lasting long.

"An eyewitness," he began, his thin voice picked up and carried away by the mild breeze.

"We can't *hear* you!" someone shouted.

Haywood turned toward his assistant, embarrassed, and shrugged his shoulders as if to say, "I never signed on for *this!*" The AP smiled a perfect smile and gave his boss an encouraging thumbs-up. "You can do it!" he mouthed.

The County Prosecutor turned back to the podium and tried again, his voice somewhat stronger this time.

"An eyewitness!" he shouted. "The *Defense* in this case seems to be relying on an eyewitness that they don't even know what they saw!"

He was certainly more *audible*, but not entirely *comprehensible* to the crowd, and Harvey expected some of them to start booing and chanting, "Laugh*lin!* Laugh*lin!*"

Haywood grasped the podium tighter and leaned forward.

"Any of you ever hear of a little thing called *the Kennedy assassination?*"

This got a response. A *bewildered* one. Harvey was getting a kick out this now, observing the puzzled expressions on the faces of his comrades.

Not grasping that no reaction at all would be better than the one he was getting, Haywood pressed on.

"Well, there were *lots* of eyewitnesses that day in Dallas, weren't there?!"

He was greeted by a confused mumbling.

"But I'll betcha they didn't find *every* eyewitness though, did they?!"

A reporter to Harvey's left verbalized what Harvey had surmised many of them were thinking.

"What the *fuck*?" he whispered.

The perfect smile of the Assistant Prosecutor froze somewhat, making him look a bit like a Ken doll who'd just had a vibrator shoved up his ass, but didn't want to let on that it bothered him.

"And *yet,*" Haywood yelled, his confident gaze confronting the crowd.

"*And yet,*" he repeated, taking a page from Laughlin's public oration handbook, though, unfortunately for Haywood, it was a page blank except for the inscription "Use This Space to Doodle" across the top.

"*And yet a jury of his peers found Lee Harvey Oswald GUILTY of that crime!*"

Haywood leaned back from the podium and beamed, mistaking the shrieks of laughter washing over him as approval.

"Jesus Christ, this is going on fucking *YouTube*," Harvey heard from a giggling cameraman behind him.

The vibrator up Assistant Ken's ass appeared to have grown barbed wire as he leaned forward and whispered into his boss' ear. Haywood's self-satisfied grin disappeared in an instant, and he gave his underling a sharp, unpleasant stare.

"What?" he mouthed.

Assistant Ken leaned forward and whispered again, this time at a little more length.

"What?!" Haywood said, this time a bit more audibly. "Somebody *shot* him?!"

A terse nod.

"They shot the guy that shot the President?"

The County Prosecutor's underling's expression now said,

"There's a vibrator with barbed wire up my ass! Somebody get it out please!"

Harvey, who had plenty of experience maintaining a professional demeanor under hilariously adverse circumstances, wondered if he was the only one in the crowd close to peeing his pants. He didn't think so. His fellow journalists were doubled over, many hysterical, quite a few crying, one actually shouting out, "Oh *God* I'm gonna pee my pants!" as Wilson County Prosecutor Haywood Brice closed his briefcase, glared at the scene below him, and bellowed at the top of his light-weight lungs.

"She's *guilty!*"

Then, saving his last malicious stare for Assistant Ken, he turned and stormed back inside.

CHAPTER ELEVEN

Six months after I turned nineteen years old, I moved from Oklahoma to Tennessee. The day I arrived, I learned how to play "Heartbreak Hotel" on the guitar.

But I'm jumping ahead a bit.

During my senior year in high school, I'd decided I was gonna be a singer in a rock and roll band. My little halfway-to-Hollywood misadventure the previous year hadn't made me give up *on being a comedian - I was* still *cracking 'em up in Drama class and at the occasional school assembly – but it* had *opened my young mind up to other options. In fact, it was* at *one of these assemblies that I first witnessed the mesmerizing and totally* awesome *power of music. Although "totally awesome" was still a good two decades from making it into popular vernacular.*

I had just got off stage, wowing the crowd with my little story about falling in love with and marrying Agatha T. Cat (the T *stood for "The") - and was standing in the wings, still basking in the just-faded laughter and applause, feeling a bit smug, when a handful of the "long-hairs" got up and played "Free Bird." Being a Barry Manilow and, yes, still an* Elvis *fan, I had never heard the song before. Looking back from the perspective of a music vet, I can only surmise that the hippies' rendition was mediocre at best, but* HOLY CRAP *did they steal the show! The crowd of probably four hundred was on its feet, cheering like CRAZY, many holding up lighters I'm pretty sure they weren't supposed to have, and I thought from my quiet spot offstage that these guys – these* musicians - *could immediately have underage sex with* any *of the luscious underage girls in the audience that morning – many of whom* I'd *fantasized about having underage sex with. Funny I say "underage." That's one of those words that, like "incontinence," doesn't even* appear *in the vernacular of a teenager. Funny I say "incontinence."*

I left school that day and bought a Lynyrd Skynyrd album, the one that was kind enough to provide the phonetic pronunciation of the band's name, and which had "Free Bird" as the last cut. I also bought the Eagles, Foreigner, Bob Seger, and Styx, and for the next six months or so spent many hours in my room trying to learn to sing in a decidedly non-*Elvis fashion. I turned out to be not too shabby at impersonating the stylings of Ronnie Van Zant, Don Henley, Bob Seger, and those guys that sang for those other groups. I forget their names.*

Over the next couple of years I tried to start a couple of bands, got laid for the first few times (the latter completely *unrelated to the former – I might've mentioned that), and developed a substance-abuse problem.*

Then out of the blue one day I got a call from my father. Then *I moved from Oklahoma to Tennessee and learned to play the guitar.*

I'd been working at a convenience store when my sister Sarah (who was by then eighteen) had called and told me she'd managed to track down our paternal grandmother, who had spent an hour grilling her for the details of the last decade of our upbringings, then another *hour absolutely* swearing *that our father's absence during that time had been not* his *fault, but* Mom's.

Being the somewhat-still-impressionable youth that we were, with the memories of Mom's potential for spiteful malignance much fresher in our minds than those of a father who had disappeared at a time in our lives when Santa Claus still seemed like a completely reasonable concept, we about half-way bought it.

Four days later, instead of reaching out to my sister, his daughter, *the one who had reached out to* him, *he called* me. *Apparently me being his first-born, and also a* son, *raised me to the top of his must-make-amends list. The male ego can be an ignorant and narcissistic creature.*

Although I hadn't heard it in over half of my life, I recognized his voice immediately. It was a soft, slightly gravelly voice, with a slight Oklahoma twang, a voice that seemed at once honest and sincere, which you also sensed had the potential for mischief, but not one which you would ever suspect could be harsh or angry.

In short, it was my *voice. So I instinctively knew that the latter part of the above description could be* misleading *at best, purposely and with mal aforethought* deceptive *at worst. But I didn't care. It was still my voice.*

He told me that he'd been a stupid young man. That sometimes it takes throwing everything away to really *appreciate what you had. I quoted Kristofferson:*

"Freedom's just another word for nothing left to lose," and he not only got *it, he countered with another quote from a song.*

"You got to know when to hold 'em, know when to fold 'em."

This was kind of fun, so I continued.

"I'm the only Hell my Mama ever raised."

He got a good chuckle out of that one. Then he got a bit more serious and Dad-like.

"You raise a lot of Hell, son?"

That was the first time I'd been called "son" by a man who actually meant it literally *in as long as I could recall. I almost cried. Then I told him about the ill-fated trip west, my ridiculous beer consumption over the last couple of years, my seeming tendency toward self-destruction.*

He told me how he could relate. How he'd always felt he had that same tendency, how it had manifested itself in his drinking and womanizing, driving away Mom, losing me an' Sarah. How, when he'd lost it all, he'd left Oklahoma and moved to Tennessee to pursue music, then never really got around to it. How he'd struggled through so many part-time jobs before landing a full-time gig at a boot factory, how by the time he'd made enough money to start sending some to Mom, she'd told him she didn't want *it if it meant letting him back into our lives.*

Funny I'd never heard that story.

Then he told me how, when I'd stepped into the side of that auto, it had made the state-wide news, and his mom, my Grandma, had let him know, and he'd flown to Tulsa to see me. And been told by Mom that if he so much as stepped a foot into that hospital, she'd have him arrested for non-payment of the child support she'd told him she didn't want.

I did cry then, finally - a mournful wail for a childhood that could have been so different, tears for the lonely chime of an un-un-ring-able bell, resounding over a landscape of lost fishing trips, ball games, guitar lessons, all existing in a desolate parallel universe of "what-ifs."

As I poured out my grief, then my hopes and aspirations, then my belief – ingrained by my mother – that dreams were unattainable for a man who was "not worth a shit" (and never would be), I didn't realize Mom was in the kitchen, quietly listening to my interstate confessions while I sat on the carpeted stairs.

When my father and I finished our conversation, promising to talk again soon, I hung up and walked into the living room, where my mother sat with a glass of Scotch, smoking a cigarette.

"Sounds like you need to move to Tennessee with your shit-ass of a father," she said quietly.

"What?"

"Because you're not spending another night in this house."

While my mother's tirades had terrified us kids throughout our lives, we also knew it was when she was quiet – like a lioness before the kill – that she was the most deadly. So I knew she was dead serious.

Those were the last words my Mom and I exchanged for three years.

I called my friend Bill to come pick me up, packed my shit, and went to his house. From there I called my father. Two days later watched Oklahoma vanish in the side-view mirror.

CHAPTER TWELVE

Like a *Starbucks* or a *McDonalds*, almost every town has a *Radio Shack*. In Wilson, Tennessee, it was located on the Town Square. Next to *Starbucks*. Mack Blevins parked his new Ford F-150 in the handicapped space in front, hauled his girth out, and lumbered inside.

The bell on the door jingled as he entered a world every bit as alien to him as a health-food store. He gave the displays of cell-phones, digital cameras, and stereo headphones barely a glance as he waddled to the sales counter, where Clay Cavett, the store's manager and sole employee, greeted him with a smile.

"How ya doin' Mack?"

Mack grunted, looking at the array of thingamajigs and whatchamacallits hanging on the wall behind the counter. He'd gone to high school with Clay, but the two had never been friendly. Clay had run with the "nerds" crowd, while Mack had been part of the "rednecks" clique (which he would've spelled "click" if he'd ever had to - but he hadn't). The closest Clay and Mack had ever come to a conversation in school was when, outdoors on cold winter days, Mack would flip Clay's exposed bright-red earlobes, and Clay would say, "Ow! Cut it out!"

Mack got to the point.

"What the fuck's a thumb drive?" he asked.

Clay flushed at the language and looked around, making sure no other customers had heard and taken offense. Since there *were* no other customers, none had.

"Uh, well." He opened the sliding door on his side of the long glass display case, reached in, and retrieved one of several types of the small plastic-and-metal devices.

"Here we go," he said. "They're also called 'flash drives.'"

Mack didn't seem to care.

"I don't care," he said. "Is that a *thumb* drive? Four giga…something-or-other?"

Clay was used to politely ignoring such small-town

hospitality.

"Yes sir. Four *gigabyte*. They're called 'thumb drives' 'cause they kinda look like a thumb." He held the device up to his own thumb. "See?"

"Yeah," Mack said. "I don't care. What do they do?"

Clay sighed, trying to figure out how to explain the technology.

"Well…basically they allow you to copy files from one computer onto another computer."

"Huh." Mack shrugged. "Oh well. How much are they?"

Clay sensed, more important than a *sale*, a rapid conclusion to Mack's visit.

"Eleven ninety-nine," he said. "But you can have *two* for twenty-four bucks," he added, instantly regretting his attempt to humor such a humorless oaf.

"You tryin' to jack up the price on me?" Mack said, glaring.

"No, no, of course not Mack. That was a little joke."

"Huh. You're funny." He seemed to consider it for a moment.

"Okay," he said. "Might as well give me two. I don't wanna have to come back in here."

That makes two *of us,* Clay thought, ringing up the sale, wondering if any of this had anything to do with what Norville had told him last week at the barber shop.

CHAPTER THIRTEEN

There's a distinct possibility I owe my success in music at least in small part to the numbing-yet-exhilarating effects of marijuana.

The day before my falling-out with my mother over the phone call from my father, I'd used what turned out to be my last check from the convenience store to buy a quarter pound of pot. My plan had been to become a dope dealer, which I figured was a much niftier way to make a living than ringing up gas and oil and beer and Coke and Ding Dongs.

All of my friends smoked it, so all of 'em bought *it. I calculated that, at forty dollars an ounce (the going rate then – referred to by cannabis users old enough to remember as "the good ol' days"), I could turn a nice profit and still maintain a personal stash.*

All those plans went up in smoke (tee hee) when Mom kicked me out of the house and I moved to Tennessee, where I had *no friends, and thus no buyers. So, beginning my first day in "The Volunteer State," I began a nightly ritual of waiting until my Dad and his third wife – a thirty-something hottie named Janine – went to bed, then getting high and learning Elvis songs on the guitar. Had I not been stoned, I'm not certain I would've been able to tolerate the significant pain that comes with pressing steel strings down as hard as you can onto the fretted wood of an acoustic guitar neck. It* hurts.

After I'd breezed (or floated on a cloud) through the Elvis songbook, picking up hard-earned calluses on my fingertips along the way, I wrote my first song. I'd figured out which chords seemed to always go together, figured out the various song structures (generally verse-chorus-verse-chorus, verse-*verse*-chorus-verse-chorus, *or* verse-chorus-verse-chorus-*bridge*-verse-chorus) *and dove right in. Though I'd been writing for as long as I could remember, I'd done very little* poetry, *which is all songwriting really is. Writing is writing is writing. It's a lot easier to find words that rhyme when you just happen to know a lot of* words.

That first one was called *"Matter of Time," and had to do with my being destined for fame and fortune. Many of my early songs had this theme. Or a partying theme. Or a sex theme. Not many love songs in that initial batch, probably because I didn't care too much about love.*

While I sang the Elvis songs with my "Elvis" voice, I found myself singing my original compositions with more of a Bob Seger-meets-Ronnie Van Zant kinda delivery. I was still a few years away from finding my real *voice, which ended up sounding more like John Prine-meets-Willie Nelson-meets-Merle Haggard. Kinda. I'm pretty sure all those fellers* met.

After nine months, I'd written quite a few songs and thought it was time to get famous. Nashville was about forty-five minutes south of where we were (near the Kentucky line), and seemed maybe a bigger nut than I was quite ready to crack. So I found a local recording studio (whose owner was also a music publisher - anyone *who can fill out a little paperwork can become a music publisher, by the way), and made an appointment to come play a few songs.*

There's a scene in the movie "A Christmas Story" where little Ralphie has to write a theme entitled, "What I Want for Christmas." Of course, what he wants is that damn BB gun, even though everyone knows he'll shoot his eye out. You've seen the movie. Ralphie writes what he thinks is not only the best theme he's *ever written, but perhaps the best theme in the* history *of themes. He envisions his teacher reading – in the midst of all the* crap *she has to trudge through –* his *masterpiece, having an almost orgasmic response to his wonderful succinct eloquence, and giving him an A++++++, which is followed by an outpouring of adulation from his classmates, who carry him victorious around the room on their shoulders. When cold, cruel reality rears its ugly head (and reality is an ugly-head-rearin' motherfucker),*

Ralphie gets a C+, along with a written admonishment that he will, indeed, shoot his eye out.

That kind of sums up the beginning of my music career.

My appointment with the studio owner (I forget both the name of the studio and the name of its owner – let's call him "Dick" and call his studio "Dick's Studio") was set for 4 that afternoon. Due to a lack of funds and opportunity, I'd for all intents and purposes been on the wagon since I'd arrived in Tennessee, although I'd've probably found a way to get beer if I hadn't had a quarter pound of weed to smoke all by myself. By this time, however, the pot stash was up in smoke and I seriously could not envision going to this appointment without some sort of mind-alteration. Fortuitously (or maybe not), I'd done some yard work for my Dad the previous day, and had a twenty in my wallet to show for it. So, I grabbed my guitar and my notebook and took off in Janine's Chevette at 1:30.

I immediately drove to the nearest convenience store and picked up a six-pack of Bud – tallboys, no less – and went to the park by the lake. It was a bit out of the way, but it's where I knew that people my age sometimes went to drink and make noise, both of which I planned to do.

I found a fairly secluded picnic table and proceeded to prepare myself for my destiny. I didn't realize it at the time, but I was beginning what would become a life-long tradition of never playing without at least a modicum of inebriation. I didn't even take the guitar out of the case until I'd finished my first beer and felt the familiar beginnings of a buzz. It had, after all, been awhile. I played through a couple of the four songs I'd selected to showcase my astonishing – almost prodigal – way with words and music during beer number two. By Bud number four I had no doubt that this would be a day that Dick and I would always remember, and which would go down in the annals of country music history.

I finished off the six-pack about 3:30, and seriously

considered whether I'd have time to pick up some more and maybe run through my set one more time. Dick wouldn't mind if I was a little *late. I changed my mind only after attempting to put my guitar back in its case backwards.* Not face-down *backwards – that would've been understandable and at least physically* possible *- but with the wide body of it in the narrow part where the neck goes. Which was just stupid.*

It was not, however, my stupidest *moment that day. Not by a long shot.*

I'd practiced driving drunk plenty of times in Tulsa, and practice does indeed make perfect. It would have been more *perfect if I'd practiced driving drunk with a stick shift. I didn't* completely *strip all of the Chevy's four gears getting out of the park, but I* did *manage to knock over a trash can, one of the picnic benches, and put a slight dent in the Men's Room door (and the rear bumper of Janine's car) before I finally got my act together and hit the highway.*

Twenty minutes later I was introducing myself to Dick. I believe my first words to him were, "Hi Jared, I'm Dick." Something like that.

His first words to me were, "Geez dude, have another beer.*"*

To which I distinctly remember replying, "Don't mind if I do." Hey, it's not my *fault the studio was right next to a Piggly Wiggly. Or that they sell beer.*

I seem to recall that he seemed anxious for me to play. Not because he figured I was the second drunken coming of Hank Williams, but probably simply because I was the first *drunken coming of* me, *and the sooner I* played, *the sooner I'd* leave.

I removed my guitar from the case (recounting to Dick the hilarious tale of when I'd last *put it* in *the case), took a long drink of beer - which he didn't so much* frown *as* scowl *upon - and played "Matter of Time."*

I performed with an honesty and heartfelt sincerity only

six-and-three-quarters tallboys could provide. Sure, I messed up a chord-change or three, and, sure, I at one point sang, "A tatter of mime." But still, it was a hell of a song. As I neared the end of my auspicious debut, I finally gathered the courage to open one eye and witness what I was sure would be an expression of absolute awe on Dick's dumbfounded features.

What I in reality witnessed was that I was awing and dumbfounding only my stupid dumb self.

I heard the toilet flush, and Dick emerged from the restroom, wiping his hands on his pants.

"Thanks for coming by," he said.

Four years previously, when I'd hit Albuquerque with only seven bucks in my wallet and realized fame and fortune in Hollywood wasn't in the cards, I'd wanted to shake my fist at the Heavens and curse the unfairness of destiny-denying Fate.

"Fuck you, Fate!" I'd wanted to scream. "You ass-wipe piece of shit slimeball motherfucker!"

I hadn't, however, and it may have been because I wasn't drunk enough. Such was not the case that day at Dick's Studio.

"Fuck you Dick!" I screamed. (Whether his name was "Dick" or not I still can't recall. I'm pretty sure that's what I called him though. And I did shake my fist.) "You ass-wipe piece of shit slimeball motherfucker!"

Then I put my guitar back in its case on just the second try, grabbed my notebook and my beer, and stormed out the door.

Where I discovered I'd locked the keys in the Chevette.

In retrospect, I guess this was a good thing, for on my first outing as a songwriter - my inaugural foray into the wonderful wicked world of the business I would come to love and loathe, to see as a blessing and a curse - I didn't get both humiliatingly rejected and a DUI. I just got humiliatingly rejected and arrested for public intoxication.

CHAPTER FOURTEEN

Harvey Boyd was not a happy camper. Not only was his morning show (which he hated doing under the *best* of circumstances) going to the dogs - he'd already read the death notice of a geezer who was put in the ground last week, announced a song by Taylor Swift as having been sung by Brad Paisley, and announced partly cloudy skies only to look out the window and see a downpour – *now* he had to deal with a dozen or so damned *kids* waiting as patiently as is typical of sixth-graders (which is to say *im*patiently) in the station lobby with their teacher, waiting for a tour. Harvey found little solace in the irony of the fact that, for the first time in as long as he could remember, he actually wished the morning show could go on just a little *longer*. But duty called, and he had always been, if nothing else, a duty-doer.

Harvey clicked a mouse and put the station on automatic pilot for the remaining ten minutes of the show, following which he'd have to come in and read the local news, do the weather, then put the station *back* on auto until the noon news, death notices, and the twenty-minute "Buy and Sell" show.

He looked through the glass partitioning Studio A from Studio B, then beyond through the back window of Studio B into the lobby, where a motley crew of he guessed mostly twelve-year-olds was staring back at him.

"Lord give me strength," he muttered, then put on a smile, exited the studio, walked down the carpeted hallway, and greeted the waiting visitors.

"Hi kids!"

There was a mixed cacophony of mumbled acknowledgements and indecipherable grunts, until their teacher, Mrs. Jameson (he'd known her since quite a few years ago when she'd been Lori Ragland and he'd briefly dated her older sister Mindy) asserted her authority.

"Children, how do we say 'good morning' to Mr. Boyd?"

"*Good MORNING Mr. Boyd!*" came a chorus of young

voices, with one anonymous "Whassup?" followed by a few giggles and a glare from their teacher.

Harvey smiled, wishing he was somewhere else. Maybe getting a root canal.

"First of all, you kids can call me Harvey." This got a quick, tight-lipped shake of the head from the former Miss Ragland. Harvey mentally rolled his eyes.

"Well, as you probably know, this is the radio station, WTOR. Can anybody tell me what those letters stand for?"

Silence.

"Kids, it's '*Wilson Tennessee's Only Radio*,'" offered Mrs. Jameson, at which point a young red-headed girl's hand popped up.

Harvey smiled. "Yes young lady?"

"No it's not," the youngster said. "My Mom always listens to WSIX. They have funny people on there."

"Now Jenny…" the teacher began, before Harvey spoke up.

"Those guys *are* funny, aren't they?" This got a nod not only from Jenny, but from probably a third of the other students.

Nice to know nobody listens to me, thought Harvey, then *said*, "Well, WSIX is actually in *Nashville*, but their *signal* reaches here. WTOR is the only radio station that actually *broadcasts* from Wilson."

Which means we actually care that you exist, he said to himself, then thought, *although right now I kind of wish you* didn't.

"Have any of you kids ever *been* in a radio station before?" he asked, hoping for and getting no response. "Well, let's take a look around."

Thankful for the conclusion of the awkward "greeting" segment of the visit, Harvey led the group back down the hallway and into Studio A. With the two computer monitors, broadcast console, and the U-shaped table upon which everything sat, there was barely enough room to hold the entire class. Harvey walked into the inside of the U, stood by his chair in front of the console and microphone, and motioned for the kids to file around to both sides of and behind him. He indicated the equipment.

"Back when I started, we used to have record players in here. Anybody know what *those* are?"

Again, silence.

"Well. Nowadays, just about everything is done with computers. This…" - he pointed to the "on-air" monitor -"is what shows what song is playing, what song is coming up next, and when the commercials are going to play."

Currently, Montgomery Gentry was singing something inane about something inane.

"See?" He turned up the volume, demonstrating to the group that what was displayed on the computer screen was indeed the song being broadcast. He had hoped for some semblance of fascination – or even *interest* - but apart from a fat kid clutching a laptop behind him, staring raptly at least in the *direction of* the flashing lights and modulating meters, he might as well have been…well, a *teacher*, such was their level of ambivalence. Their *own* teacher seemed no more attentive than *they* were. She was smiling at her phone, texting.

"What's *that*?" It was the fat kid, pointing toward Harvey's open laptop on the table a couple of feet from the "on-air" computer monitor.

Harvey laughed.

"Well, young man, you should *know* what that is. You've got one too."

The other children looked toward Willard, his laptop held tight to his rounded belly, and tittered.

"But what do you *do* with yours?" Willard asked, shyly but with an air of stubborn determination.

"What do you do with *yours*?" one of the other students asked, which got another round of giggles from the rest of the group.

"Well, *actually*," Harvey began, looking at the clock.

Three minutes to news-time. "I do a *lot* of radio station stuff on it. I write commercials, I email listeners and clients and the other folks that work here at the station, and I write the news that you hear every day."

Or the news that you don't *hear, I guess.*

"Speaking of which, I've got to go on the air in just a couple of minutes, so I'm going to let you guys go into Studio B, and you can watch through the window. Does that sound like fun?"

As soon as he asked the question, he regretted it.

"Let's go into the other studio." He looked expectantly at their teacher, who looked up mid-text and got the hint.

"Come on, children."

She herded them out of the smaller studio and through the adjoining door of the much more spacious Studio B. Harvey followed them into the room and flipped a switch on a wall speaker, filling the air with the toe-tapping strains of Kenny Chesney, who was singing about living in fast forward and needing to rewind real slow.

"This is what's playing on the radio right now, and when it's over I'm going to be doing the news!"

He said it with far more enthusiasm then he felt, and was relieved to shut first the door of Studio B, then the door of Studio A, and get into place behind the microphone. He lifted a pair of headphones from the table and placed them on his head.

Harvey left the broadcast computer on auto as Kenny's song faded then segued into the news intro, complete with the requisite teletype sound effect.

"AND NOW, FROM OUR STATE-OF-THE-ART BROADCAST FACILITY IN BEAUTIFUL WILSON, TENNESSEE, IT'S TIME FOR YOUR LOCAL NEWS WITH HARVEY BOYD...."

Harvey clicked from auto to manual mode as the sound of the teletype faded, then turned on the microphone.

The "On-Air" light above the studio door flashed on.

"Good morning, it's seventy-one degrees with scattered showers at 10 a.m. I'm Harvey Boyd with your local news...."

The top story was, once again, the ongoing trial of Angel Whaley for the murder of country singer Jared Whaley. Following a full day of opening arguments, the prosecution had opened its case yesterday by calling Vern Perkins, the Sheriff's Deputy who'd not only had to deal with the trauma of being the first responder to a scene of splattered brains and exposed genitalia, but also had to recount the event literally ad nauseum, first at the preliminary hearing, and, yesterday, at the trial itself. As Harvey reported the story (requiring the use of the terms "genitalia" and "brain matter"), he couldn't help but think the school could've requested a better day for a field trip. He *did* notice, however, that he had the little munchkins' attention.

"On cross-examination by defense attorney Marshall Laughlin," Harvey continued, "Deputy Perkins further testified that, in addition to the fatal wound, there was also a bullet hole in the wall near the ceiling, and conceded that there was no way to know if both shots had been fired by the same perpetrator. He also acknowledged that no eyewitness to the crime itself had come forward."

Harvey thought his report engaging and concise (and virtually unrecognizable from the *Democrat* story he'd re-written), yet still wondered how many listeners would say to themselves, either out-loud or silently, "Huh?"

Oh well, it was a complicated case.

"And we'll have more local news after this."

Harvey clicked the broadcast computer back on auto for the two-minute block of commercials followed by the ninety-second "Farm Report," and removed his headphones. Quite satisfied he'd given his young audience in the adjoining studio something to tell their parents about, he nearly skipped from one room to the other. He opened the door and poked his head through.

"What'd ya think kids?" he asked.

The same red-headed girl who had bruised his ego earlier once again raised her hand.

"What's 'genitalia'?"

Too enthused by their now-rapt attention to spoil it with an awkward moment, Harvey punted.

"Mrs. Jameson can tell you all about that. Gotta get back to work."

Harvey once again nearly skipped – but at a quicker pace – back to Studio A. He didn't really have anything to *do* for another couple of minutes, but busied himself pretending to do something important on his laptop, enjoying the scene through the glass of the harried teacher facing an onslaught of curious young faces and waving raised hands.

During a normal news cycle in Wilson, the top story would have been followed by something completely unrelated, probably a public service announcement ("the Red Cross is having a blood drive Saturday") re-written so as to appear to be *news* ("County officials have reported a critical shortage of blood…"), but nowadays there was nothing *normal* about the news cycle, and the coverage of the trial invariably bled over (so to speak) into the next segment.

Thus it was that Harvey continued after the break:

"In other Angel Whaley Trial news, prosecutors also called to the stand yesterday Jamie Kindle with the Tennessee State Crime Lab, who testified that the murder weapon – a .38 Smith & Wesson snub-nose revolver found at the scene and registered to the father of the accused – had the defendant's smudged fingerprints on it, and that the defendant had tested positive for GSR – or 'Gunshot Residue.' On cross-examination, defense attorney Laughlin seemed to focus on the term 'smudged', pointing out that synonyms for that word include 'defiled', 'sullied', and 'tainted', and asking Kindle if the possibility existed that someone other than the defendant had handled the weapon. Kindle indicated that the possibility was remote, as no other partial prints were found on the firearm, but conceded under pressure from the defense that it *was* possible. Following the day's proceedings, Laughlin spoke to reporters."

Harvey clicked, and Laughlin's recorded melodious intonation filled the air.

"The prosecution in this case, in its effort to attain victory regardless of the interests of real *justice*, is traipsing down the path of least resistance, bombarding the jury with that which was uncovered beneath the first stone turned. Yet we made it clear during this first day of testimony, and will *continue* to make it even *clearer* in the upcoming days, that, without our missing eyewitness, the true facts of this case *cannot* be known beyond a shadow of a doubt."

Harvey sensed that this was going to be a theme. He continued his report.

"Following Laughlin's statements, Assistant Prosecutor Ken Fleming spoke to reporters." Harvey had been *delighted* to discover on the second day of the trial both that County Prosecutor Haywood Brice's perfect-hair-and-teeth assistant actually *was* named Ken, and that his prediction that Haywood would be relieved of his media relations duties after the fiasco of the first day proved accurate. Fleming had been *immensely* more poised than his boss. Harvey once again clicked a mouse.

"The Defense in this case is grasping at straws," Fleming was heard to say. "Straws that they are trying to weave into gold."

While his *oratory* skills were no match for Laughlin's – his voice was a bit higher-pitched and not nearly as *smooth* – his *content* at least was in the ballpark.

"We believe that we showed the jury today, and will show them in the days ahead, that the principle of 'Occam's Razor' – that all things being equal, the simplest answer is most often the correct one – holds true. The defendant had motive – her husband received oral sex from another woman; means – it was *her* gun; and opportunity – we will prove in the days to come that she *was* in the room. Who this *mystery woman* was has no bearing whatsoever on this case, and the defense's attempt to convince the jury otherwise is but a masterful charade by a masterful attorney.

"There was a very famous trial years ago where a guilty defendant was set free after just such a smoke-and-mirrors defense. *That* Defense used the catch-phrase 'If the glove doesn't fit, you must acquit.' *We refuse* to allow such trickery and gimmickry to sway this jury of twelve intelligent Wilson County citizens. *Our* case rests on the simple fact that if it walks like a duck and quacks like a duck, you've probably got yourself a duck."

Harvey thought this argument *much* better than Brice's "Lee Harvey Oswald was convicted" line. Though not quite as *funny*.

He wrapped up the news by needlessly informing the listeners that the trial was continuing, then giving the weather forecast ("continuing rain"), then signing off. He put the broadcast computer back on auto, removed his headphones, rose from his seat, and walked back into Studio B.

"All right, kids, that's it for the news. How 'bout we go upstairs and see where all the *business* is done at the station?"

The oh-so-inquisitive little red-headed girl's hand shot up again.

"What's 'oral sex'?"

Harvey once again deferred to Mrs. Jameson, then led the group up the carpeted stairs to the offices.

CHAPTER FIFTEEN

The first time I went to Austin, Texas, I got there with my thumb.

My Dear Old Dad, who less than a year earlier had decided to atone for the abandonment of his family in his previous life, had, upon further consideration, come to the conclusion that perhaps a drunken wannabe-musician was more than he was psychologically equipped to deal with, either because or in spite of the fact that he'd arrived in Tennessee himself as a drunken wannabe-musician.

Following what he referred to as my "incident" at the studio, he'd bailed me out of jail and brought me home, cursing me all the way, swearing that he'd "more than made up" for bailing on me and Sarah all those years ago. I found that to be rather self-serving and delusional reasoning, and, still pretty damned drunk, told him so, which didn't exactly help smooth things over. What also didn't smooth things over was when, upon arriving back at his house, I'd greeted his hottie wife Janine by grabbing her ass and kissing her on the mouth.

Come to think of it, that may have been the reason he kicked me out.

I could've gone to Nashville. It was much closer, and had everything I figured any aspiring country star needed – record labels, publishing companies, bars to play in, a homeless shelter – but for some reason my first brush with the music business in Tennessee had left a bad taste in my mouth. I figured a cross-country hitchhiking trek to a place known more for its live music than its music business might be just the ticket to allow me to hone my skills as a writer and performer.

So I packed my backpack, stole my Dad's Fender, and split, with twelve bucks in my wallet and dreams of fame and fortune - plus the beginnings of a nasty hangover - in my head.

Hitchhiking in the eighties was a far cry from what – so I'd heard – it was in previous, more trusting decades. It took over an hour of walking down I-65 with my thumb out in the rain to get that first ride, which got me to the city limits of Nashville.

Funny dynamic about hitching with a guitar in Tennessee – if you're headed toward Music City, you're perceived as an optimistic dreamer; if you're headed out of Nashville, you're perceived as a desperate loser. I was perceived both ways the same day, and may be one of the few guitar-bearing hitchhikers to have ever thumbed it right through the city. Not sure how I was perceived while within the city limits, but it wasn't as someone who needed a ride all that bad. I ended up walking just over twelve miles, the skyline becoming a hazy outline in the distance, before I got my second ride - from a trucker headed to Mobile, Alabama. This was not only my first ride in a big rig, it was my first time to get propositioned by a man. I had a feeling that, being a fairly good-looking guy, it might happen, but a gay trucker kinda seemed to go against stereotype.

Fortunately, he didn't make his move until we got to a truck stop in Montgomery.

"How 'bout a blow job?" he asked.

As we'd just spent several hours talking about sports and pussy, this question – plus the strange lustful look in his eyes – caught me somewhat off-guard. I also didn't know if he meant that he wanted a blow job or wanted to give one, but that was just an irrelevant technicality, 'cause even if I had been gay, he would've still been way too ugly for my taste.

"Uh..." was how I answered, grabbing my guitar and backpack and hastily exiting the cab. I think he called me something unpleasant as I walked away, but, hey, I wasn't the ugly gay trucker. I let it slide.

An hour later, after the cheapest meal on the truck-stop's menu (which left me with eight bucks and some change), I found myself back on I-65 with my thumb out. I got a ride about an hour later from a half-drunk construction worker in a pick-up truck, on his way home from a late job. He also propositioned me, and I thought about the Village People, and figured at some point I'd be getting a lift from a Goddamn gay Indian Chief. He pulled over quickly upon my rejection, and I barely grabbed my guitar and backpack from the bed of his truck before he was gone.

I was, thus far, not enamored with this whole hitchhiking thing.

It ended up taking two more days and fifteen more rides (fortunately only two of which involved having to turn down advances from the non-vagina-bearing gender of the species) before I got to Austin, Texas. I was let off right by 6th Street, the heart of the Live Music Capital of the World, which, coincidentally or not, happened to be just two blocks from the Salvation Army.

What can I say about The Sally? It was a big white building with a red tile roof that attracted the most destitute drifters, dreamers, roustabouts and ne'er-do-wells one could imagine. Fortunately, I only had to stay there one night.

That day I met Wayne, a prematurely gray silver-tongued devil down from Boston due to some legal difficulties he preferred not to discuss, but which I found out about later. Wayne was nattily-dressed and seemed out of place at the Sally. After talking with him for ten minutes, I figured a more fitting environ for him would be persuading some Eskimos that they really needed some ice, and that he was just the guy to sell it to 'em. He would've made a killing.

I broke out my stolen guitar on 6th Street my second night in town, after I'd rested up from my long journey, had a couple of crappy but free meals, and used my remaining money to buy a sixer. Wayne and I had become fast friends, and, at first, I played just for him - a couple of guys havin' a couple of beers, me sitting on the window-sill of a tattoo parlor, Wayne standing idly on the sidewalk.

The police in Austin had much better things to do than hassle folks with open containers on the sidewalk, and they would rarely deign to get off their horses (yep, on 6th Street all the cops were on horseback*) unless you were raisin' quite a ruckus.*

There were musicians on the sidewalk about every hundred feet or so, just far enough apart so that we weren't drowning each other out, and you really had to do something different *(and* good*) to catch any of the passer-bys' attention for more than a minute or so. So, as I said, it was mainly just me playing songs for Wayne at first.*

I started out with my original material. This was, after all, my destiny*, the foundation upon which I would soon build my lucrative music career. Wayne was more polite than Dick in Tennessee had been (he didn't have to go to the bathroom until the* third *song), but still seemed more interested in introducing himself to the frequently-passing young honeys as they strolled from one bar to the next, than he was in hearing my music. His understated-but-unique pick-up line was, "Hi. I'm Wayne from Bwah-sten." Rarely – yet more frequently than Wayne got any response from the passing beauties – someone (and on occasion a* couple *of someones) would stop and listen for sometimes as long as two minutes before moving on. I was all in all disappointed and somewhat disheartened, but the beer made it better.*

After about an hour, Wayne paid close enough attention to one of my songs to offer some constructive criticism.

"You should play something somebody's fuckin' heard before," he said.

And that's basically how I resurrected my career as an Elvis impersonator.

The first cover song I played was the first song I'd learned on the guitar, "Heartbreak Hotel." There was a well-but-casually-dressed middle-aged couple passing by, both with the buoyant glow that epitomizes the carefree character of vacation and its inherent alcohol consumption. They stopped immediately, smiling, and listened as I played the song. My guitar skills were still rather rudimentary, but my Elvis skills were sharp, having been honed since my (it seemed then) long ago childhood. They

*enthusiastically clapped and tossed a five-dollar bill into my open
guitar case.*

*Thus, at the age of twenty, on a street in Austin, Texas, a
far cry from the desolate dream-filled yearning days of my youth in
Tulsa, I became – for all intents and purposes – a professional
entertainer.*

*After I'd played "Heartbreak Hotel," "Suspicious Minds,"
and "Love Me Tender," (and attracted a rather large crowd), I
gathered up my beer-and-applause-inspired courage and actually
stood up, threw the guitar strap over my head, and began playing
"Jailhouse Rock," this time with the accompanying jerks and
gyrations I'd perfected as a kid.*

*As my nearest competitor – a Rastafarian-looking
character three doors down – was warbling Springsteen and
Mellencamp and Bon Jovi (all artists selling millions of records at
the time) to practically no one, I was channeling a dead guy who's
last number one hit had been in the last year of the sixties to a
throng that, by "Hound Dog," was starting to spill from the
sidewalk onto the heavily-travelled street, my guitar case littered
with ones and fives and a stray ten, weighed down by quarters and
dimes.*

Tee hee. "Channeling a dead guy." I kill *me!*

*I made $89.23 the first night of my show-biz career, and,
since Wayne and I had long-since missed the last available bed at
the Sally, I used the money to get us a room at the cheapest hotel
within walking distance of 6*[th] *Street, which was an Econo-Lodge
over the Congress Street bridge (which crossed over the Colorado
River, called "Town Lake" as it ran through downtown). I bought
us a twelve-pack of PBR and a dime bag of weed from a guy we
ran into en-route, and we sat up till the wee hours, getting drunk
and high, talking about the glorious potential of our new-found
association.*

*Wayne was, as I mentioned, a natural-born salesman, and
he declared that night that he wanted to be my manager. Although*

72

I knew that I could easily make as much as $89.23 without his help, I quickly and enthusiastically agreed. I'd never had anyone have confidence in me, and I'd never had the confidence in myself to actually represent me to others.

Plus, he had some pretty good ideas. I'd worn my sideburns long since I was old enough to have sideburns, but he thought I also needed to cut my hair (Elvis never had a ponytail) and dye it from its current reddish-blond to black. He also suggested we hit the Goodwill store and see if we couldn't dredge up some sort of appropriate attire. I doubted Goodwill would have a white-sequined jumpsuit, but he figured they would have something more fitting than blue jeans and a Bob Seger t-shirt. I couldn't argue with that logic.

A part of me – the part that wanted to make it as a singer/songwriter – was a little overwhelmed with this complete reconfiguration of my dreams, and I told Wayne, but he convinced me that I'd have all my days free for writing and developing that particular not-yet-profitable talent while I made enough being Elvis to not have to get a gig at Whataburger. It didn't take much convincing.

He also told me the reason he'd left "Bwa-sten." Heroin. Apparently he'd picked up a nasty habit there, had stolen some stuff to get the stuff, and left just over a month previously, before a couple of warrants had a chance to catch up to him. He convinced me (Wayne was a convincing fella) that he was clean now, and that pot and beer were more than enough to satisfy his hungry demons. Having had no experience with the hard stuff, I believed him. I wanted to believe him.

The next night on 6th Street I by-passed playing my original stuff (and sitting down) and began right away with the full-blown thrusting and twitching and gyrating Elvis. Once again the crowd quickly grew, but this time Wayne worked it, encouraging if not cajoling spectators to toss money into the guitar case, and by the time I quit playing two hours later we'd raked in $148.52. I gave

Wayne twenty percent (we rounded it off to thirty bucks) and we got another room at the Econo-Lodge, more beer, and another dime bag. I had enough left to go the next day to the barber shop, where I got my hair cut and dyed, and to the Goodwill Store, where we found a black leather jacket and black leather pants, all for less than forty bucks. As they say in today's vernacular, the game was on.

If I needed at least three beers to feel courageous enough to so much as strum my guitar on the street, to do so in full Elvis get-up took a whole six-pack. I felt like a dork, but not nearly the dork I would've felt like sober.

I opened my guitar case, to the inside cover of which I had that day affixed a BIG-ASS TIP JAR *sign, strapped on my guitar, and played "Heartbreak Hotel." The crowd gathered quicker and tipped better with the added visual. I by no means looked* anything *like the King – I was shorter and had gaps between my teeth – but the fact that I could actually sing and move like him made me seem, compared to the other sidewalk entertainment options on 6th Street, like a Las Vegas headliner. The horseback cops that night actually had to warn people not to stand too far out in the street, but did so between shouting out requests.*

That night at the Econo-Lodge, Wayne and I got drunk and high and discussed ways I could spice up the act. Although I could impersonate his speaking as well as *his singing voice, the King had never really been known for his between-song patter, and I mainly had kept it to the requisite "Thank you very much." So I mentioned to Wayne how when I'd first started doing Elvis as a kid, I'd tried to combine the songs with comedy bits. Wayne thought this idea a hoot. Apparently, he'd missed Andy Kaufman on SNL.*

I took out my notebook and started writing:

"I was in bed with my girlfriend last night, reached for the KY Jelly and accidentally grabbed the Preparation H. Talk about your 'Burning Love.'"

"My girlfriend said she'd wear my ring around her neck. So I strangled her."

You know, that kinda thing.

Since there was no way to come up exclusively with jokes that referred to Elvis songs, I threw in a few of my old favorites:

"What's the difference between an oral and a rectal thermometer? The taste."

"What's green and yellow and eats nuts? Gonorrhea."

That kinda stuff.

By the end of that first week we were bringing in at least two hundred bucks a night. Wayne had to periodically gather up and arrange the bills and stick 'em in his pocket to keep a gust of wind from scattering them down the street.

We figured at this point we could probably afford a pretty swanky two-bedroom apartment, but neither of us had references that were worth a damn, and Wayne didn't want anybody checking too closely on him period. So, being the salesman that he is, Wayne went to an agency that worked with the Sally finding housing for the indigent. Despite the long waiting list (and the fact that we hadn't actually been staying at the Sally), he managed to convince the administrator there that we were more deserving of immediate assistance than everyone on the list ahead of us.

Wayne never told me explicitly, but I got the feeling he told 'em we were gay and under a constant threat of bodily harm from our fellow Sally-ites. Just a hunch, based upon the fact that he'd said, "I'll bet if I told 'em we were gay and under a constant threat of bodily harm from our fellow Sally-ites, we'd get bumped to the head of the list." Whatever he said, it worked, and two days later we moved into a furnished one-bedroom apartment that was ours, all bills paid, for three months.

The next few weeks flew by in a haze of beer, songwriting, beer, Elvis, beer, and pot. And beer. I'd begin each day with a couple of cups of coffee, then pop my first top somewhere around noon and start writing songs, sitting on the couch (which was my bed) while Wayne slept in the bedroom. I wrote at least one song a day, sometimes two, before it was time to take a nap, then head to 6th Street, buy more beer, and earn our daily bread. Sometimes I played more than two hours, but rarely, as I seemed to have developed a window of prime performing opportunity wherein I was drunk enough to give it my all, but not drunk enough to mess up the words. Like the King himself was known to do – via pills, not booze - during those last days before he dropped dead on the toilet.

Our "room" was bounded by 6th Street out front and Trinity a half-block to the east, and we were packing the joint. It was Wayne's job to milk our audience for as much of their money as they were inclined to give up before they got to one of the bars they were headed to in the first place to give up their money. One night we made just over three hundred dollars, but were generally happy with the hundred-eighty to two-twenty range. As we had no rent or bills to pay, much of our not-so-hard-earned funds went to enjoying ourselves, which we did immensely. The part of my eighty percent that I couldn't find a way to blow, I stuck in a savings account.

We spent our post-show hours hopping the bars, trying to get hot chicks to come back to the apartment with us (Wayne succeeded on several occasions – I never did. I might've mentioned that), then staying up till three or four or five, partying.

The sky seemed to be the limit, but limitless skies develop storm clouds. My particular cumulus came in the form of Dexter, a massive bald part-Mexican who, with his semi-attractive girlfriend Kim, moved in next door toward the end of our second month at the apartment.

Dexter happened to walk by our open door as we were having one of our regular late-night parties. He invited himself in – and no one was gonna tell him he wasn't invited – either because of my lovely rendition of a tender ballad I had just written or because we were all drinkin' beer or (most likely) because he smelled the wacky weed we had just finished smoking.

To say Dexter was strange would be kinda like sayin' Rosie O'Donnell's ugly. It captures the essence but doesn't quite do it justice. (I don't much care for Rosie O'Donnell – even if I did, she'd still be one butt-ugly broad.) Dexter was psycho. And really seemed to enjoy our company. Or our pot. Which was funny (but not in a "ha ha" way), because Dexter was a drug dealer. He didn't deal weed obviously, otherwise we wouldn't have had the honor of his presence every freakin' day.

Nope, Dexter dealt heroin. What are the odds a heroin dealer would move in next door to a recovering heroin addict? Looking back on it, I think maybe God had a problem with my Elvis.

Three days after meeting Dexter, he sat in front of our TV, high on our pot, and detailed an elaborate fantasy he had of torturing and killing his mother. Four days after meeting Dexter, Wayne stole his stash of heroin, shot up, and fucked Kim. Hours after that (wanting to be neither a witness to nor a victim of a homicide), I took a cab to the bank, then to the airport, bought a ticket, and flew the fuck out of Dodge. To Nashville.

CHAPTER SIXTEEN

Harvey Boyd was now less of an *unhappy* camper than he was a *puzzled* and *mystified* camper. A *perplexed* and *befuddled* camper. Somewhat bewildered and discombobulated even.

The Sixth-grade class from Davy Crockett Middle School had left about a half-hour earlier. It hadn't been, Harvey thought, *too* awful an experience, though he was quite grateful it was over.

Harvey had wrapped up the field trip by showing the kids the upstairs offices, introducing them to Anne, an account executive, and to Betty, who handled bookkeeping and traffic. Their offices were nothing more than glorified cubicles that just happened to have walls extending to the ceiling, so the class and their teacher had been stacked up behind Harvey in the hall as he made the introductions and Anne and Betty in turn briefly explained what their respective jobs were. Harvey got a modicum of satisfaction from the fact that the rug-rats seemed even more bored *upstairs* than they had been *down*. He mouthed a silent *"Sorry,"* to each of his co-workers as they concluded their little talks.

It wasn't until they got into station owner Jack Dawes' spacious corner office – the only one large enough to hold the entire tour – that Harvey noticed they had a student missing.

"Um…Lori," he started, then corrected himself. "Mrs. Jameson? I think we're missing one."

The teacher's mouth opened in a mixture of surprise and dismay as she surveyed the group.

"*Willard!*" she said, giving a name to the student Harvey had mentally referred to as *"Fat Kid with Laptop."*

"I'm *so* sorry…I'll go find him," she assured both Harvey and Jack, leaving the office and heading down the hall.

"Well, kids," Harvey said, "This is Jack Dawes. He owns the radio station."

Jack, a fifty-something, heavyset man with a gray goatee, a few wisps of gray hair, and a pair of bifocals perpetually perched at the end of his long nose, was kicked back in his large cushioned chair, his hands clasped behind his head, his feet propped up on his desk. Apart from the few times Harvey had seen him entering or leaving the building, this was his standard pose, although he *would* take his feet down when he had to lean forward to pick up the phone.

"So what d'ya think kids?" Jack asked the group, and received, as Harvey had expected, a mixture of noncommittal murmurs and dead silence.

"Well then," Jack said, then paused – somewhat awkwardly Harvey thought, considering this was a man *never* at a loss for words. "I *own* WTOR, which means I basically hire and fire people and sign checks."

If Jack thought this would *impress* them, their silence was disillusioning. He attempted to break the ice.

"Harvey, you're fired!" he said, then laughed.

This got some giggles from the students as they looked at Harvey, their eyes wide.

Harvey played along.

"Yes, sir. I'll pack my things."

This got a few more snickers, as Harvey headed toward the door.

"Naw, I'm kidding," Jack said, then addressed the kids. "If Harvey left I'd have *way* too much to do. He's one of our most valued employees."

Harvey stopped at the door and turned back to his boss, winking at the class.

"In that case, I need a raise."

This got some laughs and even a gasp from the now-attentive onlookers.

Jack laughed again, and was about to retort when the little red-haired girl raised her hand.

"Yes young lady?" Jack asked.

"What's 'oral sex'?"

Jack's bushy-gray eyebrows shot up and he looked at Harvey, once again at a rare loss for words.

"The report on the trial," Harvey explained.

"Huh," Jack grunted. "Great day for a field trip."

"I thought maybe her *teacher* could field that one."

"Good idea," Jack replied, then rather brusquely addressed the children. "We just *report* the news," he said. "We don't *explain* it."

With that, he put his feet down, reached across the desk for the phone, punched a button for an outside line and dialed a number, effectively concluding his participation in the field trip.

"Okay, kids," Harvey said. "Let's go back downstairs and see if we can't find your teacher."

As he ushered the class out of the office, his boss said into the phone, "Whadya *mean* we need more cooking sherry?"

Harvey led the group down the hall and reached the top of the stairs as Lori climbed the final two steps, her arm around a contrite-looking Willard, still clasping his laptop like a security blanket.

"Oh good," Harvey said. "You found him."

"He was in your *studio*," the teacher whispered.

Harvey was momentarily alarmed.

"He wasn't *on the air*, was he?"

She shook her head quickly. "No, no, no," she said, and Harvey breathed an almost audible sigh of relief.

"He was on your *laptop*."

"Well *sh...ucks*," Harvey said. He looked at Willard, who was staring silently at the floor. "God. There's some *really* important stuff on there."

He started down the stairs, the class following, Lori and Willard just ahead of him. He leaned slightly forward.

"What was he *doing*?" he murmured to the teacher.

"He was closing it up when I got in there. I asked him and he just shrugged."

They reached the lobby.

"Willard." Harvey put his hands firmly on the boy's shoulders and turned him around. Willard continued staring downward.

"I'm not mad at you buddy," Harvey said calmly. "I'm just curious what you were doing with my laptop, when you've got one of your own."

Willard looked up, finally. He shrugged.

"Dunno."

Harvey didn't see any point in pressing further. He'd find out as soon as they left.

Which he had. And now he was puzzled and perplexed, befuddled and mystified. Bewildered and discombobulated even.

He'd opened his laptop to find a Word document, thirty-seven pages in the first person, which began with a dissertation on Heaven and Hell and religion, then evolved into what seemed to be a diary or journal of some sort.

Harvey had never *seen* this before, so the conclusion was obvious and inescapable that the fat kid...Willard...had uploaded it. The question therefore was *why*? And what the hell *was* it? Clearly, the *child* didn't write it. He was probably only twelve years old, and the writing – overrun with slang and colloquialisms and a healthy dose of profanity – was obviously that of an *adult*, and a fairly bright one. This kid was *neither*.

Harvey pulled his pipe from his pocket and stuck it, unlit, between his lips. He often did this at work, comforted by the familiarity and the faint flavor and aroma of the tobacco which through years of use had insinuated itself permanently into the wood and plastic. He'd hated it when the radio station had banned smoking indoors some years ago, but figured it was probably better for him, and *definitely* more economical.

He continued to read.

Why in the world...what *in the world*...

Four pages in, Harvey's teeth loosened their hold on his

pipe, and it drooped somewhat as he read the writer (a musician of some sort) describing the beginning of his affair with a girl named "Angel."

Well that's just wacky, he thought. *That's the name of the defendant in the…*

His pipe fell from his mouth, bounced off the laptop keyboard, and clattered to the floor as he read, *"Not sure I've mentioned this, by the by, but that's my name. Jared Whaley. Pleased to me ya, reader."*

Harvey thought of something his Grandfather used to say: "What in the name of *Sam Hill?*"

Harvey paraphrased his Grandfather, out loud but to himself, alone in Studio A.

"What…the…*FUCK?!*"

He picked up his pipe, then continued reading.

CHAPTER SEVENTEEN

How ya likin' it so far, dear Reader?

I know I didn't lead the most exciting *life, though I anticipate it's not so much the life* itself *as it is the timing of the telling that's got you so interested. I was going to wait until it was done before I let my host…my* ghost writer *(now that's a HOOT!) show it around, but there's a little trial going on that may not exactly come out with the best interests of* justice *being served if I don't speak up.*

I'm maybe the only writer to ever write his life story knowing in advance how it ends. You know, specifically. *But that ending is still a ways off. I trust you'll bear with me.*

I arrived in Nashville with just over five thousand dollars and looking – despite my jeans, t-shirt, and ball cap – way too *much like Elvis. But then again, that's how I wound up with five thousand bucks.*

I could've stayed in Austin, got my own place, and continued making a helluva living on 6th Street, Wayne or no Wayne. But I felt like I had written some pretty good songs, that I had a real shot at making it as a country songwriter, and that I'd rather be Jared *Whaley than* Elvis *Whaley. Plus, with five grand, I figured I might be able to afford to live for six months, during which time I was pretty sure I could get a songwriting deal. Silly me.*

I didn't know a soul in town, so I gathered up my suitcase and my guitar from the baggage carousel and caught a cab to a nearby HoJo, where I bought a newspaper, got another free *paper* – the Nashville Scene – *from a rack inside the door, ordered breakfast, and began reading. I perused the* Scene *first, 'cause it had all the live music venues' schedules, and I figured I'd find the best club for songwriters and try to find a place near there.*

My waiter at the HoJo – with his scruffy beard and tattoos – looked like he might be a starving musician or songwriter himself, and, since the restaurant wasn't too busy (it was that quiet time between the end of breakfast and the beginning of lunch), I struck up a conversation.

"So it looks like The Bluebird Café *is a pretty happening place for songwriters."*

His nametag said "Chad," so I assumed that was his name.

"Oh dude," he said, refilling my water. "Pretty much every songwriter in town *plays there. That's where Seth Rivers got discovered."*

Seth Rivers was a country singer/songwriter who, in the two years since he'd signed with Capitol Records, *had almost single-handedly made country a mainstream genre.*

"Wow," I said, my finger trailing to the Bluebird's listings in the Scene. *"So where's Hillsboro Road?"*

"Green Hills. A few miles kind of west of downtown. You just follow 21st Ave. South, till it becomes Hillsboro Road, then the Bluebird's on the left just past the mall."

Since I'd be cabbin' it most places at first, his directions were kind of irrelevant, but I didn't let on.

"Any apartments out that way?"

Chad paused in thought a moment. There was only one other customer, a middle-aged guy drinking a cup of coffee at the counter.

"Yeah, quite a few," he said, crossing to the Bunn to grab the coffee pot and give the guy a re-fill. "But it's kind of pricey out there. Lotta rich folks."

He put the coffee pot back in its place and returned to my table.

"I just got here from Austin," I told him, "So I don't really know what 'pricey' means."

"Hmmm....," he looked at the ceiling as if there were "for rent" listings up there. "Probably a one-bedroom'll run ya three hundred a month."

I quickly did the mental math. If I paid six months' rent in advance, I'd still have about three grand to pay other bills, buy some food, and keep myself beered up while I familiarized myself with the Nashville songwriter scene. I didn't want the headache of a car (or the risk of DUI's, 'cause I knew *I'd be getting drunk on a regular basis), so figured if I got a place within walking distance of the Bluebird, I could kinda make that my home base and just catch cabs or – if absolutely* necessary – *ride the city bus. Or maybe I'd make friends with some songwriters with cars. I surmised such creatures* existed.

"Very cool, Chad, thanks," I said, opening up the newspaper to the "Apartments for Rent" section. Chad lingered a moment.

"So," he said. "You a songwriter?"

"I am indeed," I replied. "You?"

"Nah." He looked around, saw that the place was still nearly-empty. "I'm a guitar player. Moved here from Tulsa six months ago to try to get some studio work."

It is indeed a small, weird world.

"Guess where I was raised?" I asked him.

His eyes widened.

"Tulsa? No shit?!" He turned his head to see if the guy at the counter had caught his profanity. If he had, he didn't seem to care.

"Wow. That's crazy*!" he said.*

"Yep. Graduated from Edison."

His eyes widened again.

"No fucking shit!"

This time he didn't turn to see if his only other customer had heard. This time the guy had, *and gave a disgusted glance in our direction.*

"I dropped out *of Edison."*

"Jesus. Small world," I said, thinking, Jesus, it's a small world.

"You need to give me your number before I leave. We'll

have to get together and play."

"Hell yeah," he replied eagerly, then paused, taking in my sideburns and hair from underneath the cap.

"I don't know too much Elvis," he said, writing his name and number on an order ticket.

I laughed.

"That was another life."

Four hours later I was signing a six-month lease on a furnished efficiency apartment in a space above the detached garage of an old house just three blocks from the Bluebird. As Chad had guessed, the rent was three hundred a month, and even though it was smaller *than a one-bedroom, it was all-bills-paid.*

The apartment had a fridge, a stove, a microwave, a sofa-bed, and a recliner, plus an end table, a small coffee table, and a small dining room set. Everything an aspiring country star needs.

The owner of the house was a forty-something good ol' boy named Burt, who just happened to be an aspiring songwriter himself. He'd been a little leery about my lack of references, but the big wad of cash I pulled from my pocket when I offered to pay six months' rent in advance seemed to ease his mind.

"Hot damn, I'm getting a boat!" is how he phrased it.

Burt, like many songwriters, was also a pothead, so he told me up front he didn't have any problem with that. In fact, he proceeded to sell me a quarter-ounce for fifteen bucks.

I smiled, thinking how handy it would be to have a weed-dealer landlord, but not as much as I smiled when Burt's daughter came bounding down their front-porch steps, all smiles and blond hair and short-shorts and long tanned legs and a tank top from beneath which untethered ta-tas bounced in unison like a couple of fat guys on a trampoline.

"Daddy," she said in the sweetest southern twang I'd ever heard, "Who's this?"

That look of wariness of any father with a beautiful

daughter crossed Burt's face, followed immediately by a quiet sigh of resignation.

"Kristi, this here's Jared. He's gonna be stayin' in the apartment."

She assessed me with a cute smile.

"Can I borrow some blue suede shoes?"

Jesus. *I was either gonna have to dye my hair or shave my head.*

"I had a gig in Austin...Elvis impersonator. Not really my thing though."

"You a songwriter?" she asked.

"Aren't they all?" Burt smiled (revealing a space where a tooth used to be), I think to let me know that he couldn't hold it against me, but that I didn't have a snowball's chance in Hell.

"Well." Kristi smiled. "I guess I'll be seein' ya at the Bluebird."

"Ah," I said, happy as a fly on shit. "Are you a songwriter?"

She and her Daddy both laughed.

"Hell no,*" Burt answered, as if I'd asked if his daughter was a hooker (and how much?). "She's a waitress."*

"A server, *Daddy," she said, correcting him with the fairly-new non-chauvinistic term for women who bring you food and drinks while wearing shorts and low-cut tops in an effort to entice bigger tips from us chauvinists. At least I* hoped *she wore shorts and a low-cut top, and that I could resist the urge to stick a five-dollar bill in her cleavage – an urge I was resisting at that* moment.

I didn't know it then, of course, but I had just been introduced to the woman who would mother my children.

"The doors open for open-mic in about an hour," Kristi said. "You should come play."

Forty-five minutes later The Bluebird Café *and I came into one another's lives.*

Its appearance belied its reputation. It was in a strip mall, sandwiched between a dry-cleaners and a furniture store, a baby-blue awning adorned with its logo - combining a musical note and, of course, a bluebird - sticking out over the entrance-way.

I was probably the twentieth person or so in a line that stretched from the still-locked door, virtually everyone holding a guitar case, many wearing cowboy hats, most chatting it up with the person in front of or behind them. I had walked over with Kristi (she was, Glory be to God, wearing shorts and a low-cut top), but she had gone in the back employees' entrance, so I was in line solo.

I heard a voice behind me.

"So where ya from?"

I turned and faced a guy with stringy-brown hair, probably a few years older than me, a backpack slung over his shoulder, holding a guitar in one hand and a can of PBR in the other. I liked him immediately.

"Well, I actually just got here today from Austin, but I was raised in Tulsa.

"Ah, cool. I'm from Tallahassee, but I've been here four months already. Name's Gary."

He clinched the lip of his beer can between his teeth and extended his hand.

"I'm Jared, Gary. Pleased to meet ya."

Gary leaned out of the line and surveyed the entrance.

"They probably won't unlock the door for another five minutes or so. Think you got time for a cold-beer?" He said "cold-beer" as if it were just one word.

"Yes!" I said that as if it were just one word, too.

Gary sat his guitar case down, unzipped his backpack, and produced a can of liquid Heaven.

"They don't sell PBR in there, and their Buds are two bucks a pop," he said, handing me the beer.

I popped the top and took a long swallow. My first beer in

Tennessee since my eight or nine or ten that had got me in such trouble just less than three months and half a lifetime ago.

"Well, I'll be glad to buy you one once we're inside," I told him.

"I might just take you up on that. I seem to stay pretty broke."

"So how does this work?" I asked him, nodding my head toward the front door. "You just sign up and play?"

He took a drink and nodded.

"Pretty much. Just put your name in the basket. You'll get a number, and if it's less than...usually about twenty-five, you'll get to play two songs. If you don't get to play, they'll give you a stamp on your sign-up slip, which you can bring back next time. They pick the ones with the stamps first, so you'll be guaranteed to play then."

I thought I understood, but wasn't quite sure, so I just nodded and took another long drink.

He looked behind us, where another fifteen or so people had joined the line since I got there.

"I'd say we'll probably get to play tonight, but it all depends on how many people have the stamps."

At that, the front door was unlocked and opened (by Kristi herself – I felt a thrill completely unrelated to music, unless it's the kind of music you hear in a porn video), and the line quickly moved indoors. But not so quickly that Gary and I didn't have time to finish off our PBR's, depositing the empty cans in a trash bin by an outdoor ashtray by the door.

Once inside, I was surprised at how small the place was, and how quickly it filled. Gary showed me the spot to the far side of the stage where you put your guitar (mine and Gary's were among the very last that would fit), then led me to the line to the basket - on the end of the bar that lined one side of the room - where each aspiring country star wrote their name on a slip of paper (except those with the stamped slips, who just tossed them into a separate basket), then moved either to a table or a seat at the bar or one of the wooden pews located to one side of the sound board.

I signed my name, threw the slip in the rapidly-filling basket, and turned to face Kristi, her smile beaming, her blue eyes twinkling. I tried and failed to not give a quick-but-appreciative glance to her soft-yet-firm and oh-so-inviting cleavage.

"I reserved you a table in my section," she said happily, and I more than happily followed her to a small table to the side of the stage.

"What'll ya have sweetie?"

I noticed Gary waiting at the bar. He hadn't got his beer yet.

"Give me two Buds, please."

"Be right back sweetie," she said, pivoting on one heel and heading toward the bar. I kept my eyes on her ass even as I raised my voice and beckoned Gary, who turned from the bar and found me, hand waving, motioning him over.

He smiled widely and made his way through the crowd.

"Wow," he said. "How'd you get a table?"

"Our waitress is my landlord's daughter." I pointed at Kristi, now at the servers station at the far end of the bar.

"Holy Moly," he said. "She's hot!"

I heartily concurred, mentioning something about her sparkling personality and physical assets (though not necessarily in that order) until she returned with our beers and set them down, telling me she'd just run a tab.

Then the host of the writers night took the stage and everybody in the room shut up.

She was about thirty or so, a tall girl, with broad shoulders and dark hair. She began by welcoming all of us to the "Monday Night Writer's Night at the Bluebird Café," introducing herself as Beth Lloyd, and telling us that there were thirty-eight writers that night, so some people would probably not get to play, but would get a stamp, blah blah blah.

She then announced the basic rules: have your guitar tuned and ready to go, introduce yourself with your number, play two original songs (but try to keep your stage time to eight minutes), tip your servers and bartender, and shut the fuck up.

I'm paraphrasing the last part, but the Bluebird's motto – it was on their banner across the back of the stage as well as on their menus – was "Shhhhh....."

Then she read the list, with occasional applause scattered throughout, I guess for the folks who had brought friends.

I knew I wouldn't be near the top of the list, due to that "stamp" thingy, but when she got to number fifteen, I started getting nervous. I just thought it would suck to not be able to play, considering how seemingly serendipitous my day had been so far, what with the finding a place so quick and the pot-dealer landlord with the smokin' hot daughter and the what-not.

Number eighteen was "Gary Mathis," and I caught on from my new friend's reaction that that was him.

Plus, he said, "That's me."

I started to think, Well, at least *one* of us gets to play, *but before I could finish the thought, Beth read, "Number twenty-one, Jared Whaley."*

Gary looked at me and gave me the thumbs up, and I heard Kristi from across the room yell out a quick, "Yay!"

I was really hoping she felt the same way after *I played.*

Beth continued reading the list up to number thirty-eight, then said that anyone from number thirty on could go ahead and get their stamps now, or could trade numbers with someone, buy somebody's number…*(this got a few scattered laughs)…however they wanted to do it.*

Then, at exactly ten minutes after 6, the show began.

I wasn't sure what to expect from the writers in Nashville. I'd heard that it's like a 50,000-to-one shot to ever be able to actually make a living *playing and/or writing there, but I'm pretty sure I heard that from someone pulling a number out of his ass. Even though I had been playing to crowds for nearly the last three months and had now written about eighty or so songs, I still feared that – compared to the songwriters I was about to hear – I was a relative novice.*

I needn't have worried.

I coined a phrase that night I'd use many times throughout the rest of my life, whenever I heard somebody singing tortuously off-key, playing a particularly-crappy song.

"That's not just bad, *that's* Monday-Night-Bluebird-bad."

I sat silently stunned, occasionally signaling Kristi for another couple of beers, as one after another mostly God *awful wannabes – some alone, some with a back-up player - paraded onto then off of the stage, their time behind the mic filled with the discordant caterwauling of sappy songs about love or pick-ups or the farm, or love in a pick-up* on *a farm. I thought that if they were playing on the sidewalk in Austin, the cops* would've *got off their horses to get them off the street, if they could've kept the bewildered beasts from stampeding away from the horrendous semi-melodic excretions rendered by these amateurs who at some point in their lives, somewhere in the far reaches of their delusional addled minds, had actually thought moving to Nashville and trying to become a country star was a reasonable idea.*

Dang. That's just mean.

As number seven left the stage, immediately replaced by number eight, I leaned toward Gary and whispered, "Are you shitting *me?"*

Gary, in the middle of a swig, nearly lost his beer as he laughed out loud (provoking a harsh "Shhh" from a nearby table). He leaned in and whispered back.

"Some are better than others," he said. "I need a smoke. I'm goin' outside." He stood and grabbed his backpack.

Kristi was passing near our table, so I smiled at her and motioned for two more, then got up and followed Gary out the nearby front door (I heard someone mumble, "Elvis has left the building"). Number eight started a song with "If mama could just see me now, I know she'd be proud…"

"Jesus," I said, as Gary lit up, the sound from the stage now assaulting our eardrums (but at – thank God – a lower volume) from a small speaker hanging above the door. "If his mama could see him now she'd wish to God she'd kept her legs together."

We both laughed at this, and I silently prayed that Gary would be better than the performers I was so viciously castigating.

"Hey, believe it or not, some of the ones who were here four months ago started out just like this, and are actually not half bad now," he said.

I arched my eyebrows skeptically.

"Then the Devil's been buying up some souls," I said, and he laughed yet again.

"There'll be a couple of good ones tonight."

He walked down the sidewalk past the large front windows, out of sight of anyone inside, and pulled another couple of PBR's from his backpack. He opened one, held out another to me. I took it and opened it.

"Sunday nights are better," he continued. "You have to audition for those, and you get to play three songs, and there's usually some music-biz people here."

I took a drink and nodded, then asked, hopefully, "Have you done one of those yet?"

He shook his head, and my heart sank a little.

"I auditioned 'bout my third week here. I don't play 'til August."

"Very cool," I said, quite relieved. He couldn't be too bad. "When are the next auditions?"

"I think they do 'em the first Sunday of the month, so I guess next Sunday," he answered. "You should call tomorrow and get on the list, 'cause if you do pass, it'll be five or six months

before you actually get to play."

I nodded, took a drink, and changed the subject.

"You smoke?" I asked him.

He glanced at me, then at his cigarette, then got my meaning.

"Ohhh. Hell yeah. I'm a musician."

As if to further demonstrate his point, he took another long drink of beer.

"Well," I said, "I only live three blocks from here. After we're done playin', we should head over and play a few, get good and stoned."

"We are on the same page, brother," he grinned, tilting his head back and finishing the PBR.

He crumpled and tossed his can as I finished my beer and followed suit, and we walked back in. A pretty girl with straight dark hair was singing a surprisingly decent song in a surprisingly decent voice.

"See?" Gary whispered. "Some are better than others."

And they seemed to get better the more beers I drank. By the time Gary took the stage, I was pretty well lit, hoping I'd get to play before that window of opportunity between "not drunk enough" and "too drunk" slammed shut.

I made a mental note to just sip on the beer in front of me, knowing somehow that note would wind up stuck on the refrigerator door of my mind beneath the one that said, "Drink More Beer."

Even half-drunk, with that state's accompanying charitable appraisal of the talent level, I could tell that Gary was better than most. He had a comfortable stage presence, a pleasant (if not outstanding) voice, and songs that were well put-together, with some memorable lines and catchy hooks. I don't actually remember *any of those lines or hooks, but I was way too concerned with my own upcoming performance to listen as attentively as I would've otherwise.*

Shortly after arriving in Austin and beginning my short-lived-yet-lucrative career as Elvis, I'd picked up a John Prine tape, immediately smitten with his combination of depth and humor, with his Dylan-esque delivery of basically simple songs. As my songwriting evolved, I found myself trying more and more to write and sing like that, *to use my penchant for humor to communicate themes that were on their face quite serious – heartbreak, disappointment...you know, life in general.*

The first one I'd written that I thought sounded like something Prine himself would have done was called "Cat Dreams." (Remember I told you about that speech in school being about a cat? Funny how life works. I really don't even like *cats.) The song was funny, yet still somehow* serious:

> I dreamed the whole world was a big rubber mouse, I'm havin' cat dreams
> I dreamed Charlie Tuna was livin' at my house, I'm havin' cat dreams
> I felt my whole life was beginnin' to slip, I felt like some catnip
> Ain't nothin' wrong with that, just dreamin' my cat dreams

You get the idea. That song seemed to go over really well at me an' Wayne's get-togethers, and also just felt *comfortable, a melding of those aspects of my creativity I thought most worthwhile. So I began to write more and more along those lines, songs that I thought were a unique defining of my own character. I'd found my niche, I thought.*

However, a few drunk and high people at the Austin apartment notwithstanding, I'd only actually publicly *performed Elvis songs. So to say I was a wee bit nervous that night at the Bluebird would be like saying Charlie Sheen is a wee bit obnoxious.*

As Gary got off-stage (to enthusiastic applause – including my own), followed by number nineteen, as number nineteen gave the stage over to number twenty, as number twenty sang a song about Jesus being a country music fan, I tried to quell my nerves with more of the beer I'd told myself to slow down on. I'd made sure my guitar was tuned when I left my new apartment earlier, so I knew I could basically drink until right up to the moment when I had to walk to the other side of the stage, get the guitar out of the case, and meet my destiny.

Kristi came over to the table as the scattered applause for "Jesus Loves Country" died down.

She leaned over, and I stared glassy-eyed at her delicious cleavage as she asked me when I went on.

"I'm next," I whispered to her tits, then her eyes. "How quick can you get a beer over here?"

She giggled and rubbed the back of my neck, which momentarily relocated the feeling in the pit of my stomach further south.

"You'll be fine," she whispered.

And I was. Better than fine, in fact – I killed! A part of me thought, as the waves of applause from the packed room washed over me, that I was playing funny stuff after over two hours of gloom and doom, and that I'd simply provided some long-overdue comic relief.

My nervousness had disappeared when I got a big laugh following the opening line of "Cat Dreams," and by the time I'd finished the song to the loudest applause of the night thus far, I felt more in my element on that stage than I ever had singing Elvis songs in Austin.

I introduced my second song by saying, "Well, I heard that if you wanna make it in Nashville, you've gotta have a train song. This one's called 'Hit By a Train.'" More big laughs, even scattered applause, as I began singing the story of a man and a woman, alone at a bar, both jaded by love and swearing they didn't want to fall again. Then they met, and danced, and "love hit 'em like a train."

And they said, "I don't wanna get hit by a train no more

I've tried it, I don't like it
I hate the way it makes you act like a fool
I don't wanna get hit by a train no more
I've learned to live without it
But tie me to the tracks, and see what you can do"

It was a nice story, a sweet story, a "happy ever after" story unlike anything I'd ever experienced in my own life. But songwriting – or writing in general – isn't about personal experience as much as about imagined experiences, called up in vivid detail when you're sitting alone with a guitar or a piano or simply a notebook and a pen.

As I got off the stage, put my guitar back in its case, and walked back to my table, I knew beyond the hint of a shadow of a doubt that this was what I wanted to do for the rest of my life.

Later that night - after Gary had gone - Kristi knocked on my door. We slow-danced to absolute silence, then kissed, then kissed some more. She helped me get undressed as I helped her get undressed. We went to bed.

I awoke with the sunrise, thinking maybe, for the first time in my short life, true and everlasting happiness might be on the horizon.

Silly me.

CHAPTER EIGHTEEN

From the outside, it seemed like a typical Wilson, Tennessee house. The paint was faded, peeling in some places, the yard (unlike the heads of most Wilson men) shaggy and unkempt.

A boy's bicycle lay on its side near the sidewalk which led to the concrete front porch, on which sat a couple of sturdy plastic chairs, a large blue *Igloo* ice chest doubling as a table between them. In the corner of the driveway closest to the two-car garage sat a twenty-year-old Ford Ranger, dingy metallic gray, the left front tire flat and looking like it had *always* been thus, garbage bags and empty boxes piled in its bed.

It was what *else* occupied the drive that made this house differ from the others in the neighborhood: the brand-new Ford F-150 and brand-new Triton bass boat were, by Harvey's quick calculation, worth more than the run-down house in front of which they sat, the contrast stark, like the King and Queen of the Prom sitting down to lunch at a rickety picnic table.

He parked at the curb in front of the Blevins' home and shut off the engine.

It hadn't taken any real detective work to get the information. Lori Ragland-turned-Jameson had at first been hesitant, but after Harvey reminded her that this particular student had jacked with his computer only after she'd lost track of him on a field trip (possibly while *texting*), he got a phone number.

After he'd read the treatise left on his laptop, which ended with murdered country singer Jared Whaley leaving an Elvis-impersonator gig in Austin and moving to Nashville as a young man, Harvey had googled, hoping (yet part of him *dreading*) that the information - if not the actual *document* itself - was available online, and that, for whatever reason, the kid had just found it and was playing a very strange practical joke. Harvey sincerely doubted the twelve-year-old was nearly computer-savvy enough to pull off such a stunt, but nowadays you just never knew, and, at the moment, it was the only explanation he could fathom.

The name "Jared Whaley" garnered thousands of results, but the only *biographical* info Harvey could find (apart from that included in the numerous obits and reports of the murder), was a three-page bio on the record label's website. It confirmed that, yes, Whaley *had* been raised in Tulsa, *had* aspired to be a stand-up comedian, *had* spent time in Austin as an Elvis impersonator. It also mentioned that he had two daughters. The bio ended with a simple-yet-sad, *"Jared Whaley was murdered shortly before a show in Wilson, TN on Feb. 13, 2009. He was 42."*

Harvey could find no mention of the singer's aborted trip to Hollywood, no mention of a heroin-addict roommate, and *certainly* no mention of meeting a woman with a tattooed breast.

After he'd suffered through the "Buy and Sell" show, he'd called the boy's parents, then called his friend Warren at the *Democrat* and offered him twenty bucks (plus the use of his digital recorder) to tape the daily post-trial statements given on the courthouse steps by the opposing attorneys. Harvey hated to miss the briefing (and *really* hated to give up twenty bucks), but this thing was too damned *weird*, and while there was probably a simple explanation, he somehow sensed that there might be a story here.

He'd driven to the offices of the paper, dropped off the recorder and the twenty – telling Warren only that "something came up" – then returned to the radio station to call a few prospective advertisers, record a couple of commercials, and print off two copies of the "Dead Guy's Diary" (as he'd taken to mentally calling it).

As Harvey sat in his car, puffing his pipe, two manila folders containing the print-outs on the seat beside him, he wondered exactly how he'd handle this. When he'd called earlier, speaking with the boy's mother, telling her that Willard had been caught playing with his laptop at the radio station, he was at first met with an uncomfortable silence.

"He's *always* playing with his laptop," she finally said.

"No, no," Harvey clarified. "He was playing with *my* laptop."

"Huh." There was a pause as she yelled away from the mouthpiece, "Mack, now he's messin' with *other folks'* gizmos!"

Harvey couldn't quite make out what the unseen Mack had replied, but it *sounded* kind of like, "*Fuck a bird.*"

"I'd like to show you what he did," Harvey said.

More silence had followed. He heard a muffled conversation, followed by another – more distinct this time – "Fuck a bird," then Elenore gave him the address.

Harvey got out of the car with the folders, walked up the drive, down the sidewalk, and up the three steps to the porch. He saw the curtain covering the front window flutter, and, before he could knock, the door was opened by a very large redneck.

"You must be that feller from the radio station," Mack said, extending a meaty hand. "I'm Mack Blevins."

Harvey shook his hand and introduced himself, then accepted the larger man's invitation inside.

"That's a nice truck you've got there. Nice boat too," Harvey said as Mack shut the front door.

Mack's face lit up.

"Why thank you! Them's my pride and joys," he said. "Lost my big toe at the bowling alley and they gave me a big ol' check."

He laughed through Harvey's stunned silence.

"Here, let me show you."

The large man steadied himself on the TV stand (it was a large flat-screen, turned on at a low volume, airing what appeared to be some sort of reality show), and with his free hand began removing a sock.

"Oh no, no," Harvey protested. "You don't have to do that."

"Mack, he don't wanna see your skanky stub," came a voice from the sofa, and Harvey was startled because he hadn't even realized anyone was *there*.

"I'm sorry," he said, "I didn't see you."

And he wondered *why* he hadn't – she was almost as large as her husband – unless it was because she was sunk into the plush padded sofa to the point of almost seeming a *part* of it, her black hair blending into the dark vinyl, the room illuminated only by the TV screen.

"That there's my wife Elenore," Mack said, abandoning his sock removal.

"Pleasure to meet you, ma'am," Harvey smiled, leaning forward to offer his hand, which, after a moment's hesitation, she limply shook.

"Yes, sir," she said, attempting to not be too obvious as she tilted her head to the side to see the TV.

Harvey noticed and stepped out of the way.

"So do we need to buy you a new computer?" Mack asked. "I'll get my checkbook."

"Oh no, no," Harvey said again. "It's nothing like that."

Mack looked at him expectantly, waiting for him to continue. Which Harvey would have done, if he'd known exactly *how*.

"Um..." he started. "He didn't do any *damage* to my laptop. It's fine."

The expression on Mack's face remained unchanged.

"Huh," he said. "Well, *that's* good, ain't it?"

"Yes, sir. It's actually....um....what he left *on* my computer that has me a little puzzled." Harvey held up the manila folders. "I thought you two might want to read this."

Harvey momentarily expected the same reaction to the word "read" that the Wicked Witch of the West in *The Wizard of Oz* had to getting a bath.

Instead, Mack reached out his hand and took the folders.

"Elenore," he said. "I think we might finally get to see what Willard's been typin'."

Elenore's eyes came unglued from the TV.

"Shut the front door," she said.

That's when it struck Harvey. Like almost every other male in town, he got his hair cut at Norville's Barber Shop. His last time had been three weeks ago (in fact, he was due for another), and he remembered now the conversation he'd had with the proprietor.

"So whadya make of Mack Blevins' boy?" Norville had asked him.

Harvey figured he *knew* Mack Blevins, but couldn't quite put a face to the name.

"He's got 'im some sort of demon or something-or-other in his computer," Norville said. "Boy's possessed."

Harvey had chuckled at the time, thinking about how few people seemed to realize the extent to which *men* gossiped, guessing this particular rumor to not be any more or less outlandish than the one about the Richards boy being kidnapped by aliens the previous summer (he had in reality run away from home and been found two weeks later at his Aunt's house in Memphis).

"Well, I hope at least it's not interfering with his grades," he remembered replying.

Standing in the Blevins' living room, Harvey couldn't believe he hadn't put two and two together, unless it was because, like most of the town's gossip, he let it go in one ear and out the other.

"Curiouser and curiouser," he said, half to himself, feeling like Alice in a redneck Wonderland.

"Huh?" Mack asked.

"Uh...nothing," he said, as Mack reached out an arm and helped his wife from the sofa.

"Let's go in here to the table," Mack said, leading the way into the dingy dining room. He and Elenore took a seat, and Mack motioned for Harvey to do the same before sliding one of the folders to his wife.

As Harvey sat, he began to explain how Willard had got away from the rest of the class during that morning's tour of the station, how his teacher had found him in the studio on Harvey's laptop, how Harvey had then found what they held in their hands.

"I know for a fact *I* didn't do that, and I'd just been on the computer when the class arrived for the field trip. So..." he left the sentence unfinished, not wanting to make an outright accusation.

Both Mack and Elenore were already absorbed in the first page, their brows furrowed in concentration, their lips occasionally moving.

Mack looked up.

"So now...how would the boy get this stuff on your computer? He wasn't sittin' there long enough to *type* it was he?"

"No, no," Harvey said yet again. "If he did it on *his* computer, he could put it on *mine* with what they call a 'thumb drive'."

A look of disbelief crossed the big man's face, and both he and his wife looked at Harvey as if he'd just told them their microwave was broken.

"Fuck a bird," Mack said.

"Shut the front door," said Elenore.

"What?" Harvey asked.

Mack looked at his wife, then back to Harvey.

"Willard asked us to..."

"Wasn't Willard," Elenore interrupted. "It was *Elvis*."

"Uh..." was about all Harvey could respond.

"Boy broke out in a goddamned Elvis song at goddamned supper the other night, then told us we had to get him one of those thingamajigs at the Radio Shack," Mack explained. "A 'thumb drive.'"

"Wow," Harvey said. "That's...uh...weird."

Harvey, thinking about the *Elvis* portion of the story, reflected that "that's weird" might be the greatest understatement

103

since that day long, long ago when Noah said, "It looks like rain."
He sighed heavily.

"I guess you better read it," he said.

They continued.

When, after a full five minutes, they had only flipped the
page twice, Harvey excused himself to go outside and smoke.

He sat on the front porch, packed his pipe and lit it, then
leaned back and pondered this bizarre development.

There has to be a simple explanation, he thought. If this
were a movie, then of course the boy would be possessed by the
ghost of a murdered country singer. But this *wasn't* a movie, so
obviously someone was going to great lengths to play an elaborate
hoax. But *why*?

Harvey thought of Warren at the *Democrat*. This was just
the kind of thing Warren would do, but when Harvey thought of all
the effort that would be involved – the research, the typing, the
planting of the document - he concluded the notion just didn't hold
water, that even if it *did,* the laugh wouldn't be worth the work to
his old friend.

Maybe the boy was a prodigy, a creative computer genius
who had done online research on the singer and written the memoir
based on the record label bio, simply filling in the rest with
fabrication? After all, Harvey had no *corroboration* on the other
parts of the story. Not yet. He thought of the couple inside, their
lips moving as they read at a rate somewhere between a first-
grader and a trained chimp. Maybe the boy was *adopted*.

Oh well. He'd know better how to proceed after the
Blevins had finished reading.

He looked at his watch. *If* the Blevins finished reading.
But first, there was a question he *had* to ask.

He tamped out his pipe, rose, and knocked lightly before
opening the door.

"Come on in," he heard Mack say from the dining room,
followed closely by, "Shut the front door," from Elenore.

He had a feeling she was referring to something she'd just read, and not requesting that he *physically* shut the front door, but he did anyway, then walked back into the dining room.

Apparently the pair read at the approximately the same slow speed, for, right after Elenore's "Shut the front door," Mack said, "Well fuck a bird."

They both looked up at Harvey.

"Right here," Mack said, pointing to the page. "Our boy said *exactly* those words. Cussin' and all."

Harvey leaned over and saw that Mack was referring to the part where the boy (or *whoever*) had written, "*I can't believe I fucking lost my fucking capo again.*"

He was shocked on two different levels.

"You're only on page *eight*?" he said before he could censor himself, then quickly added, "Well, that's pretty *weird*."

Mack and Elenore both seemed to concur with the latter while either ignoring or not catching the former.

"Umm...do you remember about when it was Willard started typing?

Mack looked at Elenore, Elenore back at Mack. They both shrugged.

It was still winter," Mack said. "And it must have been on a Saturday or a Sunday. 'Cause the boy wasn't at school."

Elenore's eyes widened, and she smiled.

"It was on Valentine's Day, Mack. 'Cause you took me to the Shoney's and that's about all we talked about."

Mack nodded slowly, remembering.

"We was gonna take the boy, but left him here 'cause he weirded us out."

Elenore patted Mack's arm and looked at Harvey.

"We only go to the Shoney's once a year."

"Now horseshit Elenore," Mack said. "We went last November after Aunt Cousin Bertha's funeral."

"Oh, that's right."

"Does that make any difference?" Mack asked Harvey.

Harvey hated to lie. He wasn't any good at it, especially when his heart was in his throat.

"Nah," he lied.

Valentine's Day *had* fallen on a Saturday that year. He knew this because he remembered thinking the previous day had been a particularly unlucky Friday the Thirteenth for a particular rising country star.

"You don't have internet, do you?" he asked, grasping at increasingly-elusive straws.

"Inter – *who*?" Elenore asked.

Mack turned his massive frame in his chair and yelled down the hall.

"*Willard*!"

A moment later, the closed door at the end of the hallway slowly opened, and the pudgy boy shuffled toward them, clutching his laptop to his bosom. After a furtive glance at Harvey, he looked at his father.

"Yeah, Dad?"

"What the hell is this shit you put on Mr. Boyd's gizmo today?" he asked, holding up the pages.

Willard acted like he didn't know what his father was talking about.

Maybe, Harvey thought, *because he doesn't know what his father is talking about.*

The twelve-year-old looked at the print-out, then looked at his Dad, then looked at Harvey, his expression bewildered. He shrugged.

"Dunno."

"Goddamn it boy!" Mack shouted. "This here's some weird shit!"

Willard cowered from his father's raised voice.

"I dunno," he repeated, on the verge of tears.

"Now Willard," Harvey said, his voice calm, hopefully

soothing. "Do you remember your trip to the radio station this morning?"

The boy nodded.

"We watched you do the news," he said. "It was *cool*." He allowed himself a smile.

"Then after that," Harvey continued, "do you remember me and your teacher and the rest of your class going upstairs?"

Willard looked again at his father, fearfully, before turning back to Harvey.

"N-no sir," he said.

Harvey held up a hand, warding off another verbal onslaught from Mack.

"And do you remember Mrs. Jameson finding you in my studio at my computer?"

The boy's lower lip trembled and a tear rolled from the corner of his eye.

"No sir." He looked at Mack. "I'm sorry Daddy. What's he talking about?"

Mack, in a touching display, held out his arms. Willard leaned into them and started sobbing.

"Now, now, son," he said, patting the boy's back. "It's not your fault you're possessed."

Willard sobbed even louder.

Harvey began to interject. "Well, now...we're not so sure about..."

Elenore, who had continued reading throughout, suddenly looked up, excited.

"Our little boy's a Elvis *impersonator*!" she said.

"No he ain't. He's *Elvis*," Mack retorted.

"No, Mack," Elenore persisted. "He *wrote* about it."

Mack released his son and leaned over and read where his wife's pudgy finger was pointing.

"Shut the front door," he said.

Fuck a bird, Harvey thought.

CHAPTER NINETEEN

Most of the next thousand or so days in Nashville began the same – I woke up and plowed my landlord's daughter's fields. So to speak. I screwed Kristi.

There were occasions we didn't go at it first thing in the morning – we fought some, she got pregnant a couple of times (which didn't involve skipping sex as much as you might think), I stayed out late pickin' and grinnin' and crashed over at friends' houses – but all in all, we copulated voraciously. Until we didn't.

Those days flew by all-too-quickly and now seem like a blurry blink of an eye. Six months to the day after I met her we were married. Eight months after that, our first daughter, Suzie Michelle, was born.

Why have there been so many opuses, so many billions and billions of words, written about romantic love, yet relatively few written about the love of a parent for a child? Maybe it's the uncertainty and seeming randomness of the former and the unquestioning, natural, ingrained nature of the latter. I don't know. But when Suzie was born, when I saw that big melon full of red hair ("She's definitely Jared's," my mom-in-law Fran had said – not that I needed reassuring), when I held her in my arms…well, I was a writer all my life, and I can't begin to describe it.

I can say that, a year later, when our second daughter Marie was born, when she emerged from Kristi blue and limp and with her umbilical cord wrapped around her neck, I felt a pain and fear so intense and all-encompassing that I immediately, without a nanosecond of conscious thought, wished I was dead.

Moments later, when the doc cut that cord, slapped that little bottom, and I watched her turn pink before my eyes and start wailing at the top of her little lungs, I felt a relief and happiness the depth of which was never replicated in my lifetime.

But I digress.

A few hours after I awoke that first morning with Kristi, I called the Bluebird and got on the list to audition for the Sunday night writers show. I passed that easily and played there at least semi-regularly on Sunday nights for the rest of my life. I also continued playing Monday nights for awhile, because my girlfriend (and later my wife) worked there, and because it was a good place to try out new material.

I also started riding with Gary to writers' nights at Douglas Corner, *the* Commodore Lounge, *the* Broken Spoke, *and countless others – very rare was the night there wasn't* someplace *to play. Gary and I never wrote together, we were both the solo-writer types, but we spent many hours drinking and smoking and critiquing one another's work, offering the kind of mutual moral support without which it's tough to continually bang your head against the Nashville wall.*

I met and became fast friends with Sean, a comedy-songwriter and musician who also owned a recording studio. A few months later I recorded "A Fairly Decent Tape, and It's Only Five Bucks," *which contained six of the songs that had consistently got the best audience response at the writers' nights I'd been playing. (That's also when I wrote that "born in Southern California...raised in neighboring Tulsa, Oklahoma" line for the tape's liner notes). From that experience, I learned that if you've got a tape to sell, you* have *to play* at least *a couple of the songs on the tape. Every time. Since most writers' nights allowed you to play only two or three songs, I found myself doing the same stuff over and over and over, getting* really *good at those numbers (and selling a butt-load of tapes), but building up quite the back-log of tunes I felt were as good or* better.

So that's when I decided I needed a band.

The first person I thought of was Chad, the waiter from Tulsa I'd met at the HoJo near the airport my first day in Nashville. I found his number in my wallet, gave him a call, and we started jamming together on the weekends, when he could generally get off work and when there were the fewest writers nights.

Chad was a helluva lead player, and also sang harmonies, so we jammed together for a couple of months in that little cramped garage apartment I now shared with a pregnant Kristi and a baby Suzie. Kristi was still working a lot (she only took off from the Bluebird for the births of our daughters slightly longer than we took off from having sex), and there were many weekends I'd have to take breaks from playing and drinking and smoking to be a daddy. I thought this the epitome of domestic bliss.

Eventually, after Chad and I had a full set of songs down, we decided it was time to get a bass player and drummer, so I spent ten bucks and put an ad in The Nashville Scene. *It was only after I'd got twenty or so calls that I thought to ask Burt if it was okay to practice in the garage. I told him that with a band practicing two or three times a week, I'd be needing more pot. That was all the convincing he needed, so I spent four hundred bucks and bought a little P.A. And, of course, some pot.*

Nashville's a funny (but not "funny ha-ha") place – there are some absolutely God-awful songwriters who'll sell everything they have to take a chance on the dream, but very few musicians *who move out here without some chops. So it's not so much a matter of finding quality musicians to play, it's more a matter of finding quality musicians who'll play* with you. *For free. Most players are here with dreams of studio gigs or backing up major artists on the road, but often wind up making their money backing up wannabes for showcases or playing cover gigs. So it's tough to find people who believe enough in a project that they'll volunteer their time on the off-off-off chance that it'll lead to something profitable.*

Knowing this, I felt it a nice testament to the uniqueness and marketability of my music that finding back-up players came so easy. Of course, it could have been the free pot.

First we hired Dan, a bass player who also sang harmonies. The next night it was Miles, a drummer extraordinaire

110

whose hero was Neal Peart from the band Rush, and who had a similarly large drum kit. This turned out to be a real headache in some of the smaller venues we played, because Miles felt that absolutely every single piece was crucial *to his art, and so we were left with either a smaller section of the stage or no stage at all, setting up our gear and playing from the floor.*

Once the band was together, we needed a name. The rest of the guys were perfectly happy with "The Jared Whaley Band," but I thought that was boring. While I did *want my name out front, I also wanted a band name that would reflect the style of the music.*

One night - during one of our regular "let's get high" breaks - I wondered aloud if, before cows were domesticated, people actually hunted *them. Wondered how challenging that would have been. Did they have cow* stands? *And at what point in our evolution did we figure out that we could just walk up to them and hit 'em on the head with a hammer?*

Which, half-drunk and completely stoned as we were, led to a fit of giggles and a discussion of cow-tipping. No one I've ever known has actually done *it; almost* everyone *I've ever known has* claimed *they have.*

I think it was Chad who said, "Hey, we could be The CowTippers."

And thus we were. And, as rare as it is in the music biz, much less in Nashville, *those same three guys – Chad and Dan and Miles – remained The CowTippers on and off till the day I died. If they have any sense, they'll continue to milk that cow as long as my name still lives.*

CHAPTER TWENTY

Corroboration.

That's what Harvey needed. It was now obvious that Willard was involved. There were too many factors to just be *coincidence*, yet – implausible as it seemed – the boy *still* could've got the information somewhere...but *where?* And *why?* Trying to glean a rational explanation from all this was giving Harvey a headache.

Corroboration.

With this in mind, Harvey googled and got the number to Whaley's record label in New York, *Originality Records*. It was after 6 there, and a *Friday* no less, so he was surprised when the president of the label himself answered. Harvey explained that he was in possession of what appeared to be a portion of their most famous late artist's memoirs.

Phil Kearns seemed skeptical, said he wasn't aware that his recently-departed friend had been writing anything besides *songs*, but had agreed to read what Harvey had and gave him his email address.

That had been two hours ago, and Harvey was finding it hard to concentrate on writing a commercial for *Johnny's Hardware* as he sat in the studio, the station running on auto.

Line three – the news hotline – blinked, and Harvey pressed the button and picked up the phone simultaneously.

"WTOR," he answered.

Without an introduction, Harvey heard, "*Where* did you get this?"

"Mr. Kearns?"

"Our contract with Mr. Whaley states specifically that we have the rights to *any* creative property produced by him both *prior to* and for the *duration of* said contract."

Harvey was caught off-guard.

"Well, sir...I just wanted to make sure..."

"So I want to know where the *fuck* you got this!"

Corroboration.

"*Sir,*" Harvey said, trying to calm the old man down. "First of all, I want you to know I'm not *trying* to undermine your right to…"

"There must be some part of 'Where did you get this?' that you're not understanding, son," came the irate voice at the other end of the line. "Is it the nouns or the verbs?"

"I'm not exactly sure *where* it came from!" Harvey nearly shouted into the phone. "I got it…kind of…anonymously."

Which, in all honesty, was fairly accurate.

"I just wanted to know if it seemed like the real thing before I…dug further."

There was a moment of silence. Then a sigh.

"Look Harvey," the old man said. "I only knew Jared for a little over five years, and only *met* the man twice in all that time."

He seemed no longer angry. Just sad.

"But during our short friendship I got to know him very well and to think of him like a son." The voice broke then, and Harvey found himself, conversely, getting almost giddy.

"So you can verify…"

"I don't know *everything* there is to know about the man…how he felt about his parents, that he wrote little monster skits as a child…that Angel showed him her *tits* the very first time they met…*Jesus.*"

The old man paused again, as if collecting his thoughts.

"But I know Jared's *voice,*" he said softly. "And I don't have to hear it out loud to hear it *in my head.*"

Harvey sensed what was coming, but didn't want to spoil it. Besides, he was afraid that if he spoke, he'd giggle.

"I don't know if everything there is *factual,*" the voice continued. "But there's nothing there I know to be a *lie.*"

"So…" Harvey began.

"*So,* young man," the old man said. "I would swear on a stack of bibles on my late wife's grave that Jared wrote this."

Neither Harvey nor the man in New York City spoke for a moment.

"Now don't make me *sue* your ass!" the old man said, slamming down the phone.

Harvey sat stunned for a moment, debating his next course of action. He hated that it was obvious.

He googled again, then called the Law Offices of Marshall Laughlin.

CHAPTER TWENTY-ONE

Can you point to one moment in your life you wish you could take back?

Probably, you think, you could point to several. What I mean is...say you found a lamp with a genie in it...and you rubbed it...and the genie said you only got one *wish, and that wish* had *to be a moment in your life you could undo, a clock that could rewind to* one time *only, an event that you'd be willing to change, even knowing that one event led to another event which led to another which led you to here - would you take that chance? Because, as* bad *as that moment may have been, you never know if changing that one thing could lead to a future even* worse. *Would you take that chance? Or would you take a fork and stab that genie right in the eye?*

I kinda doubt that such a genie exists. If it did, *however, and if I'd discovered it while I still had hands to* rub *that fuckin' lamp, I'd take back the seventeenth time I stayed at the bar when Kristi needed me at home. Because, no matter* how *things ended up - even if I'd still got the record deal and* not *got shot in the noggin, if I'd gone on to a life of fame and fortune and sold millions of records* – none *of those things would've been worth that seventeenth time at that bar.*

'Cause that's when I lost the chance to see my girls grow up. And those are memories I'll never *have – another un-un-ring-able bell.*

Now, who's to say that seventeenth time wouldn't have happened anyway? If the genie was kind enough to allow me to change it knowing what I know now, then no prob. If, however, the changing of that moment took me back to that moment not knowing that I'd gone back and changed *the moment...although I guess I would* have *to have known I'd changed the moment or the wish would be kinda pointless...so maybe I change the moment without* knowing *I was changing the moment...or...geez, I'm getting dizzy, and I'm pretty sure dead men don't faint. I guess what I'm sayin' is that* every *life has* one *major fuck-up-to-end-all-fuck-ups, and that was mine.*

It all started when I decided to go to college.

One thing you'll learn about Nashville is that there are *no overnight sensations. There is a hierarchy, a ladder of slippery rungs grasped at by the worthy and unworthy alike, often overseen by those who climbed their way up the* same *ladder, former songwriters (*many *of whom are failed* artists*) who at some point during their tedious ascension lost their grasp on that intangible which separates* art *from* business, *yet which, in the cases of those who succeed beyond what mere* marketing *can achieve, erases that line, because deep-down every human knows what is* real *and what is* contrived.

In Nashville, reality only wins out by accident.

Me and The CowTippers *were never that accidentally lucky. We continued practicing at least twice a week, started playing gigs here and there, gaining just enough notoriety to make us think it was worth continuing the fight.*

We recorded a four-song EP at Sean's studio, had a promo pic done, and sent those to all the labels, hoping to get someone *in the biz out to some of our shows, all to no avail.*

In addition to the stuff with the band, I was continuing to write, surprising myself sometimes with songs that I thought worthy of commercial radio. I'd play those for Burt, and he'd tell me which ones he thought I should pitch (and sell me some weed). Then I'd go to Sean's, record demos, and take them to the few publisher-friends Burt had been able to get me in to see. There was always some reason the songs didn't quite *fit the standards of Music Row (I started thinking it was because they weren't* crappy *enough), but I was always encouraged to keep trying, welcomed to come back again.*

Suzie began walking, then talking, Marie crawling and jabbering. Kristi continued working at the Bluebird and paying most of the bills, and we continued making love almost every morning.

Two years after moving to Nashville, I'd finally spent my savings – mainly on beer and pot and recording - and Kristi, now our little family's sole source of income, became a little less supportive of my wild and wooly songwriter ways. I don't believe she'd lost faith in me – it was obvious when I played at the Bluebird and at the few gigs she was able to make that the crowds at least loved us – but havin' a family, combined with her rapidly-advancing maturity (she was all of twenty-two by that time), seemed to make her realize that there were many factors involved in making it in the music business aside from talent.

She suggested I get a job.

No matter what the economy's like at any given time, it's always tough for an aspiring musician whose only experience has been as a busboy/dishwasher, convenience store clerk, and Elvis impersonator to find a job.

Scratch that. It's always tough for that person to find a job if he deep down doesn't want a fucking job. Still, because I understood her position (and because I wanted her position to continue to be underneath me naked every morning), I gave it a shot.

I got a job as a water-purification system salesman (made it through a week of paid training, then quit), a telephone survey-taker (made it through two weeks of paid training then quit), a J.C. Penney telephone sales rep (another two weeks of paid training, then I quit)...I think you're probably sensing a trend here. Eventually (it took about six months), I'd run out of jobs I could get paid to train for without actually having to stay on and work.

That's when Chad and Dan told me they were going to college.

I respected and admired the guys for hanging in there with the band even after they realized what a long road we had to hoe. Chad still had his day gig at the HoJo, Dan worked as a carpenter, Miles as a computer programmer (geek!), and I understood that *they - or at least Chad and Dan - were probably growing tired of manual, subservient labor.*

So I can't say I was surprised when, after rehearsal one night as we sat around getting high and finishing off a case of PBR, Chad and Dan announced that they were filling out applications for Middle Tennessee State University, about thirty miles southeast of Nashville in Murfreesboro.

When they informed me of their plan, my first (selfish) thought was, well, there goes the band. *But that was before they told me how they would be getting grants and guaranteed student loans on top of "supplemental" loans, that they would basically be making as much (or more) for doing nothing but taking a few classes. And that* some *of these classes involved working in a professional recording studio as part of MTSU's "Recording Industry Management" program.*

Even through the haze of alcohol and pot, I sensed that they were hinting something to me.

"Hey Jared," Dan said. "You should go to school too."

I was pleasantly surprised how easy it was to convince Kristi. I think part of her was ready to live away from her parents, part of her realized my job prospects were dwindling with each abrupt resignation, and part of her saw that – if the music business didn't pan out (which was looking more and more likely) – I could have a degree *and maybe, Heaven forbid, a* career.

There were several other factors in our favor – our Honda station wagon (courtesy of her parents) got good mileage, and it was only a forty-minute mostly-interstate drive from the campus to the Bluebird; she had free babysitting (courtesy of her mother) just three blocks from work on those nights I had practice and/or gigs; and...okay, there were a couple of *other factors in our favor. Sue me, I'm writing this off the top of my non-existent head.*

Three months later we were living in a two-bedroom apartment on campus. I was enrolled as an English major, leaving the door open to just stay *in school, racking up loans, until*

I could become an English Professor. Chad and Dan (both enrolled as RIM majors) had rented an eighty-year-old farmhouse - the upstairs of which made for a perfect practice studio - on twelve acres just outside of town.

The apartment was okay, if rather industrial (the walls were made of white cinder-block), but there was a playground right outside our door, and I was only a ten-minute walk from even my farthest class.

Kristi and I quickly fell into a familiar, comfortable routine: We'd wake up, have sex, get the girls up. Kristi would make them breakfast as I got ready for school, then I'd be off to class. I'd scheduled my courses mainly from eight to one, so I could be home in time to give Kristi a chance to take a nap before heading to work. Sometimes, if the girls were also napping, I'd selfishly interrupt Kristi's nap with my penis in her vagina, but she generally didn't seem to mind, such was the bliss of our domesticity.

Wednesday nights was practice, so Kristi would pack up the girls at around 4:30, take them to her parents', then head to work. Either Dan or Chad would pick me up and take me to the farmhouse, then Kristi would fetch me at about 12:30 (my angels sound asleep in their car seats) to take me home and often give me sex.

These were good times!

Within a few months, the 'Tippers were playing gigs around town – mostly doing opening sets at a place right across the street from campus called The Boro. We went over great with the college crowd, but didn't feel like learning all the covers we'd need to play a full three-set show. We'd get a cut of the door, usually enough to pay for our beer, but were still miles away from earning anything like a living. Then again, we were professional students.

I made straight-A's my first semester without spending too much time on homework, so I was optimistic this student-musician thing was going to be a sweet deal.

Then Fran, Kristi's mom, my mother-in-law, my daughters' grandmother, was diagnosed with lung cancer. If any one thing led to another thing that led to that seventeenth *thing I mentioned earlier, that was it.*

Fran underwent chemo, Kristi cut back on her hours at the Bluebird to spend time with her, and we were left with less money and no babysitter. I knew *it was selfish and inconsiderate of me to think about how this would affect the* band, *but I've deep down never been* anything *if not selfish and inconsiderate.* Especially *during my youth. Or my life. Or even after that.*

But I digress.

Things kinda went downhill from there. Between the stress of her sick mom and motherhood and work, Kristi grew distant and less frisky (see where my priorities didn't get laid?). She needed understanding, love, and support. She needed me home.

Had I been the kind of father and husband I should've *been, had I not been so focused on the thin shred of hope that was my music career, and, truth be told, had I not started drinking every day as soon as my last class ended (except on those occasions when I took a large insulated coffee mug full of beer to my* first *class), I wouldn't have wound up divorced, separated from my kids, and, eventually, homeless.*

It wasn't a steep *hill my snowball rolled down on its way to Hell. Kristi was a patient woman, and she* loved *me. She also knew my girls loved me and that I absolutely* adored *my girls. My babies never laughed so much as when they were around their old man. But, if laughter was enough to sustain a relationship, drunken clowns such as I would never be lonely. It doesn't, and we are.*

At the beginning of my second year of higher education, I auditioned for and got the job as host of a country music video show on the student-run cable TV station. I think the show was called "Top Country" or some such thing.

Throughout my performing life – from monster skits to Elvis to high school assemblies back to Elvis and then finally as a CowTipper – I'd found it fairly easy to be on stage and make people laugh. I had a dry delivery, a pretty quick wit, and I suppose I was a likeable fella - at least that's what the student-producers of the TV show told me when they gave me the host gig.

The show was the project of the "Advanced Television Production" class, which met Mondays, Wednesdays, and Fridays from 3 - 4, ending at exactly the same time happy hour began at the Boro. Coincidence or fate? Doesn't matter, I guess.

The first few times of what became our regular post-production drunk-fest (for myself and many of the crew), I was able to maintain at least a modicum of responsibility. If Kristi had to head to the Bluebird, I'd get home by five; if she was going to go spend time with her rapidly-declining mother, I'd get home by six.

Kristi – patient, loving woman that she was – didn't mind accommodating my new foray into television so long as it didn't interfere with her much-more-important schedule, but the first time she had to call out at work because I was MIA to watch the girls (which was at the beginning of the third week of the show), she left me. That time only lasted a few days, and she came back less because she couldn't stand us being apart as because the uncertainty of my reliability was the lesser of two evils compared to the certainty of Burt's unfitness as a babysitter.

"Suzie ate some of my pot," he'd told Kristi after the first time she'd had to leave the girls in his care.

The second time she left me was about a month later and probably my tenth time to stay at the bar when I should've been home. This time it was a Friday – of course one of the 'Bird's busiest nights – and I deemed getting smashed at the Boro to be more important than fulfilling my parental obligations (and, from what I've heard, deemed stripping down to my underwear and challenging a bouncer to "rassle" more important than…uh…not doing that) - and Kristi once again packed her shit and went to her parents.

She was gone over a week this time, mainly because her Granny (Fran's mother), had driven up from Lewisburg to help take care of her dying daughter. Plus, the old lady absolutely adored *the girls, spoiled 'em rotten, and easily had enough energy (she was a freakin'* dynamo *for a gal in her late seventies), to take care of her daughter* and *her great-grandkids those nights Kristi had to work.*

I don't remember too much of that period of time, except that I pretty much stayed drunk, skipped class, and slept with Erin, my co-host on the TV show. That was the first and only time I ever cheated on Kristi, probably because the guilt of having done so lasted until we split for good.

Which was just three weeks later.

That seventeenth time I stayed at the bar when I should've been home was a Thursday.

Drunk as I was, I still recall it vividly.

We were about four pitchers into our party when Kristi called the bar looking for me. I yelled at Cody the bartender to tell her I wasn't there, but, like the dumb ass I am, yelled it easily loud enough for her to overhear. Fifteen minutes later, Erin (who had her tongue in my ear and her hand on my thigh) noticed the Honda driving slowly around the building, Kristi and my babies all peering through the windows trying to spot me before Kristi pulled into a parking space and came in.

It was Erin's idea I hide behind the booth. The rest of our party, drunk as they were, found it a hoot to tell Kristi I had just left. As I watched her storm out of the bar in a huff, get into the car and back out, the lights of my miserable life continued to stare, their wide eyes searching for their Daddy, their necks craning from their car seats, until Kristi pulled out of the parking lot and was gone.

If I'd known then what I know now – that that was the last time I'd see my girls until some time after they'd grown breasts and started menstruating – I'd've immediately gone looking for that goddamn genie.

CHAPTER TWENTY-TWO

Marshall Laughlin was a happy camper.

The case of *The People versus Angel Whaley* was going - from *his* perspective at least - swimmingly. He'd worked some high-profile cases before, but none as high-profile as *this* one, thanks in part to Jared Whaley's single continuing its climb up the charts (it was now in the Top 5). Which was due, in part, to the trial. Getting murdered was good PR.

Laughlin was – for now – the most well-known defense attorney in the land.

The prosecution was still presenting its case – today was Saturday, a day off of course, so he figured they'd rest by Tuesday or Wednesday – and he was confident that, unless they could produce the thus-far-un-*findable* eyewitness, and unless said witness testified to actually *seeing* his client fire the shot into Whaley's head, there was no *way* the jury would not be able to find reasonable doubt, regardless of the preponderance of ridiculously overwhelming circumstantial evidence.

His client was a strange bird. She'd maintained her innocence throughout, yet hadn't uttered a single syllable explaining away the evidence against her. Laughlin didn't really *care*. He could win this thing *without* her, and sometimes ignorance is bliss.

Although he hadn't even begun to present his case, he was already working on catchy phrases to use during his closing, trying to emulate his hero Johnny Cochran's famous, "If it doesn't fit, you must acquit" line.

"You can't convict if you don't know who sucked his...." Nah.

"Unless we know who was on her knees, my client must go free." Probably not.

He laughed at the absurdity of it all (and cursed his lack of meter), yet knew that, especially in the low-attention-span-theater that was today's America, you couldn't underestimate the power of a pithy phrase. He'd work on that.

Right now he had more pressing business.

The phone call he'd received that morning had been *strange* to say the least. His assistant, whom he paid well to be a gatekeeper between him and the *press* (whose existence was only validated by their usefulness as a tool), had listened to a message from the previous evening that she deemed worthy of his attention, either because it might benefit the *defense* or because it might shed light on something that might benefit the *prosecution*. A lot of *might*'s.

Hmmmm. " 'Might' don't make it right*." That* could work.

The caller, the News Director at the local radio station, claimed to have a document that appeared to be a *journal* of some sort kept by Jared Whaley, possibly up until the day of his death. The late singer's record label president – according to this small-town radio guy – had verified its authenticity, and now Harvey something-or-other was seeking further confirmation from the victim's widow that the information contained in said document seemed "true…uh…to the best of her knowledge."

Laughlin was skeptical, but curious, and curiosity won out. He wasn't one to leave stones unturned, even if this stone turned out to be a complete waste of his valuable time. On a *Saturday* no less.

Harvey had been to the Wilson County Jail, located on the basement floor of the County Courthouse, many times. Never as an *inmate*, of course. But he'd been chummy enough with past personnel – including current Sheriff Dan Dawkins, whom Harvey had known since he was just a green deputy – to be more than familiar with its somehow dank-yet-bright environ, its black-and-white tiled floors, its six twelve-by-twelve cells.

The cell doors were operated by remote control, from a panel on the wall behind the counter which separated those who were *paid* to be there from those who had less of a choice in the matter. A couple of old filing cabinets, three desks, five chairs, and a table (on which sat a coffee-maker and affiliated condiments) occupied the restricted area beyond, dusty windows along the far wall half-open to the shrubbery lining the Courthouse sidewalk. In the far corner, almost inconspicuous, was the door to the Sheriff's office, the only room in the building - apart from the two restrooms near the entrance - which had any privacy whatsoever.

Or, at least, it *had* been.

The first thing Harvey noticed upon entering the seemingly-deserted jailhouse was that the farthest cell had been *modified*, to say the least. Where there had once been only bars and thin air separating it from the adjoining cell, there was now a wall of plywood, making it appear at first glance that there were only *five* cells. Harvey had to inspect closely to discern the *sixth*, as there were also heavy curtains spanning its front top-to-bottom from inside the sliding barred door.

"How's it hangin' Harvey?" the Sheriff asked, emerging from his office. He sauntered to the counter, extending his hand halfway en route, almost as if he couldn't wait for the physical contact. Harvey felt obliged somehow to extend *his* hand early in return, so that their handshake was more like a space-station docking than a simple greeting.

"Down and to the right," Harvey replied, the same way he'd replied to the same greeting each time they'd met for as long as he could remember.

Dawkins motioned Harvey around the counter.

"Come on back," he said, then turned and headed back toward his office. "I understand you've got an appointment with our guest of honor."

Harvey walked around the counter and followed the Sheriff.

"Well, with her and her *attorney*," he clarified, entering the small office as the Sheriff sat down behind his desk.

"Have a seat," Dawkins said, motioning toward two chairs

on the other side.

Harvey chose one and sat, placing his briefcase on the floor beside him.

"You should consider yourself lucky," the Sheriff continued. "You'll be the first member of the press to have an audience with her."

"Well, actually…" Harvey began, once again feeling the need to clarify but not wanting to divulge too much. "I'm not here as a member of the press."

Dawkins arched an eyebrow.

"Um…" Harvey continued. "It's more just some information I came across that needs to be verified by…uh…Ms. Whaley."

Dawkins leaned back in his chair, his eyes narrowing.

"It's not anything that *we* would need to know about, is it?"

Harvey tried and failed to laugh the question off. What came out was more of an uncomfortable snort.

"No, no, no," he said. "Probably just somebody playing a prank, trying to stir something up."

"'Cause I'm pretty sure you could get in trouble for withholding information if it turns out you've got something that shouldn't be withheld."

Harvey had considered this before calling Laughlin, but also considered how a full disclosure to *all* concerned parties might be received:

"I've got what appears to be a journal dictated by the victim after his death."

"Huh?"

"Apparently it was written by a twelve-year-old kid."

"Get the fuck out."

Harvey couldn't imagine the scenario playing out *too* much differently. Maybe with more laughter.

"I honestly won't know anything more until I talk with Ms. Whaley," he said, honestly.

Harvey was about to offer small talk to break the ensuing silence when the sound of the front door opening did it for him.

"Hello?" came a deep, instantly-recognizable voice.

Dawkins slid his chair back and rose.

"There's your attorney."

Well, not my *attorney,* Harvey thought as he rose, picked up his briefcase, and followed the Sheriff out of the office.

"Good morning, Mr. Laughlin," Dawkins said, extending his hand once again from across the room and following it to where the mountain of a defense attorney stood, dressed casually in jeans and a short-sleeved Polo shirt, carrying an expensive-looking briefcase.

Laughlin, unlike Harvey, didn't feel the need to extend his own hand, and instead turned his gaze to the trailing newsman.

"You're the one smokes a pipe," he said.

"Yes sir," Harvey said, reaching the attorney and offering a tentative handshake, which Laughlin accepted.

"I love the smell of that thing," he laughed. "And I notice it always ensures you a front row spot at our briefings."

"Yes sir," Harvey replied. "I guess a lot of my fellow reporters *don't* love the smell. Or think the smoke's gonna kill 'em."

Laughlin smiled and shook his head. "Damn government-sponsored paranoia campaign," he said. "Another case of our elected representatives biting the hand that feeds 'em."

He finally turned his attention to Dawkins.

"Well, Sheriff," he said. "Shall we?"

"Certainly," Dawkins replied, uncharacteristically deferential, crossing to the panel on the wall and pushing the last of a row of buttons.

There immediately followed a mechanical *whirring* sound as the door to cell number six slowly slid open.

"Thank you, Sheriff," Laughlin said, dismissive, before turning to Harvey.

"Let's go see Angel."

Harvey walked around the counter, noticing out of the corner of his eye Dawkins' non-committal shrug as he shuffled back to his office, then followed Laughlin to just outside cell number six, where the attorney paused.

"You decent?" he asked loudly.

From behind the thick curtains, Harvey heard, for the first time, the literal voice of an Angel.

"No, I'm in the tanning bed," she said. "You know I always tan in the buff."

Laughlin looked at Harvey with a knowing smile, as if to say, "Here we *go*," then reached up to grab the curtains.

His hand only got halfway there before they were flung open from the inside of the cell.

Even after two months in confinement, without the benefit of makeup or even a daily *shower*, dressed in a drab county-issued orange jumpsuit, Angel Whaley nonetheless left Harvey with no doubt this was the woman described (by *whomever*) in the mysterious journal.

He wasn't sure *how* he knew. Whether it was the height or the hair or the "fantabulous ta-ta's." Or her very *essence*. But Harvey *knew*. And it freaked him out.

"Angel, this is Harvey," Laughlin said. "Harvey, Angel."

She held out a long smooth hand at the end of a long smooth arm (*just like in the diary*, Harvey thought), and shook his hand with a softness that belied her circumstance.

"Hi Harvey," she said.

"Yes ma'am," Harvey said, feeling the *antithesis* of smooth. "I mean, hi."

She released his hand, smiled, then turned and walked back into her cell. Laughlin followed, holding back the curtain for Harvey.

From the inside, her cell was not much different from the others, with the exception of the plywood wall (adorned with a

129

calendar and several pictures of Angel and Jared during happier times), and a small night-stand with a lamp - provided out of necessity, since the windowless cells were lit by fluorescent bulbs in the hallway, unable to penetrate either curtain *or* plywood. The sink and toilet were stainless-steel, the bunk a steel mesh covered with a thin sleeping pad, a pillow and folded wool blanket set on the end closest to the back wall. A single plastic chair made up the remainder of the furnishings.

Angel sat on the bunk nearest the pillow and blanket, looking at Harvey with a strange combination of curiosity and boredom.

"You can have the chair," Laughlin said, as he sat on the other end of the bunk.

Harvey sat, placed his briefcase on his lap, and opened it. He wasn't quite sure how to begin.

"Um," he said.

"I think this is all bullshit," Angel said. "No offense."

Harvey couldn't imagine *ever* taking offense at anything that came from those lips.

"Um," he said again. For a man who made his living talking, he felt surprisingly dumb-struck.

"Now Angel," her lawyer interceded. "Harvey said on the phone he was sure this was some kind of a prank. But *Phil* seemed to think it had some merit."

"Well, Phil's eatin' this shit up," she replied bitterly. "Any chance to make this *more* of a circus will only make him more money."

Harvey removed a file from his briefcase.

"Um," he repeated, then handed it to Angel.

"I just brought the parts that I thought only *you* might be able to verify," he said, finally putting together an entire sentence. "But I've got the whole thing…so far."

Angel and Laughlin both stared at him for what seemed like half a minute.

"*So far?*" they asked in unison.

"It's kinda weird…I guess," he said. Then, to Angel, "Maybe you should read it first."

She eyed him warily, then turned her attention to the file folder, removing the pages, laying the empty folder on the bunk. She began reading.

"What do you mean '*so far*'"? Laughlin repeated.

"Um…well," Harvey replied. Laughlin shook his head and studied his client, awaiting her reaction to the words.

Harvey felt a fool, watching Angel's eyes move across the written lines. Part of him hoped she would repudiate the whole thing and allow him to put it to rest.

The section he'd given her began with the mini-thesis on the nature of love and continued through their first meeting, concluding with the argument they'd had before going to what turned out to be Whaley's last gig.

"Oh my *God*!"

Angel looked at Harvey, then at Laughlin, then back at Harvey.

"This is *exactly* how we met!" she said. "Where did you *get* this?"

"Where *did* you get this?" Laughlin added, looking at Harvey with mounting suspicion.

"Um…well," Harvey said. "I think she needs to read the rest."

Angel lowered her head and continued.

"Oh my *God*." She whispered this time, her eyes racing down the page, her shaky hands flipping to the next.

Laughlin glared at Harvey again, unaccustomed to being out of the loop.

Corroboration, Harvey thought, then wondered if he even *wanted* corroboration, as the evidence thus far had only raised more questions than it had answered, had just been one step farther along a path that seemed to lead only to the unexplainable.

"Oh FUCK!"

Angel looked up at Harvey, her eyes glistening with tears –
Harvey couldn't tell whether from sadness or anger. She suddenly
stood up, thrusting the pages in Harvey's face.

"Where the FUCK did you get this?!!"

Harvey leaned back in his chair, suddenly afraid, suddenly
commiserating with the fear of her wrath implied by Whaley (or
whomever) in the journal.

Laughlin rose, restraining his client.

"Angel!" he said. "What the hell's *wrong* with you?"

Angel's shoulders slumped as she looked at the floor, her
lip quivering, barely controlling her emotions. She looked at
Harvey, her eyes questioning, almost pleading, then turned to her
attorney.

"God*dammit* Marshall," she wailed. *"Nobody* knew this!"
She fell to her bunk and started crying.

"What?" Laughlin asked her, then turned to Harvey.
"WHAT?!" he barked.

Harvey leaned even further back in his chair, fearing
momentarily the plastic legs might give way.

"I don't KNOW!" he shouted, although he had an idea.

Angel sat on her bunk and sobbed into her hands. "Nobody
knew about the *gun*."

Laughlin looked perplexed.

"Of *course* they know about the *gun*, Angel. That's
practically their whole *case*!"

She shook her head sadly. Harvey knew why.

"Nobody knows we had a *fight* that day," she said. "And
that I cleaned and loaded my gun right *in front* of him!"

She thrust the pages at her attorney.

A look of disbelieving alarm crossed Laughlin's face as he
took the wrinkled sheets from Angel, sat back down, and began
reading.

"I used to do that a lot," Angel whispered.

As Laughlin's attention focused on the printed words, Angel quietly stood. Before Harvey's befuddled senses even had time to register shock, she'd unzipped her jumpsuit and shrugged it from her pale, smooth shoulders. In his peripheral vision, Harvey saw Laughlin look up, his eyes widening. The attorney started to protest (Harvey wasn't *about* to), but muted himself as he and the radio newsman seemed to simultaneously realize what they were seeing.

Angel's bra was low-cut and black-lace, her "fantabulous ta-tas" barely confined. Just above the thinly-veiled left nipple, in sharp contrast to the silky-white expanse of lightly-veined skin, were the words MY FIRST TATTOO. In fancy lettering like that.

While Harvey's gaze remained riveted, Laughlin's quickly returned to the pages. He thumbed through them, his frown deepening, then looked back up at the tattoo. Then back down. Then back up again.

"Sonofabitch."

He glared at Harvey, whose eyes reluctantly peeled themselves from Angel.

"Huh?"

"Where the fuck did you *get* this?!" the lawyer demanded.

Harvey looked at him, then at Angel. He was disappointed to see her zipping up.

"Well." he said. "*That's* kind of an interesting story.

CHAPTER TWENTY-THREE

Ain't happiness an elusive fuckin' butterfly whose wings you wanna to pin to your heart? Sucks when it turns out it's just a goddamned dressed-up moth.

That kinda sums up my life, and wouldn't make a bad epitaph for my tombstone. The one they gave *me* – Jared Matthew Whaley 1966 – 2009 – *bores me to death.*

My beautiful butterfly's de-evolution into a moth, then into a smoldering reminder of the dangers of flying too close to the flame, began that day behind a booth at the Boro and continued downhill, through dropping out of college and moving into the farmhouse, then getting thrown out *of the farmhouse (and breaking up the band) after sleeping with Chad's girlfriend. That's how I wound up living on the streets of Nashville.*

Do I regret *screwing Chad's girlfriend? Was that one of those moments I'd ask the genie to let me change? Prob'ly. More on that later. But Amanda was a hottie. And they ended up getting married. And the band re-united. Now I'm jumping* way *ahead. While digressing. That's tough to do.*

My first homeless day in Nashville I hocked my guitar. Which sucked, but was far *from being one of my worst days over the course of the next few months. I blew most of the money on a cheap room at a cheap hotel on Dickerson Road, got drunk, and wished like hell I had a guitar to play. I didn't sleep in another bed for over three months. Quite a few* couches *though.*

The next morning, as I re-stuffed the sum total of my worldly possessions into my backpack (and it wasn't a very big *backpack), I sensed I had sunk to the lowest point of my life, yet also conceded the possibility that I might look back on it at some point with yearning nostalgia.*

"The good ol' days."

I hoped not.

The sun on that summer morning lit my own portal to Hell,

a searing spotlight on everything that was wrong with my world –
namely, everything my squinting eyes could see. I put on my spiffy
John-Lennon shades and was reminded instantly that darker don't
mean cooler, that reality is reality whether your shades are tinted,
rose-colored, or covering eyes sewn shut.

I closed the door to room 47 behind me, knowing my key
was laying on the nightstand next to the channel guide and pizza
delivery flyer, that I had no chance to change my mind and crawl
back under the covers until housekeeping banged on the door and
threw me out.

"This ain't eternity," I said aloud.

"No, baby, this is Nashville,"

The voice came from the middle-aged black woman
emerging from the room just to my left.

Housekeeping. Figured.

I was either on a bus or waiting at a bus stop for most of
the rest of that day, riding to the end of each line, getting off,
waiting for the next in-bound bus, taking it to the downtown hub,
then choosing another bus at random away from downtown again.
I re-re-read most of the Jim Morrison bio "No One Here Gets Out
Alive," and wished I had some acid.

I didn't of course. Alphabetically, it was near the top of a
long list of things I didn't have. Practically, *it was near the*
bottom.

Eight bucks had got me a week of unlimited bus rides and
left me with a ten-dollar bill, with which I intended to find a
writers night and get drunk. And maybe eat a little something.
Wasn't sure in which order.

I found a Nashville Scene *downtown and discovered there*
was a writers night at a place called Bogie's *in the* Day's Inn
Vanderbilt *right by where Broadway split into West End. They not*
only had an open-mic early in the evening, they also had a free
buffet.

I got on the #3 headed that direction for the third time that day, but this time got off at the spot where 17th Ave. N. becomes 17th Ave. S., or vice-versa. I'd showered that morning, so didn't look too homeless, which probably served me well as I walked into the lobby of the hotel. Although I still got a suspicious looking-over from the attractive young lady behind the front desk.

Just to my right, a set of double doors opened into a fairly-busy restaurant, obviously somewhat high-scale, based on the attire of the diners – to which by comparison I did look homeless. I said a little prayer that the open-mic wasn't going to be there.

To my left there was a large black door beside which hung a large framed poster from the movie Casablanca, *the black-and-white photo of Humphrey Bogart and Lauren Bacall giving them the illusion of youth and life.*

Ah. Bogie's.

The aforementioned young lady behind the desk arched her trimmed eyebrows in the direction of the bar. Perceptive of her.

As I smiled and nodded (something I have a tendency to do in the company of hotties), then turned toward the indicated door, it swung open from inside and two really *big guys came out. I momentarily feared for the buffet.*

The least-huge of the pair (still about two-bucks seventy-five or eighty), black-brown hair cascading from beneath a gray fedora, led the way.

"How ya doin'?" He seemed happy.

"Hey man." I offered a quick nod.

Following him was a Kodiak bear in blue jeans. That spoke. The bear, *not the jeans. He seemed happy too.*

"Hey man."

"How's it goin'?"

That was pretty much me and the Jones Brothers' first conversation. Later we would embellish the story, add some syllables. They would swear I was drunk.

The mountains headed out of the lobby as I entered the bar and let the door close behind me. I stood still for a moment, my

136

eyes adjusting to the subdued lighting, first taking in the small lit stage in the far corner, several guitar cases leaning against the wall to the side, the shadowy silhouettes of a handful of patrons sitting around a handful of small tables.

The room could hold maybe twenty-five or thirty people (several fewer if those big fellers I'd just met came back). Its walls were adorned with more posters from Humphrey Bogart movies – The African Queen, The Maltese Falcon, The Treasure of the Sierra Madre *– each illuminated by a filtered spot suspended above. The bar to my right, on the opposite side of the small room from the stage, sat six, although only one at that moment – and his dirty white apron and hair net belied his non-songwriter status.*

"Can you get me on about 8?" the non-non-songwriter (I should've known better than to judge) asked the bartender, a muscular long-haired guy who looked like he'd just arrived from California with a useless surfboard.

"Yep," he said, then turned to me. "How's it goin'?"

"Much better now," I answered, honestly, for I was in my element, all of my woes pushed to the periphery. Beer, women, and song on the near horizon. If there were any women, and if somebody let me borrow their guitar.

"How much is your draft beer?"

I prepared myself to do the night's most important math.

The bartender smiled a perfect smile that immediately made you want to befriend him and punch him in the face.

"A buck a glass, two-seventy-five a pitcher. We've got Bud, Bud Light, and PBR."

Three pitchers. That sounded about right. With a little left to tip. Then I'd be broke.

"PBR, definitely," I said.

"Glass?"

"With the pitcher, sure." I smiled, though not with nearly enough dazzle to make a person want to punch me in the face.

"Sure thing," he laughed, grabbing a plastic pitcher from a

shelf behind him. He held it under the PBR spigot and opened the tap. The beer flowed like a golden-haired seductress releasing her locks from beneath a ball cap. That's what I *thought, anyway.*

He filled the pitcher, then cut the flow and set the beer in front of me, along with a frosty glass he pulled from a freezer beneath the bar.

"Two-seventy-five."

I set my backpack on a barstool, pulled the lonely ten from my wallet, and handed it to him. He took the money, turned to the register beneath the lined shelves of liquor bottles, and made change.

After I'd taken the money I'd later be giving back, he held out his hand.

"I'm Justin," he said.

I laid the change on the bar and we shook.

"Jared Whaley."

"So I'm guessing you'll be needing to borrow a guitar." His accent was definitely *West Coast.*

"I'm that obvious huh?"

He smiled. "Unless you're just here for the buffet."

I slid into the padded stool beside the one where I'd set my backpack.

"Both actually." I grinned and filled my glass.

"Well, the buffet comes out in about half an hour. And I've got a Takamine you can use."

"Nice," I said, taking a drink. "Standard tuning?"

"That's generally all that's allowed in Nashville. That's why they invented capos." He turned to a guy in a cowboy hat standing down the bar.

"When's open-mic start?" Cowboy asked.

Justin looked at his watch, then surveyed the half-dozen or so seated.

"Probably about twenty minutes or so. Might wait on a few more to show up."

"Cool. Can I get a bottle of Bud Light?" I already envied those wannabes with expendable incomes.

In the next twenty minutes, I found out that Justin was actually from Ohio (but to give me a little credit, he was from the west coast of the state), that Jeff from the kitchen had a famous-songwriter father, and that I could almost finish off a pitcher of beer in twenty minutes. Although I think I might've known that. I also discovered, from Justin, that the large pair I had passed as I came in were actually brothers down from Chicago to get the blues playin' country, and that they'd probably gone out to their van to get high. Which, for some reason, made me happy.

As I poured the last half-glass of the first third of my night's allotment, I noticed that, while I had my back turned yackin' with Justin and Jeff, the room had almost filled. With the re-entrance of the affable behemoths – now somewhat glassy-eyed and giggly - it was damn-near packed. The really big one stopped at the last remaining unoccupied table and occupied it in a large way. He was about six-six, and fat, but not in a "fat-ass slob" kinda way. More in a "I'd look stupid skinny" kinda way. A reminder that every once in awhile God just makes a big boy. He eased himself into the padded chair, re-arranging his mid-section a bit to ensure a comfy fit, as the quite-large smaller fella with the hat came up to the bar to my left.

"Two Buds?" Justin asked.

"Please." He turned to me. Smiled and held out his hand. "I'm Walt Jones."

"Jared Whaley." His grip was firm, but not as firm as it could have been, and definitely not as firm as I imagined his brother's was – I had a mental pic of my handful of small bones being crushed to powder.

"You playin'?" Walt handed Justin a fiver for the beers. I nodded and took a drink. Which reminded me...

"Hey, Justin, I didn't even ask about a sign-up sheet."

Walt laughed. "Justin don't need no steenking sign-up

sheet. "

*To illustrate the point, Justin yelled to the cowboy, sitting
at a table near the stage.*

"Hey Terry, you playin'?"

"Sure."

"You wanna go first?"

"Sure."

"Okay. 'Bout five minutes. You get three songs."

*A semi-hot brunette at the table with Terry leaned forward,
revealing some not-too-shabby cleavage, and said something that
seemed encouraging.*

*"Buddy!" Justin yelled to a young long-haired kid sitting at
a table with another young long-haired kid.*

"Yeah Justin?"

"You're second."

"Okay."

"Three songs."

"Yep."

"Hey, Joe. You wanna go third?"

Joe nodded from another table. "Sure thing."

Justin turned to Walt.

"You and Stopher want to go fourth and fifth?"

Walt nodded, taking a drink of beer.

Justin grabbed my empty pitcher and stuck it under the tap.

"After they *play," he said to me, " I'll get up and play a
couple, then Jeff'll play a couple, then it's your turn. Three songs.
Jeff'll have the guitar."*

"Cool."

*"Come sit with us if you want," Walt offered, taking both
beers and turning toward the table.*

*"Cool. Thanks." Justin set the pitcher in front of me and I
slid him a fiver, watching Terry the Cowboy tune his guitar beside
the stage.*

"Stewart. You're after Jared here," he yelled across the

room as he handed me two singles and a quarter. "Elizabeth. You're after Stewart."

"Okay."

I filled my glass from the pitcher, then eyed my backpack, thinking there probably wouldn't be room under the small table, what with me and Walt's legs and Stopher's tree trunks.

"I'll put it back here." It was Justin, quickly solving my conundrum.

"Thanks." I set my beer back on the counter, heaved the bundle to him over the bar, then picked the beer back up and turned toward the brothers, who were watching me. I smiled and walked the few steps to their table.

"You homeless?" Stopher asked.

I set my beer on the table and my ass in the single remaining chair simultaneously.

"Uh...kinda. Long story."

"This is Jared, Stopher," Walt laughed. "Jared, this is my big brother."

"No shit," I said.

Stopher turned his back to look at Cowboy taking the stage, plugging in his guitar.

"I'll bet he mentions a pick-up in the first song," he said, turning back, then smiled. "Nice to meet ya."

He didn't offer to shake. It didn't bother me so much 'cause I was a little scared and, besides, he'd just read my mind.

"Wow. You read my mind."

"Great minds think alike."

He turned back to the stage as Terry strummed his guitar slowly, checking the sound.

"Can you hear that okay?" he asked into the mic.

The room was small enough that you could have heard him clearly anyway, *but nobody mentioned* that. *Instead his table-mate with the jazzy jugs whooped.*

He laughed and adjusted his hat. "Hey I'm Terry

Templeton...I'm number one I guess..."

This got another whoop from the melon mama, along with scattered laughs from the rest of the crowd. For what possible reason is beyond me.

"This first song I'm gonna play is called 'Pick-Up Lines'."
No shit.

I laughed and automatically reached up to give Stopher a high-five. He held his bottle of Bud to his lips with his right hand, and seemed to hesitate a moment before raising his left hand to meet mine halfway across the table.

It was a girl's hand. A small *girl's hand. A dainty little slim-fingered exquisite hand.*

I didn't even think before I said it.
"Wow. That's a purty hand."

I hoped he wouldn't be hurt or – worse – angry, and was relieved when he smiled.

"It's a gift from God."
I'd never seen such a physical anomaly. Boggled the mind.
"It's kinda tiny."
Both laughed as Stopher laid his freak on the table.
"It makes his penis look larger when he masturbates,"
Walt said.

"All a matter of scale," Stopher added.
"That's one of the reasons I like to fuck midgets," I said, and we all laughed out loud as Terry the Cowboy began singing on stage:

Tell me is it a Ford or Chevy?
Tell me 'bout your bed
Tell me 'bout your 4-wheel drive
I just nodded my head
I could tell from her talk
I was gonna make her mine
Chalk up another heart to my pick-up lines
And we all laughed again as Terry sang a description of his

pick-up. It sounded like a nice truck.

I leaned into the table, my voice just loud enough for them to hear.

"You know how tough it is to get a chick with a 'bus pass' line?"

"Yeah, but it rhymes with 'ass,'" Walt said.

I arched my eyebrows and leaned back, nodding. Took a drink. Started running lines and scenarios through my head for a song where a homeless guy picks up a hottie with a line about his bus pass. Which led to thinking it could maybe be a song making fun *of pick-up truck songs. Kinda.*

She's about forty feet long and I've got me a driver
We can even have a party in the back

Then a line that rhymes with driver, *then one that rhymes with* back. *Then into a refrain along the lines of:*

I won't ask for any change
We can get off anytime
See how far I get
On the bus lines

That could work. Even without *the "pass-ass" rhyme.*

Me and the Behemoth Bros chatted amiably (but at a low volume) through the rest of Terry's set, then through Buddy's, exchanging snap-shots of our inglorious lives.

They'd moved here from Chicago a couple of months previously. Walt was delivering furniture and appliances and the like for a rent-to-own place, Stopher was a telephone solicitor, peddling medical manuals to doctors' offices. They'd had a band up north, were making decent money playing cover gigs, but felt the country music biz needed some shaking up, and figured they were just the guys to do it. They were sharing a one-bedroom apartment in Antioch near the airport. I imagined it cramped.

Mid-way through Joe's first song, the pair began fidgeting and glancing furtively at the stage. Anyone who's ever played for an audience knows the feeling – regardless of your experience or

expertise, you get butterflies. You know *there's always the
possibility that* this *is the time you're going to forget every song
you've ever sung, to validate every naysayer's prognostication that
dreams are destined to die. To absolutely* suck.

Eventually, if you hang with it long enough, you learn to
revel *in those butterflies, realize it's that nervous energy and fear
which drives you. So long as you don't get so nervous you throw
up. It's a fine line which for me is directly correlated to alcohol
consumption. Whoops. " Was." Forgive me. Sometimes I forget
I'm dead. The dead live in the past tense.*

*As Joe began his third song, Walt and Stopher rose from
the table and made their way to their guitar cases leaning by the
stage. I thought they resembled a pair of water-buffalo at an
African oasis as they laid the cases on the floor, unlatched and
opened them, removed the guitars, then shut the cases and leaned
them once again against the wall. I felt bad for likening them to
water-buffalo, so I imagined them as Volkswagens instead. That
didn't really assuage my guilt.*

*Joe finished his final song – something about his mama I
think – to appreciative applause, then turned down and unplugged
his guitar and left the stage. The bovine German economy cars
exchanged brief pleasantries with him and lumbered into the
muted spotlight, the more-nimble Walter setting up the second mic
and plugging in his beautiful Martin in the time it took for his
brother to find his Ovation's jack-hole.*

"Jack-hole." That's a fun word.

*Walt did the honors, introducing themselves as "Big
Jones" (which I, along with most of the crowd it seemed, found
amusing and fitting), then broke into a mid-tempo sad song called
"Cryin' on the Shoulder of the Road." Walt had a strong, deep,
almost-operatic voice, and though his enunciation lacked clarity -
so that you had to guess about every fourth word - you could tell
from those lyrics you* could *make out that they did not lack for
depth, that they conveyed a simple honesty which so often eluded*

many a songwriter in this town.

It was a good song, well-crafted, and that, along with the sheer physical presence *of the duo, went a long way toward quelling the chatter of the throng. Yet it wasn't until Stopher took a lead break that they hushed entirely, for that's when they noticed the hand.*

There might've been an "Oh my God,*" from one of the ladies present, but aside from that subdued outburst the room fell totally silent, awed not only by the incongruity of the mitt to the man, but by the wonderfully harmonious magic those dainty little fingers conjured from those unwitting strands of taut steel, finding the exact combination of note and tone, striking exactly the right chord, managing to resonate from the soul of the song to the soul of the listener with an ease that precluded anything but nature.*

So, yeah, the big guys were pretty damned good. Stopher's vocals on his own equally-well-crafted songs were not as striking as his brother's, yet seemed equally as honest. He sang like he talked - or maybe he talked like he sang – with neither apology nor pretense, offering up his insides to be either acknowledged or ignored, the reception not nearly as crucial as the delivery. Reminded me of me. But with better musical chops and a prettier hand.

As they concluded their set – to the best applause of the night so far – Jeff rolled out the buffet cart, laden with the finest cuisine an establishment could afford to provide for free: mainly a lot of chips and dips, with a pan of miniscule chicken wings and little wieners thrown in as entrees. There was a stack of snack-size Styrofoam plates and plastic forks at one end, and as soon as my new friends had left the stage and re-packed their guitars they were there, piling on the grub as they accepted the accolades of their new fans.

I stayed in my seat and watched. For some reason, beer and impending performing have always been major appetite-suppressants. I wasn't sure where my next meal would come from, and could only hope the buffet wouldn't be picked clean by the time I felt like eating. Damned drunken butterflies.

Jeff, his kitchen duties temporarily suspended, went behind the bar to serve beers as Justin took the stage with his community Takamine, announced the upcoming line-up, then serenaded us with a song so soft and sweet as to make you want to befriend him, then punch him in the face. It was amazing he still had all of his pearly-white teeth.

I don't recall the rest of Justin's set, or any of Jeff's, or clearly remember the exchanges I had with the brothers as they sat down and commenced to devour their free food. I only recall my inner debate over which three songs to play, a debate which continued until Jeff had finished playing and I found myself standing to the side of the stage, smiling and nodding, accepting the offered guitar. I was, as always, nervous as shit.

Even though I had none of those aforementioned Fairly Decent Tapes to sell, I still decided to go with a couple of its ludicrously-familiar songs. I started with a happy little tune called "Pain." Which is just how I always introduced it. Which always got a laugh.

The slammin' door broke his nose
As his tears fell her laughter rose
But she's not completely heartless,
She slid some tissue through the mail slot
She said "If you ever come 'round here again
I'll have you hurt, I have some friends
Who will happily break every limb that you got"
Now he's startin' to think she don't love him any more

Again, it could have been my own selective perception, or it could've been the novelty of a funny song after so much beer-cryin', but I could swear I killed more than even the Jones boys had killed. And they killed 'em dead.

By the end of my "Train" song, which I played next, I had no doubt.

After the applause and whoopin' and hollerin' and the what-not from that one died down, after I'd taken the first pull from a bottle of beer bought for me by one of the tables up front, after I'd caught Justin smiling and nodding in a way that assured me I'd found a friend who served beer, I decided to try out a new one.

It was a song I'd written during those last drunken days at the farmhouse, before I'd got laid and evicted, before I'd become guitar-less and homeless. The good ol' days. I called it my "Sing-along Divorce Song."

I don't have cash, I don't have a car
I don't have sense and I don't have far to go
I don't have love or joy or success
And I don't have many prospects I know
...which is all very gloom and doom I know. But it gets better...
It may seem as if I don't have anything
But I've got a wealth of treasure
I can do nothin' with....
And this is where, with a build-up, it finally pays off:
I have all your shit in the bedroom closet
I have all your shit in the closet in the hall
I have all your shit, and you can't have it
Where is your shit you ask?
I have it all
By the time I reached the final chorus, with everybody singing along, I knew it was a keeper, and knew I'd at least for the next few minutes be the most popular guy in the room. Which I was.

Don't know for the life of me why I never recorded that song.

CHAPTER TWENTY-FOUR

"*Where is your shit, you ask? I have it all!*" the pudgy kid sang into the camera, his face devoid of emotion but his *voice* full of it.

"Damn, boy, that's creepy," his father remarked off-screen, just moments before the monitor went dark. Someone flipped a switch and the rows of fluorescent bulbs bisecting the ceiling flickered, then stayed on, illuminating the drab conference room on the second floor of the Wilson County Courthouse.

A small folding table had been set up near the door, supporting a stack of Styrofoam cups, a half-full 12-cup coffee maker plugged into the wall, small boxes of sweetener, creamer packets, stir-sticks, a couple of pitchers of water, and a small stack of napkins.

It was here that Mack, Marshall Laughlin, Haywood Brice, Ken Fleming, and Harvey congregated during the uncomfortable silence following the video presentation, all but Fleming pouring cups of coffee.

"You want coffee Angel?" Laughlin asked.

His client remained seated at the conference table, dressed for court in a conservative pale-blue dress, her long dark hair pulled back in a ponytail, her beautiful face unpainted, looking for all the world like *anything* but a murderess.

"Sure. Thanks."

She spoke quietly, her eyes down, a lone tear sliding down her cheek to the corner of her pretty mouth before being brushed absently away with the back of a hand.

"Two creamers, one sweetener please," she added.

Marshall turned his gaze to the nearly-empty pot, then paused, making an executive decision.

"Penny, why don't you fix Mrs. Whaley a cup of coffee, then make us a fresh pot?" he said, rounding the head of the table where Brice and Fleming were now settling into their padded chairs. He sat in a chair between his client and his assistant Penny, a short bespectacled redhead who was now rising from the legal folder in front of her to less-than-enthusiastically perform waitressing chores.

"Certainly, Mr. Laughlin," she said.

Marshall set his cup down, slid the folder his way, then opened it. Harvey, sitting across the table from the defense team, next to Mack, opened a similar folder.

After a pregnant pause, Fleming cleared his throat, drawing the table's attention, and gestured with his eyes toward the now-dark-and-silent video monitor facing them from the opposite end of the table.

"So *that's* why we're here?" he asked.

Brice spoke up in a thin whisper.

"Judge Way is *not* going to be pleased."

"*What?*" Marshall and Harvey said nearly simultaneously, while Mack said, "*Huh?*"

As the County Prosecutor rolled his eyes, Fleming more-voluminously elaborated.

"What Haywood's trying to say is that the Judge may not look kindly on an *emergency* recess spent watching a home movie of a fat kid auditioning for *American Idol*."

"He's just big-boned," Mack said defensively. "Like me and his mama."

Marshall's deep voice resonated clearly through the room.

"I think it would be a mistake to trivialize what we just witnessed," he chided, then added, "The show's not over just because the fat kid sang."

"Hey!" Mack objected.

"That's just an expression to illustrate a point," Harvey assured him.

"He's just big-boned," Mack nearly pouted.

What they had in fact just witnessed was over an hour of video showing the youngest member of the Blevins clan typing –

sometimes on his bed, sometimes from the dinner table - his eyes staring into space as his pudgy fingers raced across his computer keyboard, occasionally bursting forth with such non-sequitur rantings as, "That's not just *bad,* that's *Monday-Night-Bluebird-bad,*" or something about stabbing a genie in the eye with a fork, or "That's why I like to fuck midgets," sometimes spontaneously breaking into song, singing either a piece of an Elvis tune or one of the Jared Whaley songs with which everyone in the room was now familiar. Except for that last one.

"He never recorded that one," Angel said quietly to her coffee cup, which Penny had handed her before sullenly taking the now-empty pot out the door, presumably to a water source.

"But he *performed* it plenty, right?" Fleming asked.

"Sometimes."

"And there *are* recordings of some of these performances out there?"

"Yeah. Probably"

She looked at the AP, a touch of pride momentarily brightening her sad features.

"People used to bootleg his shows all the time."

Fleming paused and allowed his point to sink in.

"So *see?*" he said to Laughlin. "There's an alternate to your theory that…"

He paused a moment, briefly taking in the radio man and the boy's father before turning back to the defense attorney.

"What *is* your theory exactly?"

There was a long moment of silence, as Laughlin looked at Angel, who looked at Harvey, who shrugged.

"That country singer done possessed my boy," Mack said defiantly.

Brice laughed aloud at this, though few in the room heard, the slight sound drowned out by the opening of the door. Penny was back.

"We're just saying…" Marshall took a breath and paused.

"...that this whole thing raises more questions than it answers, and that justice would not be fully served if we didn't disclose it and allow you the opportunity to make your own assessment as to its relevance."

Brice again laughed out loud, but was this time eclipsed by the water pouring from the coffee pot into the coffee maker. Fleming's snicker was plainly audible.

Harvey understood their skepticism, and, for the millionth time, wondered what the hell he was doing. He worried that his own at-least-*respectable* news career could take a blow from which it might not recover, relegating him at the very best to a sideshow freak, aka *morning guy*. He couldn't very well expect to be taken seriously about any *real* news if this fiasco blew up in his face.

Yet...

Things had taken an even *stranger* turn when, the day after the meeting in the jail cell, Mack called Harvey.

It was Sunday, and Harvey was at the station re-writing the *Democrat*'s account of Friday's developments in the trial - namely, a parade of prosecution witnesses from the *Thirsty Turtle*, all of whom gave testimony as to where Angel *wasn't* when the shots were fired that night. She wasn't anywhere near the door, according to Melvin the doorman, although he *had* seen her and the victim enter. She wasn't at any of the three bars, according to the three bartenders. Nor was she in the ladies' room, according to Maureen Samuels, who was touching up her make-up and almost rammed her mascara applicator into her eye.

Laughlin's cross of each of these witnesses had been about the same:

"So you weren't in the dressing room at the time of the shooting?"

To which each witness had simply answered, "No."

"And you didn't witness my client firing a weapon at the

victim?"

Again, each time: "No."

"No further questions."

Harvey was just about to go downstairs to the production room to start editing Warren's recordings of the press briefing when his cell phone rang.

"Hey Harvey, it's Mack Blevins," he'd heard on the other end after answering. "Willard's got one of them thumb-whatchamacallits for ya." A few minutes later, Mack had dropped the thumb-drive off at the station.

It contained another thirty-something pages detailing what certainly seemed to be *somebody's* life. It sounded like a country song. In this installment, however, the writer began acknowledging his readers, mentioning the trial and implying that at some point he'd be revealing the truth, straight from the dead horse's mouth, so to speak. Even if the whole thing *were* a hoax, it *still* made for a compelling read.

Before he called Laughlin (he had his private number now), Harvey did some more research.

He started by googling "Kristi Whaley." Hit a dead-end. Apparently she had either re-married or gone back to her maiden name, which hadn't been mentioned.

Next he googled "Gary Mathis," Whaley's acquaintance from that first night at the Bluebird. Turned out there was a guitar teacher in Tallahassee by that name. Harvey got voice-mail, and left a brief message along with the news-hotline number. He was rewarded just a few minutes later with a call.

"Hot *damn*!" the voice said. "I was wonderin' when one of you reporters would do your homework."

Harvey had put Mathis on hold, ran downstairs to the production room, and quickly began recording. He picked back up.

"So you knew Jared Whaley?"

"*Knew* him? Hell, I introduced him to his first wife at the

Bluebird!"

Harvey was simultaneously relieved and disappointed at this first contradiction of the accounts of the journal. A *minor* contradiction to be sure, but he was both desperate and hesitant to sow his own seeds of reasonable doubt.

"How did you meet him?" Harvey knew - from watching TV mainly – to avoid leading questions.

"Very first night he played there," Mathis said without hesitation. "I had to explain how the whole process worked, told him about the Sunday night shows, drank some PBR with him in line, sat with him at a table near the stage that he snagged because Kristi was his landlord's daughter."

"Oh." Harvey didn't want to point out the discrepancy, and didn't have to.

"Well, I'll be dogged," Mathis mused. "I guess I didn't introduce 'em after all." He paused a moment. "Huh."

Harvey was shocked by his giddiness at the contradiction of the contradiction.

"And how did he feel about the quality of talent that first night?"

Somewhat leading, he knew, and guessed that if he were a lawyer in open court he'd probably have to re-arrange it a bit to avoid an objection. But no one was there to object, and, hell, Harvey was a radio-man anyway.

Mathis had laughed then. It was a laugh shaded by reminiscence, a sad laugh.

"'That's not just *bad*, that's *Monday-night Bluebird* bad,'" he said.

After the chill bumps left, after the fine-blond hairs on Harvey's arms had returned to their rightful restful place, he sat silently for a moment, shaking his head.

What in the name of Sam Hill...

He'd called Laughlin then, told him about the latest

developments, then e-mailed him the latest installment of the dead guy's diary.

A short time later, Laughlin called him and suggested videotaping the kid. He seemed almost as surprised *making* the suggestion as Harvey was *hearing* it. Yet, in the grand scheme of things, it wasn't any more bat-shit crazy than any other idea. "Bat-shit crazy" was becoming an increasingly-relative term.

"You might want to give 'em a camera with a remote," Harvey said. "They're used to remotes."

The next morning before court the defense attorney had delivered just such a camcorder to the Blevins' home, showed them how to work it (*several* times), and given them instructions to tape as much of the boy's weirdness as they could.

On Tuesday, the prosecution had rested, concluding their case with a full day of testimony from Angel's father, John Dempsey, who reluctantly testified that his daughter's and the victim's relationship had been stormy at best, and had, in fact, become downright acrimonious in the weeks leading to the murder. And that he'd given her the gun.

Assistant Prosecutor Ken Fleming then asked Dempsey one last question.

"Did your daughter ever threaten to *kill* her husband?"

The witness had looked at his daughter, staring at him sadly from the defense table. Tears welled up as he turned, silently pleading, to the judge.

"Answer the question, Mr. Dempsey."

He'd paused long enough to elicit a protest from Fleming. "Your Honor…"

"She never meant it!" Dempsey cried. "She's always had a temper…but she *loved* Jared."

"Did she ever threaten to kill him?" Fleming repeated.

"This is my *daughter*…my *baby*…" He'd started crying softly, the tears rolling down his gray-stubbled cheeks.

"Mr. Dempsey," the Judge said gently, with a touch of sadness. "You're under oath. Please answer the question."

Fleming pounced, not waiting for a response.

"Did the defendant ever threaten to kill Jared Whaley?"

"ALL THE TIME!"

He'd started sobbing, the sobs turning to a wail as he seemed to realize his words might well be condemning the light of his life.

"ALL THE FUCKING TIME!"

That night Mack Blevins invited Laughlin to his home to pick up the video.

"He seems to be *enjoying* this now," Mack said, handing over the camcorder.

The next morning the defense attorney had requested an emergency recess.

"Let's cut to the chase."

Laughlin was once again standing, addressing the self-satisfied, almost *smug* prosecution team.

"We've got reliable, *independent* substantiation that much of this testimonial is accurate," he said, his eyes meeting theirs as he gestured toward the blank TV monitor. "A *combination* of substantiated facts which on their own might be discounted as coincidence, but which, when taken as a whole, *defy* disbelief."

He paused a moment, collecting thoughts he never dreamed he'd collect. His massive shoulders slumped. He sadly shook his head.

"In all my years of practicing law, this is the most preposterous...the most *ludicrous* argument I've ever made."

He picked up his Styrofoam cup, took a sip, as he gazed down at the open folder, flipped a couple of pages almost absent-mindedly. He shook his head again, then looked back up.

"It's going to get crazier before it gets saner," he said.

All eyes in the room were on him now, the prosecution team's widened in anticipation, the widow's and redneck's and radio man's reflecting more an almost morbid curiosity.

The room was silent, save for the gurgling of the coffee-maker, beside which Penny still stood, also quietly staring.

"That country singer done possessed my boy," Mack said.

Fleming chuckled as Brice guffawed, albeit *quietly*.

Laughlin just sighed.

"And I'm going to put 'em *both* on the stand," he said.

CHAPTER TWENTY-FIVE

I swear to God I got a squirrel high one time. While this has nothing to do with the price of tea in China, I felt I had to mention it. It's too good a story, and things seem to be snowballing in such a manner, with such a damned looming deadline, that I'm going to have to pick and choose the remaining episodes of my all-too-short yet apparently all-too-long life.

And I have to tell you about the squirrel.

It was about six months after the end of my homelessness. I'd started working at the Subway on West End, about forty to fifty hours a week, and had found a room to rent about a half a mile from there – right across the street from Belmont University.

Dope-smoking was frowned upon in this particular establishment, and Lord knows I hate to be frowned upon. But not as much as I hate not smoking dope. So every morning before work, and every night after, I'd crack a window. There was a big tree right outside, and one morning a gray squirrel was just sitting there, looking in at me. So I blew some second-hand high his way.

And he FLIPPED! Literally. Got way agitated, did a back-flip, and threw himself at the window. I'd've laughed my ass off if I hadn't shit myself. Pot makes me paranoid anyway, but when a deranged squirrel barks at you and tries to come at you through the window, it's not really paranoia, is it? And I didn't really shit myself.

When I was eleven, and got hit by that car, I remember being in the hospital before my emergency surgery. They gave me a shot right below my belly-button to numb me, then proceeded to cut a hole in my side and stick a tube in there to drain out my internal bleeding. Worst pain of my life. To make a bad situation worse, they then shoved a tube up my nose till it reached the back of my throat and made me swallow till it was in my stomach. Because I was about to go into surgery, I hadn't been allowed as much as a tiny sip of water, and my gullet was as dry as a nun watching a porn flick. And equally as uncomfortable. Moments after that *excruciating episode, an intern walking by tripped on the tube, and it was yanked back out with a loud dry sucking sound and a force that pulled me to an upright position and elicited a string of profanity that would've made a drunken sailor wash his own mouth out with soap.*

Apart from that – which in total lasted but a few minutes – homelessness sucked worse than anything in my life. Up until…well, you *figure it out.*

I was flat broke the morning after my first night at Bogie's, but I had my bus pass, and Nashville has a pretty decent public library. Two blocks down from the Day's Inn parking garage where I'd slept on a concrete bed, using my stuffed backpack as an awkward uncomfortable pillow, was a place called Plasma Alliance, *where you could sell the only part of your blood that justifies bleedin'. I was* way *too hung over to consider it at the moment, but filed it away in the back of my mind as an alternative to collecting aluminum cans or standing on Lower Broad with a tin cup.*

Thanks to that place, and my body's amazing ability to re-generate plasma, I never did either. My arms, even in their current advanced state of decomposition inside a buried casket in a quaint little cemetery in Oklahoma, probably still bear the scars.

After my first visit to the library as a homeless guy among countless homeless guys (I checked out a John Lennon bio and The World According to Garp *by John Irving, using Sean's address to get a library card), I grudgingly made my way down 8th Avenue to the Union Rescue Mission, next to the Greyhound station a few blocks away. All of my hopeful notions that* this *shelter might bear any resemblance at all to the Sally in Austin evaporated upon my arrival.*

They say your olfactory sense is the one most closely linked to memory. It works both ways sometimes. Thanks to the Union

Rescue Mission that summer, I can't think about the darkest days of my life without smelling sun-baked piss on concrete.

I was one of about three white guys on the premises, not including the resident preacher, an angry old man whom I'll betcha a dollar God'll swear up and down He didn't *make in His image. This pathetic excuse for a man of the cloth tried to stack the deck in his favor by only allowing a bed to those souls so anxious to not sleep on the streets as to be willing to sit through his hour-long vomitific bastardization of the Word. I sat through it exactly once.*

The place still served three meals a day though, shitty as they were, so I was there quite a bit that first week. I spent the time between free grub (or waiting *on free grub) mainly at the library, or sometimes farther down the road at the place where on Mondays, Wednesdays, and Fridays you could take a shower and do laundry.*

It was during one of these times spent waiting on grub, sitting with my back against the white cinder-block wall of the large courtyard outside the shelter, that I developed my hatred for the homeless. I was minding my own business (like always), reading about Beatles' manager Brian Epstein's unrequited crush on John Lennon, when I looked up through my cool and beloved sunglasses to see a crack-head standing in front of me, staring down with ignorant derision, holding a two-by-four.

"Gimme them motherfuckin' shades," he slurred.

I looked around and noticed I was the only white guy in the courtyard, figured I wasn't going to get any help on this. When I saw that about half the fuckers were actually enjoying *my predicament, I simply smiled, removed my favorite pair of sunglasses* ever, *and handed them over. He grunted, put on the shades, then turned and smiled at the on-lookers, many of whom laughed, some of whom actually applauded. I pictured them battery-operated, holding cymbals.*

I comforted myself with the knowledge that this was all

temporary *for me, would one day be just a blip on a distant radar; for many of* them, *it was just another worthless phase of a worthless existence that would lead inexorably to prison or death or death in prison. I hoped that the one standing in front of me would be tortured in the slammer by neo-Nazis. Those guys are idiots too, but if they sent this particular jerk-off to his Maker by way of a fork and a pair of heated-up needle-nose pliers, I'd at least get a grin out of it. Cool and unusual punishment.*

My bus pass was expiring that day, so I went and sold plasma for the first time. The place was a lot like the shelter, but with less smoking and more security. The clientele were similarly worthless and moronic, but I was at least compensated *to tolerate their thankfully-enforced quieter derision. Fuck 'em.*

I played again that night at Bogie's, beginning what would become a twice weekly routine, on the days I sold my bodily fluid for beer money. That particular night I met Derek, a kid exactly a decade my junior, who had seen me play at the Bluebird, and thought I was niftier than sliced bread and infinitely more talented. He was my opposite in many respects – he didn't drink or smoke (pot or *cigarettes, although tobacco was something I wouldn't pick up for a number of years), and he could play circles around me on the guitar. Pretty damned good songwriter too, and I envied the wisdom which seemed to come naturally to him, which I felt I had to struggle so mightily to attain and which, looking back, I never really did.*

Walt and Stopher and Sean were there that night too, and the five of us became a band of brothers and kindred compadres, spending pretty much every Friday and/or Saturday night sitting around the Jones boys' small apartment, trading songs, inspired each week to come up with something new to impress one another's most ardent fans.

These nights, along with the aforementioned blood-financed forays onto the Bogie's stage, became the highlights of my forlorn existence, the latter because of the crowds and inherent hope I would either get discovered or laid (neither of which were meant to be during that period – I might've mentioned that), the former because of the encouragement wrought by the respect and admiration of my uber-talented comrades – for how could those so gifted be misguided in their assessment of my gifts?

The Jones' comfy sofa, which was a welcome weekly change from the concrete of the Days Inn parking garage or the park benches which were my beds most nights, was just a bonus.

One Saturday morning, hung over from the night before and high from the morning's marijuana cure, I stood on the small balcony of the Jones' second-floor apartment, watching planes take off and land from the Nashville International Airport, just two miles to the east.

The air traffic consisted mainly of large commercial jets, which after a while grew monotonous. My attention was piqued, however, when I saw a military jet taking off, relatively loudly and at what seemed to me to be a ridiculously steep angle.

It didn't get very high as jets go (I thought bemusedly that I might be higher) before there was an even louder BOOM and the jet rapidly and shakily descended away from my vantage-point, becoming a speck as it fell toward the horizon. There followed another – more muted – explosion, and I incredulously stared at a fireball rising from the distant landscape.

"Goddamn. I think a plane just crashed," I said.

Stopher was the only brother awake, squeezed into a large cushioned chair in the living room, watching CMT with the volume down. (The chicks were hot, the music was not).

"You're high," he replied, dismissively waving that small pretty hand.

Turns out a Navy pilot, hot-dogging for his parents, had taken off at too steep an angle and dropped an engine. He ejected safely, but his jet landed on an old couple having coffee in their kitchen in Wilson County, not too far from the bar where I was destined to meet my Maker. (Although, to be honest, I haven't yet met *my Maker – I wonder if this is the* reception *area. No magazines, but still a tolerable and interesting way to kill time).*

    Thus passed the season of my discontent.

    When I didn't sleep on concrete or a park bench or the Jones' couch, I crashed at Jeff's or Justin's, both of whom could tolerate me only in very small doses. I might've could've stayed a few nights at Derek's, but the one time I showed up at his and his roommate's place I proceeded to drink up a two bottles of wine and take a swig from what appeared to be a 24-ounce can of Heineken, but which was actually the roommate's chewing tobacco spit-can. Tasted like shit, and the second sip was no better. I wasn't invited back.

    When it finally dawned on me that I might not be discovered anytime in the immediate future, I sucked up my pride and got a job at Subway. It seemed the lesser of the fast-food evils – they actually had a couple of long-hairs working there, and it didn't involve asking "Do you want fries with that?"

    With my first paycheck I got that little room I told ya about where I got that squirrel high. With my second paycheck I got me another Fender, an acoustic guitar which stayed with me till my dying day, and with which I wrote probably four hundred or so songs. I'd've requested that guitar be buried with me, had I had a bit more notice about my subsequent buryin'.

    Four months or so into my new-found gainful employment, I recorded some more songs at Sean's – Derek played lead and sang harmony, Sean played bass and drums and piano and also sang harmony. I sent the demo to a half-dozen indy record labels.

    One of those – a label whose name I don't recall, but which had had enough success on the charts to actually afford them the penthouse suite in a twelve-story building near Music Row – invited me to come play for them.

    I showed up drunk with a six-pack and entertained the shit out of them for over an hour. After I'd finished, they asked me to wait outside, on their roof-top veranda, while they discussed my future. As I stood staring at the nearby Nashville skyline, I reckoned my time had finally come, and proclaimed out loud that this city was mine.

That was just the beer proclaimin'. When they invited me back in, the prez of the label (I don't remember his *name either) informed me that while they thought me immensely talented ("Better than Prine," he said), they just didn't know exactly what to* do *with me.*

I wasn't sure whether he was referring to the marketability of my music or the fact that I'd asked their receptionist if I could see her tits, but I never heard back from them. Easy come, easy go.

I started playing a place called Bell Cove just outside of town, which was hosted by some friends Stopher and Walt had introduced me to at Bogie's. Mike, his wife Marsha, and his smokin' hot sister Carol were fellow Okies, and we got along swimmingly. Mike always introduced the trio (they called themselves "Blazon Pearl") with "I'm Mike, and this is my wife and my sister. I don't know who *that chick on the end is."*

Carol was a year older than me – beautiful, smart, sexy, and talented. I knew I didn't have a shot, yet about six months later we began a torrid affair that lasted just over a year and inspired the kinds of songs that can only be wrought from deep passion and gut-wrenching heartache. We loved madly and fought frequently, both of us being damned artistic types. It eventually got to the point where I realized I had been much happier single and celibate. Which sucked, because I hadn't been very happy. Guess all that shit's relative.

I'd found out shortly after I started working at Subway that, while I was homeless, Kristi's mom had died and she'd got some life-insurance money and moved the girls to Virginia to be with a guy she'd met at the Bluebird. Not a songwriter, *thank God, but a low-life nonetheless. He'd been a car salesman when they met, but lost that job and moved back home to live with his mother. Kristi rescued him by moving to Virginia shortly thereafter, buying a house, and marrying the schmuck.*

I didn't blame her for wanting to get away. But I did blame her for getting away with my children. Anyway, when I found out about it, I got her address and phone number from Burt. After a year of calls and cards and letters going unanswered, I gave up.

It was a dark cloud that was to hang over every ounce of joy or shred of success - and my joys and successes have always come in ounces and shreds - for the next decade.

I finally got burned out at Subway. It wasn't the work, it was the atmosphere that comes with working for a conglomerate, even if every store was individually-owned. Subway policy was idiotic. Two napkins with every order, and these were napkins that aspired to be toilet paper when they grew up. Only two pieces of olive on every six-incher, which pretty much amounts to "hold the olives." You've been to Subway. You're looking through the sneeze-guard, telling the sammich-maker what you want. When someone would request olives and I'd put two little pieces on there, they'd invariably look at me like I was the idiot.

One day I was working solo, waiting on a lone customer, when a regional manager came in and asked if I'd been "certified as a sandwich artist."

The customer – a college kid – looked up at me and said, "Is he serious?"

I'd only made 50,000 or so of the damned things, so I kinda concurred.

The next day I applied at The Sub Place, a big pink-and-blue restaurant right by Music Row. Their clientele were predominantly songwriters and music-biz folk, and they served beer.

When I interviewed with one of the co-owners – a seemingly-sweet little lady named Joanie – she asked me why I wanted to leave Subway. I told her I had a problem with the corporate mentality, the "customer is always right" attitude.

"The customer is not *always right," she snapped.*
"Sometimes the customers are assholes.*"*

I liked her immediately, though I would get over that. *She hired me on the spot.*

The Sub Place *was like a breath of fresh air after emerging from the suffocating stale atmosphere of a...uh...*Subway.

I met Evan, a fellow songwriter, and Bruce, who reminded me of Mr. Clean, with his clean-shaven head and weight-lifter's build. Both would become life-long friends, though none of us knew at the time that my particular definition of "life-long" would be somewhat abbreviated. In fact, they were both at the Turtle that night. Sad I disappointed 'em.

About six months or so after I'd started the new gig, I was working the register (which I never enjoyed as much as making *sammiches – far fewer idiots to deal with) and looked up to see Chad, my old band-mate. I hadn't seen him since he'd given me a ride to Nashville after I'd poked his girlfriend and been thrown off the farm.*

"You know I'm sorry about that," I said. "What'll ya have?"

"It's okay. We're married now," he replied. "Half a chicken with swiss, all the way."

"Man, that's great!*" I was immensely relieved. "White or wheat?"*

"Wheat. With yellow mustard."
"We only have the spicy mustard."
"Oh..."
I was afraid I'd ruined our reconciliation.
"Spicy's fine."
I was, once again, immensely relieved.

It was near my break time, so I made myself a sammich, grabbed a drink, and joined him for lunch. Told him all about my homelessness, my near-brush with a record deal. Asked about Dan and Miles. He told me they'd stayed together, playing their own mixture of hard rock and blues originals, calling themselves "Big Vessel."

"You mean, like a ship? Or like the big blue vein on a penis?"

He smiled, chewing and swallowing his bite of sammich. "Yep."

He said they had some gigs coming up in Murfreesboro, but didn't have that much material, and wouldn't it be a kick if we did a set of CowTippers stuff to augment their stuff?

And thus the band was reunited.

The second go-round was much more satisfying than the first. It was like we'd never been apart, plus I had quite a few new tunes that were even more crowd-pleasing than the old ones had been. We started practicing once a week, Chad chauffeuring me back and forth from Nashville, and built up quite a following playing our sporadic gigs. We recorded some more songs in Sean's studio, made a CD, and actually started making some money. Yet despite our popularity with the college crowd, and, later, with audiences in Nashville, we still *couldn't get the labels to give us a second glance.*

"The songs are great, but we just don't know what we'd do *with you," they invariably said.*

It was disappointing, but we were having too much fun *to really care. Besides, the other guys had good jobs and actual* lives. *Chad and Amanda had a baby boy, Miles had a girlfriend and was making a bundle doing computer-geek stuff, and Dan was engaged and owned his own construction company.*

Seemed I was the only one whose hopes were pinned entirely on dreams. Crazy how long those dreams sustained me.

Things coasted on like this for a number of years. Always making some bucks and getting encouragement, yet never quite scaling that brick wall standing between us and success. *I always figured there'd come a point at which the Nashville biz would cycle around to where it was* looking *for someone like us.*

We played a gig one night at a bar on Lower Broad, and sold a CD to a burly fellow who happened to be the producer for Ruby River, one of the top-selling Nashville acts at the time. He absolutely loved us, and passed along our CD to the prez of their label, who said he didn't know what he would do with us.

I at least wasn't concerned that he was referring to my request to see a receptionist's tits.

I'd been existing thusly - always on enough of a brink of a break to not give in - for just shy of a decade when Joanie hired Amy, a skinny sixteen-year-old with braces.

I hated her.

She was an annoying know-it-all who seemed to laughingly deride any attempt I made to befriend her, who ignored any attempt I made to teach her about the business I had, unfortunately, become all too good at.

A year later she lost the braces, blossomed, and became my best friend. I fell in love.

It was not a love borne of lust. It was not a love borne of loneliness. It was instead a love borne of a gradually-deepening emotional bond that happened to coincide with her development into a lustful antidote to loneliness.

She was amazed by her metamorphosis from an ugly duckling into a beautiful swan, by her awareness of her burgeoning sexuality; I was amazed by my own capacity to ignore all of the boundaries set by society and common sense, along with my awareness of her burgeoning sexuality.

For nearly a year I denied it, channeling my un-proclaimed passion into songs, doing internet research into laws concerning statutory rape. Discovered that for someone my age she was – until she turned eighteen – jail bait in every state in the union. I had prayed there might be an exception in a state like Tennessee, where, after all, Jerry Lee Lewis had married his fourteen-year-old cousin, but it turned out the laws had changed. Goddamned progress.

Finally, just before Amy's eighteenth birthday, I said "Fuck it" and told her. Three days later she told me she'd thought about it long and hard, and couldn't do it. She loved me, she said, but couldn't deal with what her parents would think.

A month later they put up that Billy Gilman billboard and I moved back to Austin.

I never even kissed her.

CHAPTER TWENTY-SIX

Judge Myra Way was every bit as beleaguered as she was bemused. She sat behind her large mahogany desk in her high-backed leather chair, looking through the bifocals perched on the end of her slightly-upturned nose at the assortment of characters gathered in her chambers: Laughlin, the defense attorney, seated beside his client front-and-center; the prosecution team seated to Laughlin's right, looking disgusted and somewhat confused; Harvey Boyd, the radio man she'd known for years and had always respected as a serious – if somewhat minor-league – professional, sat to the left of the accused; to *his* left sat Mack Blevins, looking uncomfortable in his Wal-Mart suit; and, finally, sitting beside his father, clutching a closed lap-top computer to his chest like a security blanket, the pudgy – and slightly disconcerted - Willard, whom all the hubbub was about.

Following the emergency recess the previous Wednesday, Laughlin and Brice had shown up in her chambers, the former with a DVD and what he purported to be the victim's journal, allegedly *in progress*, amazingly (and, frankly, even *more* unbelievably) from the laptop of this twelve-year-old.

Just on its face, she'd been inclined to scold the defense attorney for wasting the court's time with such nonsense, but Laughlin was passionate and seemed sincere in his argument that, when every other conceivable scenario had been eliminated, even the most fantastical and implausible had to at least be *considered.*

This was, after all, a potential eye-*witness.*

After dismissing the pair so she could watch the video and read the document, she'd called them back in.

"You know if you pursue this…" she waved toward the folder and the disc on her desk, addressing Laughlin. "You could *ruin* your career."

The attorney had somberly nodded.

"And if I *allow* you to pursue this," she continued, "I might

169

as well go into private practice somewhere in Alaska."

Laughlin just stared patiently, Brice standing beside him with a self-satisfied smirk.

She'd thought for a moment, then resignedly shook her head.

"I hear Alaska's nice during the summer," she sighed.

"You've *got* to be *shitting* me!" Brice blurted out before he could stop himself.

"*What?*" she asked, not because she couldn't believe his disrespect, but because she honestly hadn't *heard* him.

"Your Honor," the prosecutor sputtered. "This is *insane*! I beg you not to encourage this…this…"

"Don't get your panties in a wad, Haywood," she admonished. "I'm not saying any of this'll see the light of day in the *courtroom*."

She'd given Laughlin until the following Monday – nearly five days – to put together a case strong enough to allay her skepticism, believable enough to convince her it might be grounds for appeal if she were to disregard it, undeniable enough to overcome her reluctance to turn her courtroom into an episode of *The Twilight Zone* and the center stage of what was certain to become a three-ring circus.

Send in the clowns, she now thought, quietly assessing her crowded chambers, the box of notebooks at the defense attorney's feet, the downward-cast eyes of the child (looking for all the world like he was in the principal's office awaiting his fate following a particularly horrendous episode of misbehavior).

"All right, Marshall," she said. "What d'ya got?"

Laughlin opened his briefcase and removed a stack of papers, stapled into four separate sections of several pages each, then rose and wordlessly handed one of the stapled documents to the judge, then one each to Brice and Fleming, keeping one for himself.

"Before we begin, this is the latest," he said.

Judge Way glanced at the pages in front of her, as did the two prosecutors.

"The latest *what*?" she asked.

Mack spoke up. "I done bought the boy some more of them thumb gadgets."

The defense attorney translated.

"Last night Mr. Blevins informed me that this young man here…"

He indicated Willard, who looked up, clueless.

"…had given him another installment of the memoirs."

He paused long enough to allow the readers to scan further.

"While we obviously – due to our impending meeting this morning - didn't have time to substantiate most of the elements of this latest offering to the extent with which we have verified the documents *previously* presented, I *did* find something interesting which merely required a phone call this morning to the Nashville Public Library."

As was his way, Laughlin had everyone's attention. As was also his way, he savored the moment.

"You'll notice a highlighted passage on page three," he continued, then waited as the others flipped pages. He reached back into his briefcase and removed a single sheet of paper.

"I got the head librarian to email me their computer records on the borrowing activity of one Jared Whaley," he said, then handed the page to Judge Way.

She eyed Laughlin warily as she took the sheet and quickly read the first few lines. Her brow furrowed as she compared what she'd just read to the highlighted portion of the stapled pages.

As if the words might change upon re-perusal, she did it again.

"Shit."

The defense attorney smiled as the prosecution team exchanged worried glances.

The Judge, seeming to think a *third* look might cancel out the previous two and make her suddenly-crazy world a little more sane, read both again.

"Shit," she repeated.

"Your Honor?" Brice said, his wisp of a voice cracking.

Her Honor sighed and shook her head, handing the single page to the County Prosecutor, who, with his curious AP reading over his shoulder, duplicated, then repeated, the comparison of the two documents.

"Shit," they said as one.

Harvey Boyd hadn't been informed of this latest development. Being a newsman, as well as what he considered an integral piece of this increasingly-wacky puzzle, he spoke up.

"May I?"

Laughlin reached past the silent Angel and handed Harvey his copy of the stapled papers, flipped open to the third page.

As Harvey read the highlighted passage, the defense attorney, without asking, took the single-page printout from Brice and offered it to the radio man as well.

As Harvey took it, his eyes caught Angel's. For a brief moment he forgot where he was, why he was, *who* he was. She smiled, sweetly yet knowingly, before her gaze released his and he was left with nothing but the real world, which was becoming more *surreal* with each passing moment.

The highlighted portion of the latest journal entry read:

"*After my first visit to the library as a homeless guy among countless homeless guys (I checked out a John Lennon bio and* The World According to Garp *by John Irving, using Sean's address to get a library card)...*"

The other page was a printout of an email from Molly Stevens of the Nashville Public Library, sent to Marshall Laughlin, dated that very morning. It opened with a short greeting, followed by:

"*Below you will find our records on the borrowing activity of Jared Whaley. Hope this helps!"*

There, in black and white, was the late country singer's name, along with an address in Nashville.

There was a date: June 18, 1990, in front of which were the simple words, *"Card Issued."*

Below were two titles:

"The Lives of John Lennon" by Albert Goldman.

"The World According to Garp" by John Irving.

It was this moment, Harvey would later think, when he stopped being a skeptic. When his once seemingly-objective sober rationale gave way to a vague notion that up *might* be up and right *might* be right; that two plus two just *might* equal four...but then again, it might *not*.

He didn't know *why* this turned the tide, why he'd so stubbornly held on to his doubts in the face of all which had come before. Perhaps his apprehensions had been wavering on the threshold, just waiting for a final kick in the pants to send them on their way, much as finding toys in your parents' closet on Christmas Eve finally dispelled any last shred of belief in Santa Claus. Yet, in this case, it was the fantasy not debunked but *realized* (despite all evidence to the contrary), the fat man in red asserting that he *put* those toys there, and that he'd landed his reindeer-driven sleigh on your roof to do so, the Tooth Fairy riding shotgun, the Easter Bunny perched in his lap.

"Shit," he said.

There was a long silence, during which every pair of eyes in the room met every other (save for Willard's – he just stared at the floor).

Judge Way and Brice and Fleming seemed confounded, their bewildered gazes pleading for some *sense* to insinuate itself into the moment's nonsensical midst; Laughlin seemed stunned to realize the impact his presentation had made, as if it were only the grudging acceptance of the disbelievers which had finally convinced him to buy his own arguments; Harvey seemed to forget his own sudden shift in perspective and take it in as a newsman, his reporter's mind assessing the implications of the others' reactions; Angel seemed simply, yet sadly, serene.

Mack finally spoke up, his eyes and voice reflecting a renewed confidence as he uttered words that had thus far been laughingly dismissed, but which no longer would be:

"That country singer done possessed my boy."

The next hour and a half was relatively anti-climatic, like watching David Copperfield do card tricks after he'd already made an elephant disappear. The prosecutors sat in sulking silence as Laughlin proffered the box of notebooks – found beneath a dusty set of golf clubs in a storage unit rented by the victim – comprising over two decades' worth of the victim's writings.

Whaley had apparently been a firm believer that the unexamined life was not worth living, the dated reflections of his trials and tribulations interspersed throughout the volumes coinciding with the timeline thus far presented in his apparently post-mortem chronicles.

His first song, "Matter of Time," was there, dated May 7, 1986.

So too were his excited anticipatory musings about his upcoming meeting with James Gilliam, the owner of a publishing company and recording studio, followed by his account of his arrest for public intoxication and the subsequent falling-out with his father, followed by the details of his sojourn to Austin, his months as an Elvis impersonator, his return to Tennessee.

None of these entries had *near* the detail of his subsequent manuscript, which only seemed to bolster the assertion that there was *no way* anyone else could have written the thousands of words which had so recently raised such a ruckus. The last notebook - found not in the storage unit but on the Whaley's coffee table – ended with a scrawled set list headed "**Turtle 2/13.**"

"I hate to put it in such simplistic terms," the defense attorney told the judge when he'd finished laying out his case. "But, to paraphrase a man I never thought I'd paraphrase, '*that country singer done possessed this boy*.'"

When Laughlin resumed his seat, his client reached over and squeezed his hand. He looked at her and smiled sadly, with an expression that seemed to communicate that he'd done all he could do, but that he may have only managed to condemn them *both*, albeit in *drastically* disparate senses of the word. He returned the squeeze.

"I wish y'all would stop sayin' that," Willard whispered, the first words he'd spoken that morning. All eyes turned, as if expecting the boy to levitate while his head made a 360-degree turn.

"It kinda creeps me out," he added, his gaze returning to the floor.

Brice cleared his throat. Since no one seemed to notice, Fleming cleared *his* throat.

"Your Honor," he said. "This is all very…*entertaining*. But the fact of the matter is that nothing has been offered here today which directly refutes the State's case. And, to be quite honest…"

He looked directly at the Judge, his clear blue eyes unflinching, certain that he was on solid ground.

"…the fact that we're even *having* this conversation, that *any* of this is being taken *seriously*, flies in the face of all precedent and jurisprudence."

Judge Way nodded solemnly, weighing the Assistant Prosecutor's words against the overwhelming – if common-sense-defying – arguments made by the defense attorney.

She looked at Laughlin.

"Counselor?"

Laughlin ran a hand through his thick hair, gathering his un-thinkable thoughts. He looked again at Angel, then over at the boy, who was still staring at the thick carpet.

"We think he's gonna tell us who killed him," the lawyer said, turning back to the Judge, then to Fleming.

"And that it *wasn't* my client."

Fleming and his boss tried to scoff, but seemed to no longer have the capacity.

"When?" Brice whispered.

"Yeah," Fleming seconded, but louder. "When?"

"They've got a point, Marshall," the Judge said. "Even if you proved beyond a shadow of a doubt…and it's a *big* shadow and a *colossal* doubt…that this boy is…" she motioned toward Willard.

"…is…*Jesus*…what you *contend*…it doesn't change anything unless he *testifies* to what you *think* he'll testify to."

As she spoke the words, her long and respected career flashed before her eyes, and she wondered if perhaps a practice in Alaska was too lofty an ambition.

"How are you going to swear him in?" Brice almost shouted.

His voice carried this time, and the question was met with a moment of baffled silence. Such a practical consideration had, in light of all that was so preposterous, been relegated to a spot in the nose-bleed sections of the collective conscience.

"Hmmm," Laughlin offered.

"Uh…" said Fleming.

Judge Way seemed to consider it for a moment, then merely shrugged.

"*I, Jared Whaley, do solemnly swear that the testimony I'm about to give is the truth, the* whole *fuckin' truth, and nothing* but *the goddamned fuckin' truth.*"

Seven jaws hit the floor as seven heads rapidly swiveled toward the source of the outburst.

Willard sat smiling, his right hand raised, his left flat on the laptop, his eyes with a glint that had thus far only been witnessed in person by his parents, but which the others in the room recognized from the video.

"So help me Yahweh, Allah, or God, depending on your particular religious inclination." He lowered his hand.

"Goddamn, boy, that's *creepy*," Mack said.

"*Jared?*" Angel said, tears welling in her wide eyes.

The boy looked at her and winked.

"Babycakes, tell 'em about the mole right above your heart-shaped pubic hair, and how I took a Sharpie that first night and made it one eye of a smiley face."

"Oh *God*!" Angel wailed, a sob escaping her throat as she jumped from her chair and bolted from the room.

"You people are so fucking *obtuse*," the twelve-year-old said, his Tennessee twang become an Oklahoma drawl, his eyes cold and angry. "You need to suspend your goddamned disbelief and accept some goddamned harsh *reality*!"

Mack looked from his son to Laughlin.

"What's *obtuse*?" he asked.

"Uh…" Fleming said, looking toward the door. "I don't think she's supposed to *leave*."

"Oh shit," Judge Way said, then picked up the phone.

Harvey rose from his chair.

"It's all right, Judge. I'll get her."

As the door closed behind the pursuing newsman, all eyes returned to the pre-teen.

"*You* think this is beyond belief," he said. "*You* think there has to be an explanation, something you're missing, some way to make all this fit within the parameters of everything you've ever known as real life, all that which separates cold objective fact from fantasy."

No one dared interrupt. Except Mack.

"What's a *parameter*?" he asked.

"*I* think," the youth continued, "that for some reason beyond my comprehension, I've been given a chance to tell my story, to set the record straight. I don't know *how*, I don't know *why*. I don't recall anything between the flash of a muzzle and suddenly finding myself dictating my story to this fat kid."

"He's just big-boned..." Mack began, but was silenced by a sharp look from Harvey.

"I don't know what comes after this," the boy said, then became quiet. He looked at the floor.

"I'm still not sure I believe in *God*." His eyes rose and met the judge's. "But I feel like I've been given this opportunity, and that I may just have all of goddamned *eternity* to regret it if I don't tell it right."

Judge Way held his gaze for a moment, then looked at Laughlin, then at Brice and Fleming.

Finally, she looked at the boy's father, then at the father's son.

"You can take the stand tomorrow," she said.

The dead forty-something twelve-year old smiled.

"I've gotta finish writing my statement first. Give us a couple of days."

Down the hall from the Judge's Chambers, Harvey stood outside the ladies' room, listening to the muffled sound of Angel's sobs.

He lightly knocked and opened the door.

"Ms. Whaley?"

"Dammit Harvey, come in," she said, sniffling. "And call me Angel, for fuck's sake."

He cautiously entered, aware that he was truly in "no-man's-land," figuring that if Angel had not been alone she wouldn't have extended the invitation.

"Are you okay?" he asked, allowing the door to shut behind him.

Angel stood at the sink, rinsing her face, her eyes red and swollen. He thought her a vision.

"Jesus, Harvey," she said, fighting back another onslaught of tears. "It's *him*!"

He was at a loss for words, dumbstruck by both her beauty and his own sense of impotence.

"Uh," he said. "The Judge was about to alert security."

Even as he said it he felt stupid.

She dried her face with a paper towel, then wadded it up and tossed it in the nearby receptacle.

Her eyes met his, frightened.

"It's *him*!" she repeated, then wrapped her arms around his shoulders, buried her face against his neck and started sobbing again.

"Yeah…well…it's pretty damned *weird*," was all he could muster, distracted as he was by the proximity of her body.

She pulled away, held him at arm's length, her eyes once again ensnaring his.

"I have to show you something," she said.

She was dressed conservatively, a powder-blue blouse tucked into a long dark pleated skirt.

With a yank she un-tucked the blouse and raised it, exposing a smooth tan tummy, a perfect round winking navel, then slid two thumbs into the waistband of her skirt and lowered it, revealing first the thin cotton of a pair of red panties, which she also lowered until he caught a glimpse of the uppermost portion of her downy pubis. There, unmistakable, like the Northern Star on a cloudless night, was a mole.

"That's…amazing," Harvey said, as she put her arms once again around his neck. He thought about the tattoo, and now *this*. It was becoming his favorite form of corroboration.

"It's *him*," she repeated yet again, looking deeply into his eyes as her fingers strayed to his thick hair. Time stood still for a moment, as did the earth, as did Harvey's heart. She pulled his mouth to hers.

He couldn't recall a kiss so passionate, particularly with

such a beauty, *especially* with an accused felon. As their tongues met, wrapping around one another like two snakes playing twister, she clutched the back of his shirt and propelled him against the outside wall of the nearest stall, slamming her body against his so he could feel her breasts soft against his chest, could feel her crotch against his surprisingly-sudden hardness.

She pulled away, breathing heavily.

"Fuck me, Harvey."

Every part of him, *particularly* a certain southern region, *wanted* to obey. He hadn't been with a woman in five years, so he had a feeling this would be a quickie to rival all quickies. But the risks were too great, the stakes too high. Maybe after the trial, after she was exonerated, if she was still in the mood...

"We'll get caught," was all he could say before her lips were once again on his, her hands roaming over his chest, then downward...

"Mmmm," she cooed, then grabbed *his* hand and guided it to the epicenter of her passion. Through the fabric of her skirt he could feel her heat, and knew she wasn't faking.

"Jesus," he moaned.

She tore herself away from him and, still holding his hand, led him through the open door of the stall, then closed it and twisted the lock.

"Keep your ears open," she whispered, then raised her skirt up and peeled off her red panties, laying them on the toilet seat.

"Jesus," Harvey repeated.

Angel kissed his mouth, his neck, then dropped to her knees in front of him and started undoing his belt.

"Really...we *shouldn't*," he said, even as he ran his fingers through her soft hair, reveled in her touch as she unsnapped his trousers.

Both were frozen by a voice outside the stall.

"Really, Harvey," it said, its Oklahoma drawl and pre-pubescent timbre unmistakable. "She's *trouble*."

"Oh *shit!*" Angel swore, rising quickly and grabbing her panties.

"I'm *sorry* Jared," she cried, sliding the underwear back up her long legs as Harvey frantically re-did his trousers, then his belt.

"I'm gettin' you out of quite the jam here," the voice said. "Don't make me change my mind."

The widow twisted the lock on the stall door and pulled it inward, suddenly facing the twelve-year-old, his eyes angry, his demeanor sullen.

"You're fucking *dead*, Jared," she said.

Willard looked at her, then at Harvey, then back. He shook his head.

"Dead guys have feelings too."

CHAPTER TWENTY-SEVEN

My second trip to Austin was, it seems, a lifetime and a world apart from my first.

I found my new roommates – Carrie and her boyfriend Stuart – online, and sent 'em my boxes of stuff before I caught a flight out there in June of 2001.

Carrie and Stuart were hippies, just like a lot of the young folks in Austin. Stuart made his living selling weed, Carrie spent a couple of hours a day pulling *weeds from their little backyard garden.*

Carrie was an absolute knockout, *short dark hair and a perfect body, but she, like so many hippy chicks, never shaved.*

Carrie was hairy.

That *kinda grossed me out, but ensured I wouldn't get too drunk one night and try to make a move, thus ruining a pretty swell situation. I don't think* any *amount of beer could get me to lustin' after a chick with legs hairier than mine.*

I'd arrived with enough money to keep me goin' for a month or two, so I spent my days drinkin' beer and writin' songs about Amy, my nights drinkin' beer and playin' songs at various writers nights. My fav was The Cactus Café, *on the University of Texas campus, not far from the tower where that guy shot all those folks back in the 60's. Helluva way to get famous.*

The days passed quickly, as did my funds, and I ended up gettin' a job at another fuckin' Subway. If I didn't look out the window, I couldn't tell the difference between that *Subway and the one in Nashville.*

After a couple of weeks, due to my vast experience, they made me the assistant manager, which meant a whopping quarter more an hour, but also meant I was the first person called on my precious days off when someone didn't show – which was nearly every one *of my precious days off.*

Between my beer consumption, pining over Amy, and the

constant dark cloud of my lost girls hanging over my existence, I was in quite the funk. It didn't help that my schedule at Subway fucked with my writers nights, which were the only moments I actually felt there was some point to drawing air.

I quit Subway on a Thursday, and the following Saturday I think I attempted suicide.

I say "think" because I didn't write a note, hadn't given any thought to ending it all. One moment I was drinking my seventeenth beer of the day, riding shotgun with my friend Scott on our way to the lake. The next moment I was opening the car door and exiting the vehicle.

We were doing about fifty.

Don't let anybody ever tell you that doesn't smart. Come to think of it, I can't imagine anyone would.

It could have turned out a lot worse, and I somehow don't think I'd be writing this if that had been the end of my story. My only immortality in that case I think would've been inclusion in those Darwin Files, *which make fun of people who meet their Makers in extremely stupid ways.*

Reminds me of that joke about the last words of a redneck: "Hey, watch THIS!*"*

Fortunately, I landed on my ass, and the only notable damage was a black bruise which extended from my upper thighs to my groin and made the idea of riding a bicycle completely out of the question. I didn't have a bicycle.

The next week I walked gingerly into a sandwich joint called Anthony's Deli, *on Congress in downtown Austin, and got a job.*

The hours were from 8 in the morning till 3 in the afternoon Monday through Friday – a perfect *gig for an aspiring songwriter such as myself. It was a small place on the ground floor of a high-rise office building, only had two other employees, and I could wear my bandana again.*

Another bonus was that they didn't open until 10 a.m.,

which meant the first third of each day was spent listening to the radio, doing prep work, and not *dealing with customers.*

I was developing into quite the misanthrope.

On my second Tuesday there – it was early September – I was running a few minutes late and got to the sammich shop just in time to see my co-workers, Larry and James, staring at the radio like it had a damn picture.

"A plane just hit one of the towers of the World Trade Center," Larry said.

"Dang. Hope it was a small one."

"Actually, they're both *pretty big," said James.*

"No you idiot*!" Larry growled. "He meant the* plane.*"*

"Oh. Right."

"They're not sure yet," Larry continued. "Freak accident,"

As I was putting on my apron, grabbing some tomatoes to slice, the second plane hit.

It shames me to this day to report what I then said:

"Damn! What're the odds of that?!"

My co-workers just gaped at me, obviously re-assessing their opinion of my intelligence, James probably thinking his comment a few moments ago suddenly didn't seem quite so moronic.

"Oh...oh shit*!" I said, the realization hitting me at about the same time Peter Jennings announced that we were under attack.*

The rest of the morning is kind of a blur. We were in shock, I think, upon hearing the reports that another *plane had hit the Pentagon, then that one had crashed in Pennsylvania. Then, of course, the Towers fell.*

I certainly hadn't expected that.

"Guess the planes were *pretty big," I said.*

I felt incredibly selfish for being thankful when all of the buildings within a mile radius of the Texas State Capital building (which included ours) were closed at noon, and even more selfish for wondering if this meant the writers night at the Cactus Café was going to be cancelled. It was.

The next month I was scheduled to play a Sunday night Bluebird gig. I'd been playin' 'em every six months or so since that first one, and those shows – along with too much beer and angst – were among the few constants in my life.

There's nothing like a Sunday night at the 'bird. I never played a single one that wasn't packed, nor a single one where I didn't kill. *Those first few I'd played solo, but most of 'em I did with the CowTippers (when we were together), minus Miles, since drums weren't allowed.*

I always had something to sell, from those early "Fairly Decent Tapes" through the several CDs me and the 'Tippers had recorded at Sean's, and I don't recall a single night not sellin' enough to at least pay my bar tab – sometimes a good deal more than that. Although, to be honest, I don't recall every *single night.*

This was to be my first Bluebird gig as an Okie from Nashville livin' in Texas, and since my finances wouldn't afford me the luxury of flying, I had to take the Greyhound. What was scheduled to be fourteen-hour bus ride became, thanks to a couple of break-downs, a twenty-six hour journey through the bowels of Hell, and I got to Nashville just in time to catch a ride from Chad and Dan to the Bluebird, chug four beers, and take the stage.

Even though I had only slept two hours, and even though we hadn't played together in about five months, we pulled it off without a hitch and sold enough CDs to cover our beer tabs and *about half of my bus fare.*

I freakin' love *the Bluebird!*

On the return trip, I sat next to a twenty-something hot senorita from Honduras (not sure where that is, but I know it's south) *who spoke about as much English as I spoke Spanish. We wound up making out during the middle-of-the-night ride between Memphis and Dallas, and if the damn bus would've broken down* then *I wouldn't have minded.*

I gave her a CD and signed it "To my angel hermosa," which means "my beautiful angel" I think. Wrote a pretty cool song about it. They've been playing it quite a bit on the radio. I guess Greyhound's not all *bad.*

But I digress.

Honestly, I'd like *to include every single* moment *of my life, to recreate every incident, not to leave a damned thing out. Who* wouldn't *in my situation?*

Yet, to be honest, aren't most lives 99.9 percent boring as shit? We just suffer through the monotony in the hopes that the rest is something to write home about.

Not that I ever wrote *home. Rarely even* visited. *I think I* meant *to, once I was successful enough to prove Mom wrong about her prognostication that I'd "never be worth a shit." Day late and a dollar short on* that *one. Not entirely certain she wasn't right.*

Mom mellowed out as she got older. Our telephone chats a few times a year were nice (that one really drunk call I mentioned earlier notwithstanding), my trips to Oklahoma every few years full of laughter and love.

My sisters grew into beautiful, fairly-well-adjusted women, my brother into a handsome philosophy professor. I love them dearly, and wish I'd spent more time earlier talking about them.

But I didn't, and my deadline looms.

They've got me an' Willie in a hotel room, an armed guard stationed outside the door. Not so much to keep us from escapin' *I think, as to keep nosy reporters away and make sure we've got few distractions as I finish this thing up.*

Apparently, from what the fat man tells the fat kid, we're famous.

If life *is* funny, *death* can be shit-in-your-pants *hysterical. If somewhat sadly ironic.*

A few days after my return to Austin following I think my third trip to play the Bluebird (and I *flew* after that first one — fuck *Greyhound), I struck up a conversation with John Paxton, a large, jovial type who'd been eating lunch at Anthony's almost every day since he and his partner had rented an office on the fourteenth floor a couple of months earlier. They owned a radio production company with a couple of syndicated blues and country-music shows on a few stations around the country. He was as close to being in the biz as anyone I'd met there, so of course I mentioned that I was a singer/songwriter and told him all about my latest trip to Nashville, how many CD's we'd sold at the Bluebird gig, what a damned hit I was.*

I gave him a CD.

The next day he said he wanted to pitch me to some labels.
I said "okie dokie."

A few days later he told me he'd had a chat with this fella from New York, Phil Kearns, whom he'd met the previous night at a symposium given by various heads of various independent record labels. Phil ran Originality Records, *which had had enough success with one of their artists, James Matlock, to actually stay afloat and start looking for new talent.*

Phil, John said, was interested.

A few nights later, I had a phone interview with Phil, who was back in New York. He wanted to know my story and my goals. For some reason, he also wanted to know how much I drank. I was completely honest and forthright about the former, a little evasive concerning the latter.

He said if he signed me, he'd want my publishing (the rights to everything I'd written) as well. I'd studied the biz voraciously ever since I'd decided I wanted to be a country star, so I knew this was fairly typical. He said he wanted me to record a couple more songs, have those plus the ones from the latest CowTippers CD mastered professionally, and that he wanted me to go to Nashville.

I told him Nashville was a nice place to visit, but I'd prefer to stay in Austin.

He told me he'd give me a five-thousand-dollar advance, plus pay my moving expenses.

I said, "When do I leave?"

Two months later, after I'd got two contracts – one for recording, one for publishing – via registered FedEx, after I'd gleefully signed the contracts and sent 'em back, after I'd received a check from Phil for five grand, I was on a plane back to Nashville.

May the circle-jerk be unbroken.

Last time I'd got off a plane in Music City from Austin, my hair had been dyed black, I'd had about five thousand bucks, and the dreams of a delusional youth were spread out before me like a drunk sorority chick in no real hurry to get anywhere.

This time my hair was reddish-brown streaked with quite a bit of hard-earned gray, I had about five thousand bucks, and the dreams of a delusional youth had somehow weathered the storm and were spread out before me like a drunk sorority chick lookin' at her watch.

It was my time.

Not in the same way, obviously, as it was my time *a few years later in a dressing-room at a bar in nearby Wilson.*

In a good *way.*

Whereas my first arrival back in Nashville from Austin had been greeted by no one but a cabbie, this time I had a welcoming committee: Dan and Chad and Miles were there, as was Sean, as were Evan and Bruce, my friends from the sammich shop.

It was a reunion full of camaraderie and hope, and we wound up at Windows on the Cumberland *on 2nd Ave. The 'Tippers had played there a few times, and the owner, Boots, bought the first round as we celebrated what we all were certain was the beginning of the good times. After all, I had a freakin'* record deal.

I rented an apartment not far from Music Row, and spent my days drinking and recording, my nights drinking and playing.

We recorded several more tracks over the next couple of months and sent 'em to Phil, who picked two out and sent 'em - along with what we'd already recorded for the last 'Tippers CD - to a guy in Austin who'd won a Grammy for mastering a couple of Willie Nelson records.

I personally couldn't tell that much difference from the tracks we'd recorded and the tracks Willie's guy had mastered, but Sean was kind enough to point out to me that the LED meters were more consistent during the playing of the latter.

I figured it must be worth it, though I knew that the cost (a couple grand) was coming out of my future royalties.

"Recoupable" is such a dirty word to a recording artist, but, like "Goddamn," "Shit," and "Fuck," an integral part of the vernacular.

The first CD was entitled "Funny Ha Ha, Funny Strange."

For the cover, Phil paid a model to dress up like a clown and stand behind me, gazing on wantonly as I sat at my kitchen table with my guitar and an open notebook. For the back cover, she was behind me reaching into the fridge for a beer. That photo shoot cost nearly a grand and was, of course, fuckin' goddamn recoupable. Shit.

Sure looked *cool, though.*

The CD was released in March of 2004. We had a CD-release party at Douglas Corner, then Phil flew me and the boys to Austin for a second *CD-release at the* Saxon Pub. *The airfare was, of course, recoupable.*

Goddamn. Shit. Fuck.

I didn't care. Being the blurry-eyed record-deal novice that I was, I was certain that my royalties would be so staggering that a couple grand here and there represented only a drop in a very large bucket of soon-to-be gotten gains. That it mattered like a single teardrop matters to the ocean, like a single prayer matters to God.

During the Saxon Pub *gig, the battery for my acoustic guitar's fancy-schmancy pick-up died toward the end of our opening song, and I had to banter while I loosened the strings, reached into the sound-hole, replaced the battery, then re-tuned the guitar.*

I don't recall exactly what I bantered about, *but it must've been entertaining, 'cause nobody left and afterwards I was told by a few folks in the audience that the whole thing was* hilarious.

Thank God I'm such a funny fuck.

One of the tracks from the CD got put into regular rotation on XM Radio, a satellite radio service which was all the rage at the time. I had no idea why they chose that *particular song. It was a crowd-pleasing little ditty, but I generally ranked it toward the bottom of the CD's repertoire.*

Oh well, different strokes for different folks. I wound up gettin' a couple hundred bucks from ASCAP (they're the performing rights organization I'm...I mean, I was, *affiliated with that pays songwriters when their tunes get played on the radio) - mailbox money which only came every six months but was always a welcome surprise, and which* wasn't *goddamned fucking recoupable.*

I imagined that Phil would follow up that airplay with a whirlwind of promotion, figured it'd be nuts for him to invest all that he'd invested thus far only to let our modicum of momentum stagnate.

But that's just what he did. I don't think he spent another recoupable dime pushing the record.

Looking back – which is all I can do now – I think I would've rather he spent some of that money hiring a record promoter or taking out an ad in Billboard *(or both), but he didn't, and hindsight's 20-20. And I* did *have a good time with that advance money.*

Six months into my return to Nashville the money dried up.

Like I said earlier, Phil would grudgingly send me checks to keep me from bein' homeless again, but I finally had to resort to goin' back to the sammich shop on Music Row, donning my apron and matching bandana, putting mayonnaise and mustard and meat and cheese to bread.

I got a little more respect - many of the music-biz patrons now knew who I was - but I was never quite certain whether, when their eyes met mine, I was seeing admiration or hunger.

At least the beer was free.

2005 was a wonderful tragic year.

The day after New Year's, I returned home from a trip to Oklahoma to find an email from Kristi. After all those years, she'd decided it was time for me to once again be a part of my daughters' lives.

If I had eyes to cry, they would still get misty at the memory of that email.

Three days later, I heard my angels' voices for the first time since they'd told me so long ago that they loved me, but wanted more juice.

Suddenly my frustrations with the music biz didn't seem like that big a deal, for the dark cloud that had been following me for a decade and a half had suddenly lifted, and all my angst and disillusionment was bathed in the bright light of once again being a daddy.

Two months later, shortly after I'd bought my plane tickets to go to Marie's high-school graduation that coming June (the day before Father's Day no less), Phil called and informed me the label was exercising their option to have me record a second CD, and that this time they wanted to bring in some heavy-hitter guest musicians.

Sean would be producing again, and the 'Tippers would remain my core band, but Phil was determined that no expense would be spared to make this a record that could compete with what the major labels were putting out.

I had plenty of songs to choose from (by this time I'd written around five hundred or so), and I spent the next two months recording acoustic/vocal demos of the tunes I felt had the most commercial potential, might actually get played on the radio.

In mid-May, just a few days after I'd sent Phil demos of forty songs to choose from, I got a call from Mom.

My baby sister Bella's oldest daughter – a sweet fourteen-year-old named Allison – had been killed in a car crash on her way to the convenience store with her sixteen-year-old boyfriend to pick up a two liter bottle of Coke.

A drunk driver had swerved into their lane, and the boyfriend – being the novice driver that he was – had swerved off the road, then over-compensated getting back on, and the pick-up truck he'd been driving had flipped.

He came out of it with a broken arm, my niece with a broken neck, my sis with a broken life.

I gave God a good cursing that day, wondering why He would finally bless me with the overwhelming joy of having my daughters again in my life only to turn around and take *one from my beloved Bella.*

As much as it pained me to even entertain *the notion, I would've preferred He kept my girls safe strangers than to deal so crushing a blow to someone so dear.*

My mind could not conceive *the agony my baby sis was going through – I don't imagine* any *mind can, for we're simply not* wired *to imagine a life we bring into the world leaving it before us.*

Phil bought me a round-trip plane ticket to Tulsa. I didn't ask if that *was recoupable. It was the farthest thing from my mind.*

All I cared about was being there for my sister, hoping the presence of those that loved her so deeply would somehow render the overwhelming sorrow of her loss at least a tiny bit more tolerable.

I don't know how much it helped her, but it helped keep us, I think, from feeling completely useless.

The preacher at the funeral was a complete jack-ass.

In his eulogy, he actually relayed a parable in which a young girl had died not because of a moron who'd had too many beers, but because of her own sins. My Mom and Uncle thought it lovely. Us kids thought the preacher should've been wearing a clown suit and shot out of a cannon.

Bella was distraught, of course, and I couldn't bear the thought of returning to Nashville while I felt she still needed the presence and comfort of her loved ones, so I extended my stay.

Joanie, the sammich shop's co-owner, accepted this with all the grace and equanimity of a three-year-old and threatened to fire me if I didn't get back there and resume my rightful place behind the counter.

I told her to fuck off.

Probly woulda been fired if not for Bob, the joint's other owner, who happened to control fifty-one percent of the establishment. I thanked him for exercising his two percent, and made it back to Nashville the next week. Joanie didn't speak to me for a month. I was glad.

Father's Day weekend I flew to Virginia to reunite with my babies.

I hadn't seen so much as a picture of them since that day a sad lifetime ago when I'd hid behind that booth because I hadn't felt like interrupting my drinking with pesky fatherhood. Suzie had been three, Marie two.

I knew they'd grow up beautiful – mainly 'cause of their mother – but I was unprepared for these visions that greeted me upon my arrival at the airport in Norfolk.

My breath left as the tears came, and I held them to me and cried like an old woman as they haltingly returned my embrace, their eyes assessing the surrounding throng to see if perhaps they were being watched, wondering just how embarrassing this could get.

I couldn't blame them. We were virtual strangers, connected only by blood and memories – theirs fuzzy at best, mine locked away to preserve my sanity.

It came slowly, but by the time I left three days later, after tearfully watching Marie get her diploma, Suzie by my side, I felt that we were on the road to re-forming a relationship I swore I'd never allow anything but my departure from this world to hinder.

And I didn't. Until it did.

By the time I got back to Nashville, Phil had chosen fourteen songs out of the forty I'd sent him, and two weeks later we began work on the second CD, which I'd decided to call "Songs About Life and Girls (but mostly girls)." It took damned near a year to finish, mainly because we had to schedule around my work and the various projects of all those involved.

We hired Tony Nielson to play keyboards. He'd been in a band in the seventies that'd had some big-time hits and were now a staple of Classic Rock radio. He was a big fat white-haired blind guy, like Santa Claus with dark shades and a cane. Me and Sean had to go to his studio for each of those sessions, where he played the bejesus out of his baby grand, charged Phil four hundred bucks a pop (recoupable), and drank most of my beer (non-recoupable). It was worth every penny and PBR though, 'cause he played the piano like Paris Hilton plays the skin-flute, but with less slobbering.

We also hired Jelly-Bean Jackson and Fats Murphy, a couple of session players whose real names were neither Jelly-Bean nor Fats, and who had played harmonica and fiddle (respectively) on some of the biggest country songs of the last decade.

Nashville's like that – the same few guys play on almost every record. Might be hard to believe, but you've probably got a better shot at making it as an artist *than as a studio musician, especially if you're a cute teenager or look like a GQ model.*

Fuckin' town.

By the end of the next summer we'd finished recording. All that was left was the mastering, the artwork, the release, and, hopefully, the promotion and the critical and commercial success.

I celebrated by getting my first tattoo which, if you'll recall, was **MY FIRST TATTOO**. *That same night, I bought my first pack of cigarettes. Don't know what possessed me to do either. As far as the latter goes, I guess I figured that - considering the lifestyle I'd led and that I was starting the habit so late - surely something would kill me before the smokes did.*

Rather prophetic of me, don't ya think?

CHAPTER TWENTY-EIGHT

Marshall Laughlin *loved* being a lawyer. He loved the verbal jousting, the strategy, the closing arguments, the nervousness in the pit of his stomach awaiting a verdict - akin to that which he imagined a rock star feels before taking the stage, knowing there's a *possibility* of failure, but that it's highly *unlikely*.

Laughlin also loved his wife, his kids, his mistress, his houses, his cars, and his filet mignon. But what he *really* loved - what he *lived* for – were press conferences.

And this was going to be a press conference like no other.

Following the bizarre outburst by the youngster that morning in Judge Way's chambers, after the kid had left the room to go pee, the Judge granted Laughlin's request for yet *another* continuance – two days – to, as she put it, "give the boy…or ghost…or *whatever* the fuck he is…time to finish his diary or memoir…or *whatever* the fuck he's doing."

The prosecutors, Brice and Fleming, had feigned outrage, yet there was a sense that – win or lose – they were pretty damned curious themselves to see how this was going to play out.

They went through the motions of asking the Judge to at least order Laughlin to keep a lid on it – a request that was granted – but they all knew the odds of the defense attorney remaining silent were roughly the same odds as those of Vanderbilt's football team winning a national championship.

It wasn't going to happen.

Laughlin and Mack Blevins had met up with a once-again-normal Willard and a slightly-disheveled Harvey and Angel in the hallway outside. As a sheriff's deputy left with the defendant to return her to her cell in the basement, the attorney had suggested to the boy's father they put him up in a hotel.

"He'll have privacy to get this thing finished and, to be honest, it's going to get kind of crazy."

Harvey and Mack looked at the lawyer with an expression

that indicated that *that* particular horse had left the barn some time ago and was now disappearing in full gallop over the horizon.

"I get to miss school?" the child asked.

"They got cable?" his father asked.

Laughlin shook his head.

"No cable. No internet. No chance for anyone to say he got his information from any outside source," he told Mack.

"I get to miss school?" Willard repeated.

"You may not be going back to school for awhile," Laughlin told the boy, who had smiled for the first time that day.

"I don't have to *stay* there with him then?" Mack inquired.

"I'd prefer you didn't."

Laughlin had used his cell phone to make arrangements, then directed the father to take his son to the Holiday Inn on Highway 231 south of the town square, the same hotel where *he* was staying.

After the boy and his son left, and after Brice and Fleming finally emerged from the Judge's chambers, giving the attorney a baleful stare as they passed him in the hallway, Laughlin took Harvey by the elbow and guided him into an empty office. He shut the door.

"I'm calling a press conference for 4 o'clock this afternoon," he told the radio man. "By dinner time you're probably going to be famous."

"Uh…"

"And you're going to have to take a few days off from the station."

Harvey hadn't even *conceived* of that possibility, and started to protest. Laughlin cut him off.

"You're *part* of this story. You can't waste your time reporting it to a bunch of hicks when you'll be talking about it on national TV."

"But…"

"Believe me, the hicks'll know."

At precisely 4 o'clock, Laughlin stood behind the podium on the courthouse steps, his familiar silk suit unwrinkled, his longish thick gray hair unruffled.

Mack and Harvey stood looking on from behind.

The crowd wasn't as big as it could have been, what with most of the out-of-town press at home awaiting the resumption of the actual *trial*, (which was the reason there'd been no problem getting the *boy* a room), but the *Nashville* media had made it, as had most of the TV stations from Knoxville, Chattanooga, and Memphis.

In this age of instant communication, a dozen cameras were as good as a thousand.

"I'm going to tell you a story," Laughlin began, then paused until he was sure everyone was listening.

There were murmurs among those gathered, mainly whispered speculation about the local radio guy being *behind* the podium. A few expressed relief that at least he wasn't smoking that goddamned *pipe*.

"This story," Laughlin continued, "may stretch the boundaries of imagination and credulity, and many of you may perceive it as just another ploy by a desperate attorney to muddy the waters of what seems to be a clear stream of facts flowing inexorably to a sea of guilt for my client."

He had their undivided attention now, even if many had no clue what the fuck he was talking about.

"What the fuck is he talking about?" someone muttered, which annoyed those cameramen present who would now have an additional edit to make.

Several hands in the crowd flew up, but Laughlin simply shook his head, and the hands lowered.

"Not long after this trial started, Harvey Boyd..."

He acknowledged Harvey, who just stood there wishing he could light his pipe.

"...came into possession of a diary, a *journal* if you will, which it soon – after meticulous scrutiny and substantiation – became obvious was written by Jared Whaley, the victim of the crime for which my client is now on trial for her life."

The murmuring began anew, and Laughlin once again waited a moment for it to die down.

"Now, ordinarily," he continued, "the existence of such a journal would be *interesting*, but not necessarily have any bearing on the case."

He paused yet again, although the smallish throng was for the moment hushed.

"What makes this particular document *more* than interesting, and what *does* give it bearing, is that in it the late Mr. Whaley refers to his *own* murder."

Hands shot up once again and the chatter reached a level such that the attorney had to raise his voice.

"And what is even *more* astounding, what stretches the bounds of imagination and credulity..."

He hesitated before continuing, not only to allow the babble to quell and to ensure his next words were heard (and *recorded*) without the slightest impedance, but also because he knew that once they left his lips those words could not be retracted. There would be no do-over, no chance to annotate, elucidate, or extricate his way out of what many would construe as the ranting of a madman, the beginning of the downfall of a once-respected litigator.

Pure poppy-cock. He finished.

"...is that in *this* journal the victim refers to his murder in the *past tense*."

Laughlin thought he knew crowd psychology. He'd expected pandemonium.

He'd misjudged.

There was only silence, as if the audience had tip-toed to the bounds of imagination and credulity, looked over the edge, and decided the drop was too far.

He felt his stomach lurch, felt a rare moment of defeat. Saw his career flash before his eyes.

A single hand, from a reporter about halfway back, hesitantly raised.

He nodded toward the attractive bespectacled blond he recognized from the Nashville CBS affiliate.

"Uh…" she began. "How did he do *that*?"

Laughlin heard the muted voices of the others:

"That's a good question…"

"What the hell is he *talking* about?"

"Is that hair for *real*?"

The attorney straightened up to his full height. He looked the CBS reporter dead in the eye.

"He didn't," he said, and was met by a couple of dozen blank stares. He might as well have been speaking Chinese.

He sighed and plowed ahead.

"*This* journal was written by twelve-year-old Wilson resident Willard Blevins."

As those gathered shook their heads in bewilderment, not quite knowing how to respond, afraid to justify the words *with* a response, Laughlin also found himself momentarily and uncharacteristically speechless, unaccustomed as he was to having to come up with something to top a bombshell.

From behind him, Mack leaned forward toward the expectant faces.

"That country singer done possessed my boy!" he said.

Though no one realized it at the time, those seven words would be replayed ad infinitum, beginning that evening and for several weeks – and even years - to come, the sound-bite to end all sound-bites, a crudely-eloquent synopsis of what would inevitably transform the history not only of jurisprudence but of the debate over mortality and the essence of life itself.

At the time, it just seemed *weird*.

Someone laughed, which opened the floodgate of expressed disbelief.

"He's lost it."

"This is nuts."

"I drove two hours for *this*?"

"No, really. Look at that *hair*."

"I *believe* him!" Laughlin shouted, all seriousness and somber righteousness, his convincing tone and the weight of his stature - not only physically, but as one of the nation's most respected and successful barristers - finally pacifying the onlookers into at least a semblance of deference.

"And two days from now, when I put the boy on the stand, you'll believe him *too*."

And *that's* when the shit hit the fan.

CHAPTER TWENTY-NINE

There are three things in life which are certain:
1. *There's always shit.*
2. *There's always a fan.*
3. *Always at some point the twain shall meet.*

I guess one could reason my own personal poop began it's doomed journey toward those whirring, shit-sucking blades that night at the Sutler when I met Angel.

In truth, I think it began years earlier, when I slept with Chad's girlfriend Amanda.

But really, who's to say *when my fateful feces took flight? Maybe it was when I first* met *Chad, or when Chad first met* Amanda, *or even when Chad came into the sammich shop that day, leading to the reunion of the CowTippers.*

Take away any single one of those moments and the crap might've remained constipated deep within the blessed bowels of unlucky breaks, and my brains in the confines of my stupid skull, instead of splattered on the wall of the Thirsty Turtle.

Fuck it. Maybe it was karma. If so, then karma's a cocksucker.

How many times did I say, over the course of my time as a living, breathing, walking, talking, drinking, smoking, cussing, fucking human being, *that I wished I had a* life?

Well, my friends, I wish I had a life.

I wish I had a beer and a cigarette. I wish I had a headache. Anything *to remind me that time flies when you're having fun, and that* everything *compared to* nothing *is* fun.

I get no satisfaction from this telling of my story. It only makes me sad and ashamed, and words cannot express how mere words cannot express it.

I told my brother the philosopher once, when he was going through a particularly rough spell, that the true measure of one's life cannot be gauged by any particular moment in time, that it ain't over till the fat lady sings, when you can look back and determine whether the good times outweighed the bad, whether your existence left the world better, worse, or indifferent.

I was as full of shit as the fan my shit hit.

Life, I now realize, is nothing but our only option. We do our best to justify it, but in the end we're just a pebble in a pond, praying futilely that our miniscule ripples can somehow manage to capsize a cruise ship.

They really can't. *And if they* could, *would it really be a ship worth* sinking?

If I'd never been, my girls would've never been. My songs would've never been. What difference would it have made? My girls would've never been aware they never existed, my songs oblivious to the fact that they were never heard, funny little trees falling in an uninhabited forest.

We are the means to our own ends. We are the reason we are *as well as the reason we're* not.

In just over two hours, this poor innocent kid is going to put on a brand-new suit, and the two of us are going to tell the world exactly how I wound up dead. It's a long story, one which probably won't come out anything like what folks're expecting. But I can sum it up in just a few words:

A bullet in a brain.

A pebble in a pond.

CHAPTER THIRTY

The circus was in town, and the residents of Wilson, Tennessee weren't quite sure just who the *clowns* were.

Some surmised it was *them*, that the highfalutin lawyer from the big city had somehow managed to hold them all down and apply the make-up, the red nose, the funny hat, the too-big shoes, all while they had simply been minding their own business. They hadn't *asked* for this trial, and they *certainly* hadn't given their permission for the erection of such a massive big-top.

Others - those with more pride - asserted it was the lawyer *himself*, the clown as ringleader.

All one had to do over the past two days was turn on a TV or pick up a newspaper to see the snappily-dressed attorney, usually accompanied by their own Harvey Boyd, talking with a reporter or splashed across the front page.

They'd been – via satellite from one of the Nashville TV studios - on CNN with Larry King and on Fox News with Bill O'Reilly. The former had inquired if Laughlin had been examined for a brain tumor or diagnosed with a mental disease, the latter had brought in a priest to discuss the procedures for a church-approved exorcism.

Every interview, every article, every news story included video, audio, or a quote of Mack's now-famous line:

"That country singer done possessed my boy."

The New York *Times*' banner headline read "SÉANCE IN THE COURTROOM," while the *National Enquirer*'s simply read "WE COULDN'T MAKE THIS SH!T UP!"

Skeptics and believers alike flocked in droves to Wilson. It was a windfall for the small town – exponentially more so than when this was a simple *murder trial* - but, as with an inheritance resulting from the death of a loved one, most agreed they'd rather have just stayed poor.

Judge Myra Way was sitting alone in her chambers, wishing she'd just stayed in private practice.

She gave the hot-shot from Nashville an inch and he took a mile. She gave him a length of rope and he made a noose big enough to hang them all.

She'd *expected* him to blab to the media. They *all* had. But what was supposed to have been merely a two-day recess had become a damned *media blitz* for the lawyer, who'd announced to the whole freakin' *world* that he was gonna put a *ghost* on the stand.

The pages Laughlin submitted to her the previous day had really shed no new light on anything pertaining to the *case,* but now she realistically had no choice.

She could, of course, shut the whole thing down, but figured that would be *worse*, make her and the town *more* of a laughing-stock, than just rolling the dice and letting the chips fall where they may.

Either way, she calculated that the odds of maintaining a *shred* of dignity, much less getting *re-elected* in the coming fall, were roughly the same as the odds of monkeys flying out of her butt.

She laughed out loud and shook her head.
This is lunacy.

"This is lunacy," Marshall Laughlin muttered as he finished reading.

He was standing in Willard's hotel room, Harvey and Mack lingering to the side.

The attorney was holding two single pages from the printer he'd hooked up to the boy's laptop the previous day. He'd been less-than-impressed with the output *then* (basically a recounting of the last few years of the singer's life - getting a record deal, re-uniting with his daughters, burying a niece, yada yada yada), but had nonetheless delivered copies to the Judge and Prosecution, promising them that the next day – in court – he'd deliver all that was promised and *more*. He knew they really had no *choice*.

He looked at the boy.

"This is *it*?"

Willard, sitting on the side of the bed, looking in his suit and tie like a mini-Mack – and equally as uncomfortable - just shrugged.

"Dunno."

"Jesus Christ on a fuckin' Ritz cracker," Laughlin swore, quickly re-scanning the pages.

"This is *supposed* to be the *end* of the thing. We're *supposed* to know who the fuck should be on *trial* here!"

He thrust the pages at Harvey, who took them and began reading.

"All I can tell from *this* is that the guitar player and his girlfriend *might* or *might not* have something to do with it," the attorney muttered. "And that the dead guy's fucking *depressed*."

"I'm sorry," Willard said, looking at his father, his eyes welling with tears. "I wanna go to school."

Mack spoke up in his son's defense.

"The boy's scared shitless," he said.

Laughlin rolled his eyes and shook his head.

"*He's* scared? Fuck. My *career's* on the line here. My *reputation*!"

He walked to the window and stared out. It was a beautiful day.

"Fuck," he repeated.

There was a moment of silence as the lawyer stared, Harvey read, and Mack wished they hadn't taken the damned TV out of the room.

Finally, the lawyer sighed and turned away from the window.

"I think I might puke," he said.

Harvey looked up from the print-out.

"Seems he's going to finish the story on the stand," he said.

Laughlin's face turned a shade of gray, and he bolted to the bathroom and slammed the door. The sounds of retching could be heard from within.

Harvey looked at Mack.

"I think this is getting to him."

"I sure hope he don't get none on that *suit*," Mack replied.

"You are such a fucking PUSSY!" It was Willard – or *not* Willard - yelling toward the bathroom.

The up-chucking suddenly ceased and the door was flung open, Laughlin standing there pale, eyes wide, a towel in his hand, a rivulet of discolored vomit running down his chin.

"You missed a spot," Mack said, touching his own chin.

Laughlin wiped his face with the towel, not taking his eyes from Willard.

"What did you say to me?"

"You heard me," the boy drawled. "You're a *pussy*."

He rose from the bed and stood toe-to-toe with the much larger attorney, looking up with a sneer.

"You want everything wrapped in a nice neat little package. You want to know everything in advance. You don't care about Angel as much as you care about *winning*."

"Listen here, punk," Laughlin snarled, looking down, returning the menacing stare. "*Winning* this thing is could be the difference between life and death for your so-called '*soul-mate*'. It doesn't *matter* what my *motives* are!"

The youngster's vehemence died as quickly as it had begun.

"You are a *very* large man," he said.

"And *you're* a fuckin' pain in the *ass*."

"Relax, Marsh," the boy said. He patted the large man on the belly.

"I'm not gonna disappoint ya."

The attorney seemed to find little solace in the reassurance.

"Besides," the chubby possessed kid added. "The other guys don't *know* what you don't know."

Laughlin's features softened as he considered this.

"Fuck a *bird*!" Mack yelled from the bathroom. He poked his head out and looked at Laughlin.

"You didn't flush," he said.

The line outside the Wilson County Courthouse had begun forming nearly forty hours previously, shortly after the first reports hit the airwaves that a witness unlike any other *ever* was going to be called to the stand two mornings hence.

There were tents pitched on the lawn, sleeping bags on the benches, vendors on the sidewalks.

There were network vans with huge satellite dishes perched on their tops parked at the curb, preachers with bullhorns, psychics with booths.

As Laughlin eased his Lincoln Town Car – carrying Harvey in the passenger seat and Mack and Willard in the back - through the crowd toward his assigned parking spot near the front steps, he was reminded of the scene from the Jodie Foster movie "Contact," shortly after it was announced to the world that we had finally received a "Howdy-do" from a distant galactic neighbor.

This seemed more far-fetched.

The gathered media, recognizing the car, swarmed toward them, pounding on the windows and shouting questions a couple of hundred feet before the attorney finally parked.

"Kinda like the Beatles, ain't it?" the boy drawled.

"Don't say a goddamn word," Laughlin warned, their eyes meeting in the rear-view mirror.

"Huh?" Willard asked meekly.

"That's more like it."

The lawyer waited until the sheriff's deputies arrived, pushing reporters out of the way as they formed a barricade around the rear passenger-side door, from which emerged what appeared to be merely a frightened child.

Laughlin and Harvey and Mack got out next, the lawyer doing his best to draw attention away from the others as they quickly made their way up the courthouse steps.

"People, *please!*" he shouted. "We'll have a statement for you when we're done!"

With that he ignored the shouted questions, using his briefcase as a battering ram, parting the sea of humanity until he, too, was safely inside.

For the first time in the history of Wilson County, a camera was going to be allowed in the courtroom. Not necessarily because previous Judges had been intent on preserving the dignity and decorum of the proceedings, but because there really just hadn't been anything worth *taping*.

Obviously, things had changed.

Thus it was that the entire country - and much of the *world* - saw the grand entrance, through the courtroom's double doors, of defense attorney Marshall Laughlin, followed closely by Harvey Boyd and Mack and Willard Blevins, the latter clinging to his father's arm like a bride that most definitely did *not* want to be given away.

The courtroom was hushed for the most part, although a few whispered murmurs could be heard from the gallery, as well as from the jury box, where twelve Wilson citizens sat collectively wondering if *this* was the reason they'd been – without any warning or explanation – sequestered two nights ago.

They therefore had no *clue* what the hell was going on, but, based on the crowd and the camera and the general air of excitement, figured they should pay close attention and maybe even take notes, because you never knew when something like this could lead to a *book deal*.

Laughlin strode down the aisle, exuding almost-regal confidence, giving no hint that he'd just an hour before lost his breakfast.

He stopped short of the wooden gate of the railing separating the on-lookers from the principles, and motioned his three followers into three front-row seats, the only empty seats in the room save for his own at the defense table beside his client.

Angel was turned in her chair watching the entrance, gazing at Harvey.

It was the first time he'd seen her since just after their near-assignation in the ladies' room, and Harvey was momentarily overcome with such a longing and lurching in the pit of his stomach that he was glad he had *skipped* breakfast.

He sat directly behind her, their eyes meeting, but only briefly, before she turned back toward the front.

Willard sat to Harvey's right, then Mack settled into the last seat on the row, next to his frightened son.

The boy just stared at the floor, while his father took in the gallery, seemingly thrilled at the stares and whispered finger-pointing from those in the pews.

"That country singer done possessed my boy!" he shouted with a grin, which got some laughs and scattered applause from the audience, while only serving to further confuse the jury.

They looked at one another and shrugged.

Laughlin, from the other side of the railing, looked toward the vaulted ceiling and sighed, shaking his head, then fixed Mack with an icy stare which immediately wiped the smile from the latter's rotund face. Reprimanded, he joined his son in staring at the floor.

From the Prosecution table, Brice and Fleming exchanged a disgusted look, then stared toward the defense attorney with quiet retribution as he laid his briefcase on his own table and took his seat.

His butt had barely touched the chair when the uniformed bailiff, a squat fellow in his forties who seemed like he'd rather be fishing, cried out in a voice resembling Gomer Pyle's:

"ALL RISE!"

Laughlin bounced back up with the others. He looked at Angel and smiled, then turned and looked at the three behind him and gave a reassuring wink.

The bailiff continued.

"The Criminal Court of Wilson County, Tennessee is now in session, the Honorable Judge Myra Way presiding. All having business before this Honorable Court draw near, give attention, and you shall be heard."

Judge Way, wearing a customary black robe, entered from the anteroom to the side, climbed the two steps and sat at her throne behind her bench, beneath the Seal of the State of Tennessee.

She couldn't help but think it should be a seal balancing a ball on its nose.

"Sit down."

Everyone in the room complied, save for the bailiff, who stood off to the side of the bench, and the reporters and spectators lining the walls from the railing back to the courtroom doors.

They were going to be standing for awhile.

The Judge looked over the heads of the Court reporter and Court Clerk seated in front of and below her at their two small desks, and surveyed the scene before her - the attorneys at their respective tables, the packed gallery, the jury box to the side and the questioning expressions of the twelve within.

She shook her head, exasperated, then looked at Laughlin.

"Is the Defense ready to proceed?"

The attorney stood, looked down at some papers lying on the table in front of his open briefcase.

"Defense calls Mack Blevins."

As Willard's father lumbered to his feet and opened the wooden gate, Fleming rose.

"Your *Honor*," he said. "We'd like to formally object to what the Defense has planned here today. It demeans the integrity not only of the Court, but of our entire system of *justice*."

The Judge glared at him, yet seemed unsurprised.

"Your objections were duly noted in chambers. Now they're part of the transcript. I don't want to hear them again."

Fleming, looking down at Brice with a shake of his head and a shrug, resumed his seat.

Mack nervously made his way to the witness stand, in front of which stood the Court Clerk, holding a Bible. He placed his right hand on it and swore he wouldn't fib, then squeezed his massive girth into the small seat behind the small microphone.

After asking him to state his name for the record, Laughlin inquired where he was employed.

"I'm on disability," Mack said. "Bowling accident."

This got some laughs from the gallery, but a scowl from Judge Way sufficed to quickly restore quiet.

After establishing that the Blevins did indeed have a twelve-year-old son named Willard, Laughlin then proceeded to guide his witness through a re-telling of the strange events of the past couple of weeks.

"That country singer done possessed my boy!" Mack concluded, which got more laughs and scattered applause from the gallery, and which caused the jury (now enlightened as to where this was all *going*), to begin furiously scribbling notes, each hoping that *their* recollections would be the ones published in hardback, then paperback, then made into a movie.

Judge Way banged her gavel for the first time.

"Hey!" she shouted. "We are *not* in a comedy club! If restraint is *not* exercised in my courtroom, you'll *all* be watching this trial on TV."

Fleming stood once again.

"Your Honor…"

"Shut up!"

Fleming sat.

Laughlin had no further questions.

On cross-examination, Fleming tried to impugn the credibility of the witness, referring first to his affinity for alcohol (the "bowling accident"), then to his affinity for attention ("that country singer done possessed my boy").

Laughlin skillfully objected to both lines of questioning, citing relevance, pointing out in regards to the latter that it had sprung *from* the sworn-to events, not led *to* them.

Both objections were sustained, and Fleming gave up.

"No further questions of this witness."

Mack's testimony had taken just over an hour, and clearly mesmerized the gallery and the jury (as well as the *television* audience, which was already approaching the numbers recorded at the height of the O.J. trial, and made the ratings for the last Olympics look like those for a late-night infomercial).

Not one to squander momentum, Laughlin immediately called Harvey to the stand.

As he held open the gate to allow Mack to pass through, Harvey tried to catch Angel's eye again, hoping for at least a brief re-assuring connection, some comfort, before he faced what he surmised would be the most terrifying ordeal of his life.

But he couldn't see through Mack.

His right hand shook noticeably as he placed it on the Bible and took the oath, then took the stand.

After the necessary preliminaries, he began recounting the events of the last week.

During portions of his testimony, he caught Angel looking at him with what *he* perceived to be a subdued longing borne perhaps of a combination of desire and admiration, but which could have been a nervous unease borne of a combination of fear and boredom.

Harvey had never been good at gauging women.

At one point when his eyes met hers, he thought he saw in his periphery Brice noticing the exchange and frowning, then leaning over and whispering something to Fleming. Or *shouting*

213

something to Fleming.

Same dif.

Either way, the moment passed as quickly as it had begun, and he didn't sense that anything had come of it.

When he got to his telephone conversation with Phil Kearns, Fleming of course objected that it was hearsay, at which point Laughlin requested to introduce into evidence- as "Defense Exhibit A" - Kearns' sworn affidavit. The request was granted, the objection overruled.

"And while we're at it, Your Honor," Laughlin said, removing a large stack of documents from his briefcase, "I guess this is as good a time as any to go ahead and introduce Exhibits B through T, which consists of everything written by young Mr. Blevins, as well as sworn affidavits from virtually all of the principles named in the aforementioned journal, attesting to its accurate depiction of the victim's life."

Fleming jumped up.

"Your Honor," he wailed plaintively. "The State would like to renew its objection to these shenanigans…"

"What did I tell you about that?" Judge Way asked.

Fleming, aware that he'd thus far been shut down by the Judge at every turn, and that there were possibly *millions* watching his discomfiture, pressed on.

"There is not one *shred* of evidence in *any* of these documents which even *approaches* refuting the State's case."

The Judge sighed and looked at Laughlin.

"Well, Counselor?"

"Oh yeah." Laughlin reached once again into his briefcase.

"I meant to mention that he wrote some *more*. Just this morning in fact."

The gallery was once again abuzz as Brice jumped up.

"Objection!"

Judge Way pounded her gavel until the commotion from the spectators subsided.

"Did you say something Haywood?" she asked.

"Crap," the County Prosecutor muttered, shaking his head, resuming his seat. Fleming, still standing, repeated his boss' objection.

"The State requests a chance to read these documents before you make a ruling on our previous objection as to the admissibility of *any* of the Defense's exhibits."

The Judge smiled.

"Nice try, Ken. The evidence is admitted."

Fleming started to protest, but Judge Way cut him off.

"*However*," she added. "I *will* give you a brief recess to look over what the boy wrote this morning."

"It's only two pages, Your Honor," Laughlin said, looking over to the Prosecution table as Fleming sat.

"But it speaks *volumes*," he bluffed.

"Ten minutes then."

She was about to pound her gavel when she realized Harvey was still on the stand. She looked at the defense attorney.

"Uh…do you have any more questions for this witness?"

Laughlin knew Harvey had more to tell, but figured the newsman had laid a good foundation for what was to come, and didn't want to get greedy.

"I do not Your Honor."

She looked at Fleming.

"Does the State wish to cross-examine now or wait until after the recess?"

Fleming whispered something to Brice, who quickly nodded. Fleming stood.

"We've just got one quick question for the witness, Your Honor."

"Proceed."

Just one question? Harvey thought from his seat on the stand. *This was easier than I thought.*

"Mr. Boyd," Fleming began. "I know it must be quite an

ordeal sitting up there, the eyes of not only a packed courtroom but the entire *world* scrutinizing your every word."

"It's not been too bad," Harvey replied. "I've kinda got used to it the past couple of days."

This brought some sympathetic laughter from the gallery. Judge Way glared and they shut up.

"I'm sure you have," Fleming chuckled. "I'm sure you *have*."

He strolled over to the table, pretended to be looking over some notes.

"You're kind of the big fish in a small pond now, aren't you?"

Harvey was slightly taken aback, wondering exactly where this was leading. His nerves returned.

"Is that the 'one question'?"

More laughter from the spectators, this time sustained long enough to prompt Judge Way to bang her gavel.

"Shut up!" she snarled, then looked at Fleming.

"You *did* say 'one question.'"

"Oh right, right," the Assistant Prosecutor acknowledged. "Okay then."

He made his way from the table, turning to Laughlin and smiling snidely en-route to the front of the witness stand.

If Fleming's grin disconcerted the defense attorney in the slightest, he didn't show it. Everything had gone his way thus far. What harm could a single question do?

"Mr. Boyd," Fleming said, his hands casually laid upon the wooden bar of the stand. He looked toward the jury box, then at the Judge, then back at Harvey.

He smiled again.

"Would you mind telling the Court…are you having an affair with the defendant?"

It was the loudest outburst from the crowd thus far. Harvey felt like he'd been kicked in the balls by a midget. Who played soccer. A midget with a helluva kick.

Why does it have to be a midget? he thought, such was the state of his discombobulation.

Laughlin was stunned. As Judge Way banged her gavel, he heard someone behind him say, "I *told* you he wasn't gay," followed by, in response, "Some fellers are just late bloomers."

"*Objection!*" he roared, leaping to his feet, watching his momentum scamper down the aisle and out the double-doors.

"The State's implication is not only *completely* groundless but *totally* irrelevant to these proceedings!"

Fleming wheeled from the stand and faced Laughlin, his face a mask of contorted incredulous rage.

"*Irrelevant?*" he shouted. "It takes a lot of ball…" he looked at the Judge, who arched her eyebrows. He re-phrased.

"It takes a lot of *nerve* for you of all people to even *utter* the word *relevance*! This whole damned *morning* has been *irrelevant!*"

The Judge banged her gavel, then pointed it at the Assistant Prosecutor.

"You're coming *dangerously* close to a contempt citation, young man! The only one who decides what's *relevant* in *this* courtroom is the bitch with the robe! And last time I checked, *that bitch is me!*"

Judge Way couldn't believe she'd lost it like that, and watched her hopes for re-election – like Laughlin's momentum - scamper down the aisle and out the door.

As she banged her gavel again, this time to quell the uproar she herself had caused, she wondered exactly how *cold* it got in Fairbanks.

"The witness will answer the question," she said.

"Your Honor," Laughlin spoke up. "I'd like to take that recess now. I need to…uh…confer with my witness."

"The witness will answer the question," she repeated.

Harvey was like a deer frozen in the headlights of a Mack

truck with venison on its mind. He looked toward Laughlin, then couldn't help but stare at Angel, who looked at him and slightly shook her head.

Oh great! he thought. *Like nobody saw* that.

In fact, the cameraman, through the lens from his spot near the front of the gallery closest to the jury box, *did* see that, which meant that everyone *watching TV* saw that.

It was *not* the Defense's finest hour.

"We…uh…I've only known her for just over a *week*."

Harvey knew he was speaking the truth, but, as they say, not the *whole* truth and nothing *but* the truth.

"I'd like to remind you you're under oath, Mr. Boyd," the Judge calmly said.

Harvey thought back to that moment just moments ago when he'd thought this a cakewalk, certain he was about to end the ordeal with his dignity. That moment was now a lifetime away.

"We made out in the ladies' room," he muttered.

"Sonofabitch," Laughlin said loudly as the courtroom once again erupted.

The Judge pounded her gavel, considering whether the defense attorney's utterance of a profanity she'd only moments ago uttered *twice* warranted remonstration, then decided to let it pass.

"I am *so* close to clearing this courtroom!" she shouted instead.

Harvey watched his career scamper down the aisle and out the double-doors, held open by Laughlin's momentum and Judge Way's hopes.

He didn't know *why* he said that. But it *was* the whole truth and nothing *but* the truth. Even so, he figured it was *way* TMI.

Laughlin seemed to concur.

"Son of a *bitch*!" he repeated.

Judge Way hadn't used her gavel this much in as long as she could remember, and hoped it didn't break. She didn't have a back-up.

When the commotion quelled, she asked Fleming if perhaps he now had *more* questions.

"Just one more, Your Honor." He walked to the stand, leaned in toward the witness.

"Mr. Boyd," Fleming said, then turned to face the jury. "Are you in love with the defendant?"

Harvey looked at Angel. She returned the stare, her face a calm mask.

"I don't know…" he started. "Maybe…"

Angel looked away as the gallery erupted again.

"Sonofabitch," said Laughlin.

"And Mr. Boyd," Fleming continued, his voice above the din. "Didn't you concoct this entire charade as a way to get the girl?"

"Good *Lord*!" Laughlin exclaimed from the table, feigning outrage but not even bothering to object.

The crowd became suddenly quiet, articulating a collective "*Huh?*"

Harvey shook his head, as if he were trying to awaken from a bad and ridiculous dream.

"*What?*"

"No further questions."

Fleming walked back to the table, content to let the proposal, however preposterous, insinuate itself into the collective consciousness of the already-confused jury. History had proven that juries could be *idiots*.

"Re-direct, Your Honor," Laughlin said, rising from his seat. He smiled inwardly, silently congratulating his opponents on the subterfuge. He'd have done the same thing himself.

"Harvey," he said. "Did you ever *meet* Jared Whaley?"

"No sir."

"Prior to that field trip to the radio station, had you ever *met* Willard Blevins?"

"No sir."

"And when did you first have knowledge of Angel Whaley?"

"Right after the murder."

"So it's not a likely scenario that you'd research the victim's life story to the extent that you could write a detailed memoir so accurate that it would convince his record label president, his friends, and even his *widow*? And that you'd then be able to coax a twelve-year-old into pretending he was *possessed* by the victim? All to get a *date*?"

Harvey thought a moment.

"Doesn't seem like that'd even be *possible*," he said. "Even if I *didn't* already have a full-time job."

This got some laughs, but the Judge let the disruption die of its own volition.

She was worried about her gavel.

CHAPTER THIRTY-ONE

When a man thinks with his dick, dick *is generally what he gets. That sounds like a country song.*

You're probably thinking I'm referring to Harvey and Angel and that fiasco in the courtroom, but I'm really *thinking of guys and dicks in general. Myself included.*

So after Harvey got off the stand (I noticed how dejected he looked when Angel refused to make eye contact with him – he tucked his tail between his legs and slunk out of the courtroom), it was close enough to lunch time that the Judge extended the recess to an hour, and the rest of us went to that same room upstairs where Marsh had first played our video.

Appropriately enough, that's where Marsh announced he was gonna play the video, that he'd decided to introduce it into evidence.

He hadn't wanted *to, he said, hadn't wanted to diminish the impact of* my *testimony, but figured he needed to prime the pump, so to speak, since Harvey and his dick had allowed the prosecution to diffuse his precious momentum.*

So it was that, when court re-convened, everybody got to see a show.

A warm-up act, if you will, of the show to come.

Judge Myra (she's a spirited *old gal, ain't she?) said she'd allow the video to be viewed, but warned the cameraman to put his feed on a delay so that the networks'd have time to edit out all the cussin'.*

Ken protested, of course, but his heart was no longer in it, and I have a feeling he might-a been lynched if he'd kept on with his whinin'.

Seems the Judge thought the same thing, 'cause she ordered the lights dimmed while Fleming was still yammering about "relevance" and "a travesty" and the what-not.

I don't think a single person in that courtroom got up to so much as take a pee during the course of the next hour and ten minutes, mesmerized as they were by the video of me an' Willard typin', me an' Willard rantin', me an' Willard doin' Elvis.

By the time we sang the chorus of "All Your Shit" (my "Sing a-long Divorce Song"), I think even the most skeptical of the bunch were converted, and highly *anxious for the* real *show to begin.*

So me an' the boy weren't the only ones pissed when, after the lights came back up, the Judge announced we'd all seen enough for the day, and that my *day in court was gonna have to wait.*

Shit. It was only two o'clock.

Me an' the fat kid, all dressed up with nowhere to go, 'cept back to the hotel for some more quality writin' time.

I've been commanded to come up with something a little more substantial than my last outing, and it still amazes me that Marsh thinks he has any control over this situation, or over me.

Silly mortal.

However…in the interest of my own entertainment, and maybe to keep my wife's attorney from blowin' chunks again…

What if I said it was Chad's wife Amanda in the dressing room with me that night? That she was puttin' some lipstick on my dipstick when Angel came in and caught us? That my wife pulled that damned gun out and was about to blow my brains out when Chad came in, tried to grab the gun, and it went off accidentally, putting a hole in the wall? That they continued *struggling until it went off* again - *hitting me right above my right eye?*

Would ya buy that?

Or would you wonder why Angel or Chad or Amanda hadn't just told the cops this?

The human psyche is a weird thing.

It's kinda like an onion, each thin layer existing only to preserve and protect the one beneath, objectivity and subjectivity alternating without really knowing which is which or why is what, the only true reality lying somewhere between. I think that's the part that makes ya cry.

I might be dead, but I ain't omniscient.

My guess would be – hypothetically speaking, of course – that Angel would-a known that the cops would buy every bit of her story but the part that contained the word "accidentally," and that she figured she'd be better off not admitting to anything, *on the chance that her daddy's money – and the fancy lawyer it bought – could get her off.*

Most likely, Chad would-a thought the same thing, as far as no one believing it was just an accident. *Just imagine – two people in the same small room with a motive to* kill *my happy ass. Color me popular.*

As far as Amanda *goes, I figure she kept her yapper shut to protect her husband, since it was* her *yapper – in a non-speaking role – that had kinda been responsible for the whole disastrous state of affairs.*

Now I ain't sayin' that's the way it went down.

But I ain't sayin' it ain't.

CHAPTER THIRTY-TWO

"Get yer fuckin' hands off my BOY!" Mack screamed, then hurled his enormous bulk against the back of the prestigious attorney, who was in the process of strangling a twelve-year-old.

Willard gasped for air, then started crying, as his father's charge dislodged the former editor of the *Vanderbilt Law Review*'s strong fingers from around his pudgy neck.

The momentum carried, and both men crashed against the nightstand, toppling the lamp and printer, before rebounding off the wall and into the floor.

Marshall Laughlin shook his head, wondering – ironically enough – what had *possessed* him. How it had come to *this*.

"Jesus."

He looked at the boy's father, struggling to regain a sitting position beside him, like a Weeble wobbling but not being able to get up, then stood and helped Mack to his feet.

"Mack. Willard. I'm sorry," the lawyer said, patting his wrinkled silk suit.

"Fuck a *bird*," Mack panted. He looked at his son, who had retreated to the far side of the large hotel-room bed. "I wish I'd never got you that goddamned computer."

Laughlin had just moments before finished reading the latest pages. His hopes had soared as he read, and he wished he had time to subpoena the guitar player and his girlfriend. Didn't matter. He could call 'em later. If that was even *needed* to convince the jury after the kid told this *amazing* story. He'd almost kissed the print-out. Then he got to the last lines, and all of the doubt and frustration of the last couple of weeks had hit their breaking point. He'd lost it.

"'*I ain't sayin' it ain't*'?! You're yanking my goddamn *chain*!" he'd bellowed, then pounced.

Now he felt like crying. Or puking again. Or both. In just over an hour they were due in court, and he'd hoped for an inkling of a clue how it was going to go.

If the victim hadn't already been dead, he'd damned sure have killed him.

"I wanna go to *school*!" the youngster cried.

"Fuck you, fatso," the lawyer growled. "You're testifying."

Mack once again sprang to his son's defense.

"He's just big-boned," he said. "Like me an' his mama."

When the courtroom had reached its absolute capacity the previous day, many of those unlucky saps who had come so close but so far from making it inside for the spectacle had simply shrugged their shoulders and gone home to watch it on TV. Maybe take a nap.

A few foresighted souls, however, had reasoned that - even if they missed the horror show - there would still be more *trial*, and besides, what was another twenty-four hours?

So they stayed in line and won the lottery.

Movie stars, television celebrities, rock stars, and people famous mainly for being rich-and-famous descended upon the small town through the night and into the early morning, sending their surrogates to purchase places in line for as much as $100,000 each.

All of the networks were broadcasting live from the lawn near the crowded sidewalk, and all had timers on their respective video feeds counting down the hours, then the minutes, until court re-convened.

There were relatively few outside the *back* of the courthouse, however, and this was where Laughlin and Mack and Willard entered.

As they walked into the packed courtroom from the side door, Laughlin noticed that Harvey's seat was empty, and was briefly disappointed.

He assumed the radio man's pride had suffered too much of

a bruising the day before, and that he was probably locked in his house, drinking a beer and watching the proceedings on TV. He mentally pictured him sitting, unshaven, wearing only socks, underwear, and a tie, his bleary eyes maybe tearing up at the sight of Angel sitting demurely at the table wearing a plain blue dress, her hair once again pulled back in a pony-tail, her un-made-up face devoid of emotion.

Laughlin assumed wrong.

At precisely that moment, Harvey – wearing pants *and* a suit and tie - was knocking on a door in a large apartment complex in Murfreesboro, about a forty-five minute drive down Highway 231 South from Wilson.

While he *had* been crushed by the previous day's debacle, he was *more* disturbed by unanswered – and, it seemed, un-*asked* – questions, one of which had bugged him since he'd read that print-out the previous morning at the hotel. Even through his public humiliation, it gnawed at his subconscious, and he'd gone straight from the Courthouse to his laptop.

Three "Google" searches netted him the results he needed, and he'd made a phone call.

The party on the other end hadn't seemed exactly *enthusiastic* about speaking with him, said they really wanted to put the whole nightmare behind them, but Harvey persisted, said they might want to *know* some things, and they'd invited him over that morning.

A moment after he knocked, he heard muted conversation from within the apartment, and the door opened a crack. Harvey stood smiling at the unsmiling face assessing him from the other side.

"Hi Chad," he said. "Let's have a chat and watch some TV."

It was later confirmed that this was the most-watched

broadcast in history.

Virtually every home in the world with a television had it tuned to one of the numerous channels airing the event, and those *workplaces* without TV's reported absenteeism at record levels.

The moon landing four decades earlier had garnered less of a buzz. Sure, it was cool that we'd made it there, but everyone knew there was a *moon*.

Not only did *this* promise to be proof of *life after death*, it had the added attraction of being a *murder* trial, and many debated the point of capital punishment if the condemned could merely find another *body* to occupy. Made a strong case for *torture* instead.

That, many opined, would be *awesome*.

Obviously, though, not just *any* spirit could occupy just *any* body. Otherwise, this cat would have been let out of the bag a long time ago.

Many questioned how it was that this fairly-obscure musician had just happened to be the one designated to prove to the world that we were not necessarily confined to our fragile mortal shells. Which inevitably led to comparisons to a certain fairly-obscure carpenter two thousand years ago who'd had pretty much the same message.

The Atheists were kind of perturbed about this line of reasoning, but countered that *after-life* didn't necessarily mean *eternity*, argued that all this might conceivably prove was that there *was* a human spirit (they hesitated to use the word *soul*) separate and distinct from our bodies, and wouldn't concede that it had anything to do with either Heaven or Hell. Until they saw *that* on TV.

Which, like the moon landing, could be faked.

Marshall Laughlin was not a part of any of these debates, was oblivious to any ratings, didn't give a flying shit about the moon landing.

All of *his* attention was focused, as it had never in his life been focused before, on the absolute, incontrovertible moment.

Court had been called to order. The Judge was on her perch, the jury in their box.

Now he had to make a decision as to a particular *phrasing*, decide whether to utter a few words that could either doom him to perpetual laughing derision or elevate him to a place in legal history not merely alongside, but head-and-shoulders *above*, such names as William Jennings Bryan and Johnny Cochran and F. Lee Bailey.

In for a penny, in for a pound, he thought.

"Defense calls Jared Whaley."

The courtroom went nuts – the gallery, the jury box, the prosecution table – as did more than a billion spectators world-wide, gathered anywhere there was a TV set, all eyes turning to whatever widened eyes were next to them, some mouthing the words, some saying them aloud:

"Did he just say what I think he said?"

"Fuck a bird," Mack muttered from his seat.

"Fuck a duck," Judge Way growled under her breath, banging her gavel until the head broke from its handle and flew (thankfully) behind her, bouncing off the Seal of the State of Tennessee and falling harmlessly to the floor.

She reached down and grabbed the back-up she'd borrowed from the traffic-court Judge (who rarely had occasion to use it), and resumed banging.

"*ORDER!*" she yelled, almost simultaneous with the "*OBJECTION!*" shouted from Fleming, on his feet next to Brice, who echoed his assistant, although nobody heard.

The courtroom grew gradually silent, not so much because they were ordered to as out of an inquisitive reverence.

"Approach," the Judge said. Laughlin and Fleming strode to the bench, the Assistant Prosecutor with a self-righteous, indignant air, the defense lawyer as if taking a walk in the park.

"Your Honor," Fleming whispered harshly (sounding rather like a pissed-off *Brice*, the Judge thought). "We've already crossed a line here. If you allow *this*…" he searched for the right word. "This *mockery*…this *kangaroo court*…to sink farther into the muck of absurdity than it's already sunk…"

The Judge interrupted, pointing at the younger man again with her gavel.

"You call this a 'kangaroo court' one more time and I'll hop over this bench and whomp you on the head with my mallet."

She looked at Laughlin.

"But he has a point. We've already left precedent in the dust here. If I allow you, on the record, to call the *victim* of a homicide to the stand…I'm just not sure it can be done."

"Your Honor," the defense attorney calmly asserted. "It's just a matter of semantics. Everyone here…" he half-turned and motioned toward the packed courtroom, then turned back. "Hell, everyone *everywhere* knows who we're expecting to testify."

He turned again and looked past his table to the child sitting just beyond, staring at the floor with a sullen, unhappy expression, looking in his ill-fitting suit like a kid at church on the first Sunday of summer vacation.

Laughlin faced the Judge and leaned in.

"And it isn't *him*."

The Judge thought a moment.

"Seems I read about a case where one of a set of Siamese twins was called to testify at a trial. They only swore in the one, but, of course, *both* took the stand."

Laughlin smiled. Fleming silently fumed, shaking his head.

"We'll approach this from that angle."

She looked at the defense attorney and momentarily wondered why his suit was so mussed.

"Which means," she said, "that nothing the *boy* says will be admitted."

"But it'll only be *the boy* up there," Fleming protested.

"Not even *you* believe that," she scolded, then looked at

both.

"We're done here."

The men retreated, the AP to his table next to Brice, Laughlin to the railing, where he leaned over and addressed Willard.

"It's time," he said.

In a living room in neighboring Rutherford County, Harvey, Chad, and Amanda sat silently on the sofa, watching TV with the rest of the world as the chubby kid shuffled, head hanging, to where the Court Clerk stood with her Bible.

"Raise your right hand, son, and put your left hand on the Bible," she said softly.

The boy looked at her hesitantly, then down at his shoes, then complied.

"Do you swear that the testimony you're about to give will be the truth, the whole truth, and nothing *but* the truth, so help you God?"

Willard looked toward his father, his sad eyes pleading.

"I want to go to *school*," he whined.

There were audible groans of disappointment from the gallery on TV, but Harvey could've swore he heard a sigh of relief from the couple sitting next to him on the sofa.

They'd just made small-talk for awhile after he arrived, even talking about the *weather*, until Harvey finally worked up the nerve to get around to the reason for his visit: he was *pretty* sure they were somehow connected to the murder. He'd been hesitant to voice his suspicion, was unaware of the more specific quasi-theoretical charges contained in the most *recent* journal entry. It was more of an intuitive stab in the dark, based on his familiarity with Jared's *voice* and the reference to the couple in the entry from the previous day.

Harvey's stab in the dark seemed to strike home. Amanda had burst into tears, bolting into the bedroom and slamming the door. Chad momentarily fixed Harvey with an icy stare, then muttered, "*Shit*," and followed his wife.

Harvey heard more sobbing and inaudible sounds of consolation coming from behind the closed door, but resisted the urge to get close enough to hear the particulars. He didn't need to. He had his corroboration.

A few minutes later they'd emerged, Amanda drying her eyes, Chad's expression set firmly.

"Let's just see how it goes," he'd said.

It now appeared they would be content to remain silent on the subject, and Harvey wasn't quite sure whether to be disappointed or relieved. He genuinely *liked* the couple, and unfortunately knew firsthand how traumatic involvement in this case could *be*.

But he also thought of *Angel*, wondered (probably unrealistically) if perhaps *they* might be a couple, if only she were acquitted. If only he helped.

A pipe dream, he knew, and dreamed of smoking his pipe.

There was only silence from the *TV* as well, punctuated by an occasional cough or clearing of throat, as everyone wondered what would happen next. The boy still stood with one hand raised and one on the Bible, his face wrenched up as if he was trying to keep from crying. The Clerk looked toward the Judge, seeking guidance on how exactly to proceed.

Finally, the Judge spoke up.

"Um…" she said.

There followed another awkward pause, broken by a cackle the familiarity of which made Harvey sit bolt upright, the hairs on his arms suddenly erect and tingling.

"Don't get your panties in a wad folks," the boy - suddenly smiling, a mischievous gleam in his eye - said with an unmistakable Oklahoma drawl.

"I was just tryin' to build up the suspense."

He looked at the Court Clerk and winked.

"Of *course* I'll tell the truth."

From the sofa in Murfreesboro, Chad simply said, "Oh *shit*."

Amanda started crying again.

CHAPTER THIRTY-THREE

THE PEOPLE OF THE STATE OF TENNESSEE
VERSUS ANGEL WHALEY, THE HONORABLE JUDGE
MYRA WAY PRESIDING.

OFFICIAL COURT TRANSCRIPT.

MR. LAUGHLIN: Could you please state
for the record your name, age, and
occupation?
    (witness laughs)
    WITNESS: The name's easy. Jared
Whaley. The age? I would've turned forty-
three March 9th. Didn't get around to that
though. (witness laughs) The occupation?
I guess I'm still a recording artist for
Originality Records in New York. At least I
guess I'm still earning money. (witness
laughs) Ain't spending none though.
    (laughter from the gallery)
    JUDGE WAY: Order!
    MR. LAUGHLIN: And are you the same
Jared Whaley who was murdered in this
court's jurisdiction on the evening of
February 13, 2009?
    WITNESS: Shot right in the noggin.
(witness laughs) Only stung for a second
though.
    (commotion from the gallery)
    JUDGE WAY: I'm warning you!
    MR. LAUGHLIN: And could you tell this
Court who it was that shot you?
    (louder commotion from the gallery)

JUDGE WAY: I don't care how much money you paid to be here. I <u>will</u> clear this court!

MR. FLEMING: Objection, Your Honor.

JUDGE WAY: Shut up.

(witness laughs)

WITNESS: You're not going to get off that easy. I'll tell you. Eventually.

MR. LAUGHLIN: Request the Court to direct the witness to answer the question.

WITNESS: Or <u>what</u>?

JUDGE WAY: He makes a valid point, Counselor.

MR. LAUGHLIN: Did my client shoot you?

(witness laughs)

WITNESS: Maybe. Maybe not. We'll see.

MR. LAUGHLIN: Your Honor.

JUDGE WAY: Don't look at <u>me</u>. <u>You</u> started this.

MR. LAUGHLIN: Where do you currently live? Strike that. Where do you currently <u>reside</u>?

WITNESS: Right here.

MR. LAUGHLIN: By "here" do you mean in Wilson County?

WITNESS: By "here" I mean right here.

MR. LAUGHLIN: Inside this child you're now speaking through?

(witness laughs)

WITNESS: You know that. I know one of the rules of being a good lawyer is that you're supposed to know the answers to your questions before you ask them, but this is kind of silly, isn't it?

JUDGE WAY: The witness will refrain from....never mind.

MR. LAUGHLIN: Let's talk about how you got here then.

WITNESS: Let's.

MR. LAUGHLIN: Well?

WITNESS: I don't know. One minute I was getting a hummer and a headache, the next I was looking through a fat kid's eyes, typing shit on his computer.

(commotion from the gallery)

MR. BLEVINS: He's just big-boned.

(laughter from the gallery)

MR. BLEVINS: Like me and his mama.

(laughter from the gallery)

JUDGE WAY: Shut up.

MR. LAUGHLIN: And how, in your opinion, did you wind up here?

MR. FLEMING: Objection. Relevance.

JUDGE WAY: Shut up. Overruled.

WITNESS: That's a good question, Marsh, and one I've had quite a bit of time to think about. I've got a theory.

MR. LAUGHLIN: Continue.

WITNESS: I think that I had a story to tell, some wrongs to right, and that I've always been a restless soul. I think I probably just landed in the first body who's spirit wasn't strong enough to defend its territory.

MR. BLEVINS: You calling my boy gay?

(laughter, commotion from the gallery)

JUDGE WAY: Damn it! Bailiff, please

remove that man from the courtroom.

    (Mr. Blevins is escorted out)

    MR. BLEVINS: That country singer done possessed my boy!

    (laughter, commotion from the gallery)

    JUDGE WAY: Order!

    WITNESS: I'd love a burger and some fries.

    (laughter from the gallery)

    JUDGE WAY: How about you all just watch this on TV?

    (laughter from the gallery ceases)

    JUDGE WAY: I thought so.

    MR. LAUGHLIN: You mentioned that you had "some wrongs to right." Were you referring to your murder?

    (witness laughs)

    WITNESS: No, I was referring to the Publisher's Clearinghouse. They kept saying I might already be a winner. They were lying.

    (laughter from the gallery)

    WITNESS: And that "Free Credit Report dot com." Their whole goddamned <u>name</u> is a lie. Their offer only applies with enrollment in "Triple Advantage." Which ain't free. Lying fuckers.

    (laughter, commotion from the gallery)

    JUDGE WAY: All right, that's it. We'll take a recess while I decide if I'm going to let this go on. Counsel, in my chambers.

    WITNESS: Where'd my dad go?

CHAPTER THIRTY-FOUR

"What the fuck was *that*?" Judge Way screeched, directing her wrath at Laughlin, who looked at Willard, who just looked at the floor.

"Well," she continued, "I don't give a good *goddamn* that the whole *world* is watching this shit. I'm going to shut it down!"

"That's a good idea, Your Honor," Brice softly concurred. "The State would have no objections to your declaring this a mistrial. We've got more than enough evidence to try this again without the...shenanigans distracting from the facts."

"That's *another* word – along with 'goddamned' and 'fuckers' – I don't want to hear in my courtroom again!"

Brice glared at Fleming.

"That was *his* word," he said, thrusting an angry finger at the young attorney.

The Judge, her malevolent attention now on Laughlin and his star witness, turned back to the County Prosecutor.

"Did you say something, Haywood?"

"Forget it," he muttered.

"I think I should talk to him alone," Angel said, her first words of the morning drawing undivided attention.

"Talk to *who*?" Laughlin asked his client.

"My husband," she said quietly.

There was silence all around.

"Okay. I'll bite," the Judge said. "Why?"

"He loves me," was all she replied.

"Why didn't you come forward?" Harvey asked Amanda after they'd recovered from the shock of what they'd just watched on TV.

She sniffled and rubbed her nose with the back of her hand, then looked at her husband beside her. Chad patted her leg reassuringly and nodded.

"It was such a *nightmare*," she said. "At first I was in total shock. I couldn't believe I'd managed to get out of there alive. Then, when the police questioned me, they seemed pretty clueless. So I lied."

A tear rolled down her cheek.

"They *were* clueless," she added.

"And later?" Harvey asked.

"Later?" Amanda asked, not quite getting the question. "Later, they never asked me about it again, and she was in jail. I didn't think it mattered anymore."

For the second time in as many days, Harvey was glad he'd skipped breakfast. A prescient nausea was beginning to envelope the lining of his stomach, creeping upwards, winding its way around his lungs, making its way toward his heart.

"Wait a minute," he said, hoping for a clarification that would lead *away* from what he feared was coming. He looked at Chad.

"From what I gathered from his last journal entry, he was implying that *both* of you were somehow involved."

The couple seemed mystified.

"You're kidding, right?" Chad asked.

Amanda shook her head violently. "Chad wasn't there," she said.

As Harvey's world collapsed around him, he somehow had the presence of mind to pull out his cell phone and dial Laughlin's number.

Angel dimmed the lights in Judge Way's chambers, then took the twelve-year-old by the hand and led him to the sofa against the back wall.

"Jared, we need to talk," she said, fluffing up the cushions, gently pushing the boy to a seated position. She sat next to him and draped an arm around his shoulders.

"Baby, I'm not sure I'm comfortable with how this is

going," she whispered in his ear, then softly kissed it.

It was like kissing a warm cadaver, such was the lack of response. Come to think of it, she *was*, in a sense, kissing a warm cadaver.

It'd hadn't taken much convincing to get this time alone. She'd smelled the desperation in all of them, knew they felt that *anything* at this point was worth trying if it meant a chance at some resolution , knew that this was too big a deal to throw in the towel just because the witness was being *belligerent.*

She also knew that belligerence and obstinacy were part of Jared's character, a downside to his irrepressible *charm,* but that he always told the *truth.*

She should have known better than to think he'd get her out of this.

"Baby," she repeated, releasing her pony-tail, undoing the top buttons of her dress, parting the fabric, showing her inviting cleavage. "I need you to *help* me here. You know I can't do *prison.*"

She kissed him again, his ear, then his neck, then his lips. This finally got a response.

"Uh...ma'am?"

She rose quickly from the sofa, her anger flaring.

"God*damn it* Jared!" She stomped her foot. "I *know* you're fucking with me now!"

The boy's eyes, which *had* been staring straight ahead, dim and frightened, suddenly lit up and snapped towards hers.

"*I'm* fucking with *you*?!" he whispered harshly. "You fucking *shot* me, Angel! Not just a *flesh* wound either!"

He stood now, his eyes level with the top part of her open dress.

"You splattered my brains on the fucking *wall*! Do you know how much that hurts a guy?!"

"I knew you would make this about *you*!" she retorted, looking down at the angry young face. "You once told me that you would rather *die* than to be with another woman!" She crossed her arms and smiled. "You got your wish."

"Un-fucking-*believable*," the pint-sized entity moaned, looking at the ceiling, then back into her familiar taunting eyes.

"Now you're a goddamn *genie*! Well, I wish you could grant me the wish of having fucking *pubic hair* Angel! Although I'm not certain I *don't* have any. 'Cause I can't even see my *dick*!"

He turned and kicked the sofa, then turned back around.

"So could you grant me the wish of having pubic hair, being able to see my dick, and having been sick the night we *met*? Could ya do *that*? That's *three wishes*, Angel! Then you can go back into your fucking *bottle*!"

Angel calmly waited through his outburst.

"If I granted you the wish of being sick the night we *met*, you wouldn't have to worry about having an unseen hairless dick."

He laughed then, eyeing her less with anger than with a grudging affection.

"Goddamn, baby," he said. "It *sucks* being dead. And it *really sucks* being a fat kid."

"Oh, baby," she cooed, pulling the twelve-year-old into her arms, stroking his hair, whispering into his ear.

"You're just big-boned," she said.

"Are they having an *argument*?" Brice whispered in the hallway outside the closed door of Judge Way's chambers.

"Kinda *sounds* that way," the Judge replied.

"I hope she talks some *sense* into the sonofabitch," Laughlin added.

"I think I just heard a *moan*," said Fleming.

As Harvey sped up Highway 231 North, recklessly passing slower vehicles on the two-lane road, he wondered how he – and even *Laughlin* – could have been so *stupid*.

The rule of Occam's Razor. What could be more simple

than a jealous wife killing her husband? It happened a hundred times a *day*. Open-and-shut case.

Yet from the beginning, or at least from the beginning of the *weird* shit, they'd assumed that the dead guy was on a mission to save his innocent widow from a *wrongful* prosecution, that he was a knight in shining armor come from the grave to rescue his damsel in distress. It never *dawned* on them that this seemingly kind-souled entity might be out for *vengeance*, and that he wouldn't be satisfied unless he drove the stake in the bitch's heart *himself*.

But hadn't Jared *always* sought the spotlight? Even *dead* leopards sometimes can't change their spots.

Harvey wished Laughlin had answered his phone. He wasn't worried about the *case* – it had been the defense attorney's *own* lust for glory that had taken him down this path, and it was his lust for glory that would be his undoing. He was worried for the *kid*, the most innocent of pawns in this dangerous, ridiculous game. He figured the best way to exorcise the demon now fucking with the boy's life was to shut off the spotlight, and there was no quicker way to do that than to convince Laughlin it was *not* going to shine favorably.

Besides, he thought. *That Angel's a killer. Be better for the boy to not be fuckin' with* her *at all.*

Jared had always thought that make-up sex with Angel was the best sex he'd ever had. Even in death - even in the body of a big-boned pre-pubescent - he still stood by that.

Sometimes it was *good* to be a twelve-year-old, especially when a sexy woman twice your age had just hopped up and down on your pogo-stick like a…pogo-stick junkie long-deprived of…pogo-stick.

Not exactly the most poetic analogy, but he wasn't exactly thinking straight.

"*Jesus, baby, that was good,*" she murmured into his ear,

laying on top of him, her breasts pressed against his doughy young flesh.

Jared was glad to know that the sexual attraction, the *spark* between them, transcended the mere *physical*, that he could still turn her on even with the body he'd been dealt.

It doesn't matter, he thought, smiling in a haze of post-coital bliss. *Love is blind*.

So he was rather surprised, to say the *least*, when Angel took the sofa cushion from beneath his head and placed it over his face.

"You think we should check on them?" Fleming asked after a couple of minutes had passed.

"He probably went back into 'dumb-kid' mode," Laughlin scoffed, shaking his head.

"I hope she talked some *sense* into the little twerp," the Judge said.

At that moment Angel walked out, looking disheveled and shell-shocked, her hair hanging loose, her dress in disarray.

She shut the door behind her.

"What the *hell* is going on?" the Judge asked.

"Are you okay?" Laughlin asked.

Angel just stood there, staring at nothing, before she finally spoke.

"He tried to rape me," she said in a monotone.

The moment of stunned silence was so profound that when Brice said, "No shit?" everyone actually *heard* it.

Angel broke down and began sobbing.

"That little sonofabitch!" Laughlin said, heading toward the door.

"Fuck a duck," Judge Way said.

Laughlin grabbed the door knob and twisted.

"It's locked," he said, then looked at the Judge.

"Where's the key?"

"In my purse," said Judge Way.

Laughlin stopped rattling the knob. He looked at the Judge. "By my desk," she said.

The defense attorney just shook his head, wondering why women couldn't keep shit in their *pockets*. Like *guys*. Then briefly wondered if the Judge's robe *had* pockets. Didn't matter now.

"Perfect," he muttered, then started pounding.

"Willard!" he yelled.

Then pounded.

"Jared!" he shouted.

Then pounded some *more*.

He took a few steps back, preparing to use his substantial weight as a battering-ram. He looked into the stunned eyes of the Judge, then at Brice and Fleming, then at his client. Angel slid slowly down the wall, inconsolably wailing, one arm covering her eyes.

"I fucking *killed* him!" she screamed.

Her words hung in the air for a silent moment, then hit home, their impact like a sledgehammer on a soft-boiled egg.

Both prosecutors and the Judge, their faces registering horror and shocked disbelief, simultaneously shouted "*NO!*"

Laughlin too stood open-mouthed, eyes wide, staring at his client.

"Angel, what have you *done?*" he cried, then hurled himself at the door.

Which, at precisely that moment, opened.

Like a scene from an old slapstick comedy, Laughlin's momentum carried him through the doorway and across the Judge's chambers.

He tried to stop, but he'd thrown all his mass into the charge, and it wasn't until he slammed into the large desk, then over, that he finally came to a rest, landing on the carpeted floor on the other side, his face inches from the Judge's open purse.

He noticed her keys.

The twelve-year-old's head poked around from the other side of the door. He looked back toward the desk, from behind which the attorney was slowly rising to his feet, then back at the group in the hallway, all stunned, speechless.

None more so than Angel, who looked like she'd seen a ghost.

He smiled.

"That was *cool*," he said.

CHAPTER THIRTY-FIVE

THE PEOPLE OF THE STATE OF TENNESSEE VERSUS ANGEL WHALEY, THE HONORABLE JUDGE MYRA WAY PRESIDING.

OFFICIAL COURT TRANSCRIPT.

JUDGE WAY: The witness is reminded he's still under oath.
(witness laughs)
WITNESS: For what it's worth, Your Honor, I'll keep that in mind.
MR. LAUGHLIN: Mr. Whaley. In the last entry of your journal, which I've introduced as "Defense Exhibit U," you give an account of the night of the murder.
(commotion from the gallery)
JUDGE WAY: Order!
WITNESS: I tell a story.
MR. LAUGHLIN: Permission to treat this witness as hostile, Your Honor.
(commotion from the gallery)
JUDGE WAY: Shut up! Are you sure, Counselor? This is your witness.
(witness laughs)
MR. LAUGHLIN: I'm sure Your Honor.
JUDGE WAY: Request granted.
(commotion from the gallery)
JUDGE WAY: Shush!
MR. LAUGHLIN: Mr. Whaley, just before we re-convened, I received a message from Harvey Boyd, who has spent the morning with the couple you claim in your journal were

present in your dressing room that night. His message states that they disavow your account of the events.

(commotion from the gallery)

JUDGE WAY: You people are starting to get on my <u>nerves</u>.

(witness laughs)

WITNESS: What would you <u>expect</u> them to say?

MR. LAUGHLIN: So you stand by your version? That the defendant caught you in a sex act with your band-mate's wife, that she pulled a weapon, that the aforementioned band-mate then entered the room, that a struggle for the gun ensued, and that in the course of that struggle you were fatally wounded?

(commotion from the gallery)

JUDGE WAY: Order!

(commotion from the gallery continues)

JUDGE WAY: I said, 'Order!'"

(witness laughs)

WITNESS: Do you <u>really</u> want me to answer that, Marsh? I might not say what you want to hear.

MR. LAUGHLIN: To be honest, Mr. Whaley, at this point I'm beyond caring. You've manipulated me as far as you're going to manipulate me! I may get disbarred, I may be forced to retire! I don't <u>care</u> any more! This circus has gone as far as it's going to go! I don't want glory, I don't want fame – I want the <u>truth</u>!

WITNESS: You can't <u>handle</u> the truth!

(commotion from the gallery)

JUDGE: Counsel approach the bench.

WITNESS: Come on! That wasn't a bad Jack Nicholson, was it?

(laughter from the gallery)

(Mr. Laughlin and Mr.'s Fleming and Brice confer with Judge Way)

JUDGE WAY: The witness will answer the question.

(witness laughs)

WITNESS: I'm growing weary of this whole thing anyway. Time to wrap it up.

MR. LAUGHLIN: Good. Now answer the question.

(witness laughs)

WITNESS: I'm just a little scared, I guess. I don't know what happens next, and even if this is getting boring, I can't imagine <u>anything</u> more boring than <u>nothing</u>.

MR. LAUGHLIN: Just answer the goddamned <u>question</u>!

(commotion from the gallery)

JUDGE WAY: Order! Counsel will refrain from using profanity!

WITNESS: You <u>really</u> want me to answer that Marsh? You <u>really</u> want me to spill the beans?

MR. LAUGHLIN: <u>Tell</u> me, you obnoxious little punk!

(commotion from the gallery)

WITNESS: Fine! (witness stands and points at the Defendant) That bitch killed me <u>twice</u>!

(commotion from the gallery)

DEFENDANT: Jared, you're a fucking asshole!

WITNESS: And you're a fucking cold-blooded psychopath with a great set of tits!

(commotion from the gallery)

JUDGE WAY: Order!

MR. LAUGHLIN: I beg your pardon?

(commotion from the gallery continues)

JUDGE WAY: Order!

WITNESS: I said she's got fantabulous ta-ta's.

(laughter, commotion from the gallery)

MR. LAUGHLIN: I meant what did you mean by twice?

WITNESS: You'll see.

(commotion from the gallery)

DEFENDANT: I'm firing my attorney!

(commotion from the gallery continues)

JUDGE WAY: Goddamn it! Recess! Counsel in my chambers! Now!

(commotion from the gallery continues)

(witness exits stand)

WITNESS: Fuck your recess Judge! I'm out of here.

(commotion from the gallery)

(witness collapses)

CHAPTER THIRTY-SIX
The Wilson Democrat
MISTRIAL DECLARED IN WHALEY MURDER TRIAL
AFTER STAR WITNESS IMPLICATES DEFENDANT,
DIES
Story by Warren Stills

In what seemed more like a scene from a movie than a court
proceeding, Judge Myra Way declared a mistrial Tuesday in the
first-degree murder trial of Angel Whaley, accused in the shooting
death of her husband, rising country star Jared Whaley. The
proceedings were halted after the Defense's star witness - 12-year-
old Willard Blevins – tragically collapsed and died moments after
implicating the defendant not only in the murder in question, but
also in his own death.
Preliminary findings from Wilson County Medical Examiner
Roger Humphries indicate the boy died from suffocation, and – in
a bizarre twist among many bizarre twists – that Blevins' body
temperature seemed to indicate he had expired prior to his
testimony.
"This is some weird (expletive deleted)," said Humphries.
The case gained national and even world-wide attention when
defense attorney Marshall Laughlin announced that the Blevins
child would be testifying not as himself, but as Jared Whaley, the
victim of the crime. Many – this reporter included – were
skeptical of the Defense's gambit, a skepticism which faded upon
witnessing a video presented into evidence of the youth speaking
and even singing in a voice and dialect not his own, and
disappeared completely upon the witness taking the stand.
Following the declaration of a mistrial by Judge Way, the
defendant was remanded into custody at the Wilson County Jail
pending not only a re-trial on the original charge, but an inquest by
a Grand Jury into a possible indictment for the subsequent murder

of the witness.

Said County Prosecutor Haywood Brice, "The circus might be in town for awhile."

Defense attorney Laughlin was not available for comment.

EPILOGUE

A month after the nightmare, Harvey Boyd was still haunted.

He felt responsible for Willard's death, felt that if he'd been viewing the whole damned thing with an objective newsman's eyes, he could have foreseen the danger the boy was in.

He'd tearfully apologized to Mack and Elenore at the funeral, but they rebuked him, alluded in their own simple way that they couldn't help but feel that if he'd approached the situation from the perspective of anything *other* than a newsman, their only child would still be alive.

"Wasn't that damned *ghost* that killed 'im," Mack had said.

That hindsight is 20-20 is a given, but what's often left unacknowledged is that it's usually a clarity of vision blurred by tears.

Harvey often these days found his vision so blurred.

Following the abruptly-cancelled trial, he returned to work, did his best to bury himself in the daily mundane grind that is small-town radio.

Of course, things were different.

If he'd previously been – as Fleming had stated that day in court – "a big fish in a small pond," he was now a whale in a salt-water-filled shot glass.

Since he was going to be a witness not only in Angel's re-trial but also in her trial for the murder of Willard, Jack Dawes had deemed it prudent that he be at least temporarily relieved of his duties as News Director. Harvey's friend Warren from *The Democrat* had been hired to fill that role, although Dawes was savvy enough to keep Harvey on as host of the morning show.

And the ratings had never been higher. Curiosity may kill cats, and sometimes, inadvertently, innocent children, but it also sells radio spots.

One of which – for a local used car dealership – Harvey

was in the middle of writing on his laptop when he'd drifted away.

He'd been trying to come up with a clever way of saying that "Wilson Auto Sales" would take anything with wheels as a trade-in. It was the kind of thing he used to be able to knock off in just a few minutes, but which, looking out his office window at a sun which seemed to have lowered noticeably toward the horizon since he'd last touched the keyboard, he feared might now be a major undertaking.

I suck, he thought, then looked at his computer screen.

A feeling of dread washed over him the likes of which made all he'd suffered thus far seem like a walk in the park, like a child's fairy tale.

He'd started a new document, one which had nothing to do with used cars.

He knew what it was.

He *feared* what it was.

He silently prayed to a God he felt had, if not an inkling of compassion or an iota of benevolence, at least one *helluva* sense of humor.

Harvey forced himself to read the screen:

When I was 12, a dead guy tot me to tipe. Then his wife kilt me. Now Im dead to. Don't be afraid Harvy. Your my frend....

AUTHOR'S NOTE

This is a work of fiction. However, many *parts* of it are *not*.
Which is why I've skipped that whole "any resemblance to persons
living or dead..." Yada yada yada.

Much of Jared's journal is in fact my own. That's what's so
freakin' *cool* about writing a novel. Those parts which *are* true are
true from a perspective that is solely my own. Those parts which
are truly *false* are from that same perspective. Those who truly
know me will know which is which, and either forgive or condemn
me based upon their own perspectives of the same quasi-fictional
truth.

But my love will never die. Until I'm dead. Which has thus far
not *really* happened.

ABOUT THE AUTHOR

Ty Hager is a veteran broadcaster, recording artist, and songwriter. His humorous songs have been heard on *"Dr. Demento," "Bob and Tom,"* and several other morning shows nation-wide.

His non-fiction book, *"Nashville Songsmiths – In-Depth Interviews with #1 Country Songwriters"* is also available on Amazon.

If you enjoyed this book, please be so kind as to review it on Amazon or Goodreads. If you *didn't* like it, feel free to keep that to yourself.

Hager's two country-comedy CD's are available from Winthrop Records at WinthropMedia.com.

He currently resides in Oklahoma with his girlfriend Kimberly and their dog Kenzie.